The Podcast Chronicles Copy

Kathryn Dodson

Renegade Reads

Contents

Chapter 1

S ue aimed her phone at the stovetop, where a pan of scrambled eggs with scallions sat next to another filled with crispy hash browns. Her friend Paula had chastised her for making breakfast for high schoolers, but with college looming, Sue grabbed every minute of time she could with the boys. One click, and she texted her two youngest sons, now several years older than the images on her screen. Upstairs, stomping and doors slamming confirmed the text's receipt.

She poured a second cup of coffee, enjoying the rich aroma and settling into the warmth of her kitchen. Soon, the boys clomped downstairs, eyes sleepy and hair askew. "Hi, Mom," they each managed while loading their plates with food.

Sue joined them at the table, but god knows, not for the conversation. The ravenous hunger of teenage boys left little room for talking. As she watched them devour breakfast, a twinge of sadness for the lonely mornings ahead passed through her. Jaxson was a senior and Chase a sophomore. With her other two boys gone already, time would pass in an instant.

The boys finished quickly, grabbed their backpacks, and headed for the door. "Bye Mom," echoed through the now empty house.

At the sink, she turned the water on high and created her own noise. But dishes only take minutes. The quiet pushed her toward the barn.

Maybe by the time the boys left, Gabe's work travel would slow, and they could have coffee together on the back porch and watch the sun rise over the mountains. Although, since he owned the company, he could probably travel less now. Maybe she'd look for a job to fill the time. If only she could figure out what she wanted to do after a couple of decades out of the workforce.

On her way out the door, she picked up the local magazine that kept her up to date on gossip and happenings in town. She could look at the jobs section while the horses ate.

The brisk autumn morning chilled her fingertips and cheeks, and she pulled her jacket tight. The sun had just crested the ridge of mountains, and it would be a few minutes before the valley warmed. She couldn't imagine a better place to live. Whatever else happened, this would always be home.

Samson greeted her with a soft nicker. She fed him first. The smell of horses and hay in the quiet morning filled her with the contentment of life in a small town. Twenty years ago, they'd left the bustle of Seattle behind. Instead, she had the soft muzzle of a horse against her hand, birdsong, and days full of family.

She picked up the magazine and read about the proposed Worth Winter Wonderland Resort and Theme Park. Who on god's green earth thought something so tacky belonged in Durango? Sue scanned the article, which explained how a New York developer had his sights on her valley. Her blood pressure rose at the description of a roller coaster just down the road. Would the comforting sounds of horses rustling and birds chirping be replaced by rickety gears and screams of terror?

She imagined hundreds of hotel guests let loose on the neighborhood's quiet roads. How bad would it be? She wished for Gabe. He always knew the happenings in town, but work travel had taken him away. Again.

Just when things had started to slow down in life, something like this came along. She tried to shake thoughts of the theme park from her head and went to the feed room to get Samson's bridle and saddle. If she rode up the high trail, she'd have a bird's eye view of the development site.

As soon as Samson had eaten, she saddled him and headed for the mountains. The big chestnut gelding struggled up a steep incline, then topped out on a ridge with sweeping views of Colorado's Animas River Valley. She'd chosen this route for a better look at the planned development site. The craggy forested mountains and a valley studded with patchwork fields and cozy houses usually brought gratitude. Now, she only thought about loss.

The wind kicked up the ridge and blew her curly hair across her face, disrupting her view. She pulled a hair tie from her wrist to control the unruly mess. Even with her view unimpeded, she could barely picture roller coasters and big hotels near the homes nestled in the last patch of grass before the Rockies rose steep from the valley floor. Her eyes moved to the twisting, turning river splitting the valley on its journey from snow-capped peaks. This was already a mountain wonderland, that's why they'd moved here.

The first kayakers of the morning, small in their bright colored boats, shared the river with beaver lodges and trout. Trees hid the train tracks beyond the river. The narrow-gauge railroad was another wonder of the valley, shuttling tourists on an almost three-thousand-foot climb between Durango and the now touristy ex-mining town of Silverton. In a few months, when the snow was too deep to ride up the ridge, the train would transform into the Polar Express, a trip she'd taken every year when the boys were young. The memories etched into the landscape warmed her heart.

She threw a leg across Samson and slid to the ground. The horse turned his head toward her, and she gave the white blaze running down his copper face a pat. Holding onto the reins, she approached the edge of the ridge where her home lay nestled below with the other houses and ranches dotting this side of the river. One or two had been added each year since she and Gabe left rainy Seattle for the sharp, thin air and clear skies of Colorado. Despite the growth, their neighborhood had kept its small-town personality.

The highway that stretched along the far side of the river had changed the most, growing from two lanes to four and adding a few shopping centers and hotels along its edges. Even with the changes, Durango remained an outdoor wonderland with hiking and biking in the summer and skiing in the winter. Why would you bring something that sounded like Disneyland to a place like this?

Samson pawed the ground and snorted, seeming to mirror her frustration, though he probably just wanted to keep moving. Irritated, she could hardly clamber back on the horse while thinking about Mountain Disneyland ruining the town and bringing all those tourists to her doorstep. She wanted to protect this peaceful valley, to scream and fight to keep the development out.

Yes, things changed. She knew that better than anyone. She'd changed so far from the career woman she thought she'd be that she hardly recognized herself. That change she'd accepted, even welcomed at the time. And things would soon change again. The boys would be gone. A quarter century into her marriage with Gabe, that relationship had changed also, as he spent more time in Denver growing his company. Some days these thoughts made her want to roll back time, or at least slow it down, but she'd been watching change approach for decades.

The land spread before her had become her touchstone, the thing that kept her true to her deepest self, the person who wasn't important because she was someone's mother or wife. Up here she was just Sue. To lose the valley to an overblown, hundred-acre tourist attraction was too much. This change she would fight.

Beneath the anger, buried deep, a hard, shiny, long forgotten part of her took root. She recognized it from when her old firm used to send her into companies to save them. Usually, the executives couldn't figure out where their money had gone. As a forensic accountant, a good one, each time she walked in a new door, she'd known she'd find the answers. Sometimes it was theft, sometimes poor management, but she always discovered the problem and set things straight.

The Winter Wonderland Resort was a different challenge. No one had asked for her help this time, and she needed to stop something, not fix it. Once, she could stride into any office and take control. She'd have to find that Sue again if she wanted to save the real wonderland.

Her thoughts spun as the horse made his way down the ridge. Who was this Harold Worth anyway, and why had he chosen her valley for his development? The article mentioned the hundred acres needed for the project. The City of Durango owned the twenty-five acres with access to the highway. Surely, city officials wouldn't let this happen. Tourism had already pushed Durango beyond its limits. Traffic snarled on roads built for fewer people, and crowds made it almost impossible to eat or shop on Main Street. There was no way the small mountain town could accommodate such a huge resort.

It surprised her when Samson stopped in front of the barn. The trip home seemed quick, trapped as she was in unhappy thoughts. She unsaddled the horse, then brushed his coat until he shone like a new copper penny. When she turned him into the paddock with her husband's rarely ridden quarter horse and the family donkey, he headed straight to the dust patch and rolled in it until his coat was dull and dirty. What a brat.

He reminded her of her sons. Despite her best efforts, they were going to be who they were going to be. Because of this valley, they had grown up strong and a little wild, with a firm love of nature and fast friends made in a small town. That gave her another reason to fight the development. They might not return after college, but if they decided to raise their own kids here, they needed the real thing, not a theme park.

Chores waited to consume her morning. The house needed cleaning, the vegetable garden picking and pruning, loads upon loads of laundry waited—not to mention grocery shopping and a large lawn to mow. It never ended. Normally after her ride, she'd garden while listening to her favorite podcast. Today was different. Her valley needed her.

She snagged the magazine from the hay bale and took it to the small built-in desk in the kitchen. Kira Sutton, an environmental attorney with the American Lands Organization wrote the article. Sue reread it carefully, taking notes and looking things up on her laptop.

What she learned made her stomach ache. She needed share this misery and come up with a plan. She called Paula. "Have you seen the latest issue of *Durango Magazine*?" Sue asked the moment her friend picked up the phone.

"Yes. They had a whole article on Mindy Copeland, this year's homecoming queen. They didn't do that the year Cara was queen."

"No, Paula. The article about Worth Winter Wonderland."

"Hold on, I've got it right here."

Sue heard papers shuffle but couldn't wait. "I've been researching this guy, Harold Worth. He's a real estate mogul from New York City. He's got a global empire of golf courses, casinos, and theme parks. You should see the images I've found online of these opulent, gold-encrusted resorts. They don't fit with Durango. And room prices are astronomical."

"It sounds fancy. Maybe Durango could use something like that."

Sue wanted to shake her friend through the phone line and get her to focus on the project's issues. "Paula, you've got to find the article. It's not just a fancy hotel. This guy wants to put a theme park here, like Disneyland. And worse, he has a record of ignoring environmental concerns, paying meager wages, and bringing in foreign workers without housing or benefits. It's horrible."

"Okay, slow down. I've got the article here. Well, a roller coaster seems a little absurd. What are they going to do with it in the winter?"

"They're talking about buying one hundred acres. That's huge. Some of the websites I've seen tell how this guy's developments leave communities to deal with a slew of negative impacts. A cliff slid into the ocean after he ignored warnings about where to place a golf course. In that case, he tried to sue the city for damages. Another website showed a casino he built that went bankrupt. Today it just sits on a vacant lot like a huge animal carcass, rusting away."

Paula's sigh came heavy through the phone. "I can tell this means a lot to you. How can I help?"

Sue took a deep breath, relieved to hear the concern in her friend's voice. "I'm worried this development will jeopardize everything I love about our town. I can't imagine losing its friendliness, safety, or the gorgeous environment."

"I hear you," said Paula. "I'll talk to Denny about it when he gets home. He tends to have strong opinions on stuff like this. Does the article say what we should do?"

"It says the development has to go before city council as part of the review process." Denny might be a big help. Paula's husband owned the local Ford dealership and considered himself a community leader.

"Then we should probably contact the city representatives and some of the other politicians," Paula said.

"That's exactly what I was thinking. Want to go down to city hall with me this afternoon?"

"Sorry, no can do. Lainey is getting her cast taken off, so I'll probably be down at the hospital for hours."

"Darn. Well, wish her the best for me. How about tomorrow?"

"We're going up to Denver for the gymnastics regionals."

"Shoot." Sue debated whether to wait for her friend to return or just go by herself. Paula had run the PTA and led half the fundraisers in town. Sue usually followed her lead.

"Look, this is important to you. Go on down there and let me know what happens. Maybe we can strategize next week. I'll see what Denny says."

As soon as she was off the phone, Sue went back online. She couldn't find any statements from local politicians about the development, but she knew most of the city council members. Durango only had twenty-thousand people, and sometimes it seemed like she'd met almost everyone. The politicians seemed normal, just like everyone else. Surely, they'd hate the development as much as she did, or at least they would if she showed them what she'd found online.

Sue listed everything she could do to prepare for the meeting. As she reviewed the boxes waiting to be checked off, a jolt of excitement hit her, the anticipation of item-by-item progress. She'd certainly never been this excited about laundry. For the first time in a long time, she had something important to do that didn't involve her husband and kids, although ultimately, they would benefit. Today the laundry could wait, she was going to city hall.

Chapter 2

Freshly showered, Sue dressed in her best pair of dark jeans, a black V-neck tee shirt, one of the few that hadn't faded, and her brand-new fleece jacket. She never wore suits and silk blouses anymore. They'd been donated to charity years ago, but she needed to look as professional as possible. She'd visited city hall several times before, when her kids' sports teams received awards and once when they needed permits to build the barn, but it had been a while. Today, success depended on convincing people the development would hurt Durango. The pressure made her more than a little nervous.

It took ten minutes to drive downtown. She parked in the small lot and steeled herself to walk through the glass doors of city hall. Approaching the receptionist, she asked for Buddy Travis, the mayor. She had met Buddy at several events but didn't know him well.

"Do you have an appointment?" the receptionist asked, barely looking up from her computer.

Darn it, she should have known better and called ahead. The local politicians prided themselves on being available to the public, but they had to know when you planned to visit.

"No," Sue admitted.

"He's not available," the receptionist said without offering any options.

Sue hated the amateur move of arriving unprepared. Determined to get something out of the trip to town, she asked for Mike Cavanaugh, the city manager.

"Do you have an appointment?" The receptionist's now sullen eyes stared back at her.

"I don't, but I hear his voice." Mike had been the city manager in Durango for at least a dozen years. One of her favorite hockey dads, he had a child in her second oldest son's class.

"He has a staff meeting right now. Would you like to make an appointment for another time?" The woman folded her hands under her chin, her hard face chiseled like granite.

Sue had run into gatekeepers before, the kind of person you wanted protecting you at the front desk and not who you wanted to go up against if you needed to talk to someone. The woman, Carla Borelli according to the plaque at her desk, had long blonde hair that looked younger than the lined face that accompanied it. She'd have been great at Apple or Google, but her attitude was a bit much for a small-town city hall. Sue likely wouldn't meet with either man today.

Sue gave in. "I'd like to make appointments with both of them about the Worth Winter Wonderland development."

"Our assistant city manager, Amanda Payne, is handling that issue. Would you like an appointment with her?"

"I guess, but I would also like a meeting with the mayor." Sue's words came out testy. The unfriendly receptionist probably wanted her gone so she could return to a fantastic set of cat videos or an eBay shopping spree.

"Carla, I'm here. I'd be happy to speak with her now." The voice came from behind a wall meant to hide the offices from the prying eyes of the public.

"Would you like to see Ms. Payne now? Ms. . . . ? I'm sorry, what is your name?" the receptionist asked in a voice Sue would have used with unruly children.

At that moment, a woman in her mid-thirties came around the wall and opened the half-gate into the rest of the offices. She had thick, straight brown hair that fell below her shoulders and friendly hazel eyes. The woman's white blouse and gray suit jacket topped fashionable burgundy skinny jeans. Sue wished she'd worn something other than frumpy mom clothes, but the woman welcomed her and actually gave an eye roll toward the receptionist as she reached to shake Sue's hand.

Sue took a deep breath, relieved to get beyond the wall of bureaucracy. Thankfully, someone friendly had shown up. Sue followed the woman to her office, a tiny room cluttered with a desk and credenza. She motioned for Sue to sit in the lone chair facing the desk.

"Welcome to city hall. I'm sorry if Carla was a little off-putting. How can I help you?"

"Thank you for seeing me, Ms. Payne. My name is Sue Cleary, and I live in Durango, out north in the valley. I read the article in *Durango Magazine* about Worth Winter Wonderland. I'd like to understand where the city stands on this and, frankly, what I can do to stop it." There was no reason to beat around the bush. Sue didn't know how much time she'd get, and she needed information.

"Please call me Amanda. I'm glad you came in today. This project is on a fast track, and council members will vote on it within ninety days. Any incentives provided to the developer will also go before the city council for a vote."

"Is there actually a chance they might approve that monstrosity?" Sue asked. "And what incentives?"

That the city council would consider giving Harold Worth money or tax breaks to bring in a theme park seemed ridiculous. Surely, the community wouldn't support it. Sue had worked on committees at the kids' schools and had always thought the other moms were a lot like her, happy to be raising their children in a quiet, small town.

"I'm not sure how the council will vote." Amanda's voice brought Sue out of her thoughts. "We've just received the application and are still gathering information. Regarding incentives, the developer has asked for tax abatements, improvements to Highway 550, and assistance with purchasing the portion of land within the city limits."

"He wants the city to buy the land for him?" Sue's voice was too loud, but she couldn't control it or the disbelief surging through her. This guy wanted the taxpayers to give him land and fund his development? No way.

"I know it seems like a lot. I'm personally leading the team doing the analysis. The company says it will bring lots of jobs to the area."

"Is that a good thing?" Based on her morning research, most of the jobs at Worth resorts weren't great.

"Most cities want a robust economy, and that tends to be based on good jobs."

Sue stared at the woman. Did she really not know? "I've done a little research, and Mr. Worth isn't known for paying decent wages or providing benefits. Are those really jobs the city wants to attract?"

"Ms. Cleary, I promise you we will do a full analysis."

"Well, what can I do? Don't the residents get to vote on something this big?"

"Not automatically. It is slated to go straight to the city council. However, you do have the right to gather signatures and submit a petition for a public vote."

"That sounds complicated." Sue had known it would likely take more than one trip to city hall, but this sounded daunting. She didn't know how to lead a community-wide effort. Maybe the woman who wrote the article would help. Her unease must have shown on her face because Amanda got up, closed her office door, and pulled her chair closer to Sue.

I understand how you feel." Amanda's voice had lost its professional tone and sounded worried, even a little urgent.

"What can we do about it?" Sue whispered. The conversation felt secret, making her dizzy and warm, like a hot flash.

Amanda didn't whisper, but her voice softened. "When they vote on this, they'll want to know where the voters stand. I'm sure they'll hear from Worth Company, so they ought to hear from their constituents as well."

"But I'm just one person."

"Yes, and it's going to take a community effort to fight this development." Amanda looked at Sue with expectation.

She'd come here hoping the people leading the government would feel the way she did. Amanda made it seem like the elected officials wanted the development. How could a housewife fight the hired guns of a wealthy real estate mogul? The room grew hotter still. Sue took off her jacket.

"Listen, I can't tell you what to do," Amanda said, "but elected officials listen to voters. If there are enough people against the development, it might make a difference. The council will want to do what's right for the community."

"If they want to do what's right for the community, they won't even consider this."

"They have a legal obligation to consider the application, but that doesn't mean they won't listen to the people, if the people stand up to be heard."

The weight of the other woman's words shifted onto her shoulders. Did she care enough to carry this burden? Sue straightened in the chair and remembered standing on the ridge, her ridge, that morning. The sun had been strong, taking away the September chill. The smell of pine sap hung in the air. More than home, Durango represented a beautiful part of the American West. It shouldn't be destroyed for greed.

The city council would vote before the new year. The kids and Gabe didn't need her the way they used to. Maybe it was time to prove she could achieve something beyond the family, the way she had when she worked. It might not be a familiar fight, and she wasn't positive she was up to the challenge, but she had to try. The valley was worth it.

Sue looked at the earnest woman across from her. Why wasn't she fighting this tooth and nail? Maybe she had to toe the political line. She did work here, after all. And she'd told Sue what needed to be done, even if she'd coated it with a layer of spin.

"Thank you for your time. You've been very helpful," Sue said.

"Anytime, and if you have additional questions, feel free to call." Amanda grabbed a business card from a holder on her desk. "Here's my email and cell number. This is an important issue for our region."

There was that earnestness again. Something told Sue Amanda had a deeper connection to this issue than she let on. Hopefully, she'd become an ally, but Sue would need to get to know her better.

"Thank you." She stood and shook Amanda's hand. "I'll be in touch."

On her way out of the office, she stopped at the receptionist's desk to tell Carla she wanted to meet with the mayor at his earliest convenience. If she was going to save an entire valley, she couldn't let the first receptionist she ran across stop her.

Chapter 3

On the way back home, Sue stopped at PJ's market for a bag of salad. She had too much work to do to worry about dinner. She needed to put together a plan that would rally the community around saving the valley.

She'd wanted something to do with her time now that the boys didn't need her so much. Having this much purpose take over her life in one day excited her. Striding into the market, Sue made quick work of her purchases. She set the salad and a jar of dressing on the conveyor belt and recognized the long-time cashier.

"Hey, Bertie did you read that article in *Durango Magazine* about the huge development that might go in here?

"Is that the Magic Winter Kingdom place?"

A nerve of excitement ripped through her. Bertie saw hundreds of customers a day. If she dropped a few well-placed negative words about the development, it could make a difference with the locals. "I think they're calling it Worth Winter Wonderland, but that's the one. It's named after some rich New Yorker."

Bertie scanned the groceries without taking her eyes off Sue. "I didn't read the article, but this nice-looking fellow stopped in earlier and told me about it. He bought two Cliff bars and an iced coffee. It sounds like it's going to be great for Durango."

Oh, no. Bertie gave her the total, but Sue kept her wallet closed. She needed to turn this around. She glanced to her left. Only one man with a few things in a basket waited behind her.

"I've done some research on Mr. Worth, and he does not have a good reputation. I think this development could be terrible for Durango. Who told you this was a good thing?"

"I hadn't ever seen the man before, but he seemed really nice. He said there would be all kinds of new shops and that more people would shop at our store. I hadn't heard about it before then. That will be twelve seventy-two please."

Two more people had joined the line, and Sue couldn't stall any longer. "Maybe you shouldn't say anything about the development to customers until we know a little more about it." Sue regretted the guilt-inducing words the second they left her mouth. She didn't have any right to tell Bertie what she should say to people.

"Well, I don't know." Bertie looked flummoxed, and with good reason.

"I really appreciate your telling me about what this person said. Honestly, I just started looking into this, but I'm sure we all want what is best for the community. If I learn anything new, I'll let you know." She gave Bertie her biggest smile, one that disappeared the second she left the market.

She'd give anything to talk to the man and figure out what made him like the project. Bertie said she'd never seen him before. Maybe he was a tourist. Or perhaps he worked for the developer and had come to scope out the site. And put a positive spin on the development.

Sue had to prepare to deal with people on all sides of the issue. The next test would be her family. Gabe and the boys would be home for dinner.

She texted the boys to pick up pizza on their way home. Then she hesitated, thinking she should cook them a meal from scratch. The return text simply read, "Awesome."

It would be good to have Gabe back in town. She'd meant to talk to him about all the time he'd spent away the last few months. With him gone so much, it had been hard to find the time. Or at least that's what she told herself. She didn't want to be the kind of wife who nagged her husband. At least tonight, she had something interesting to talk to him about, the development.

She waited until everyone had settled at the table, plates loaded with pizza, salad in a large bowl. For the first time, she noticed how far away Gabe seemed. The table still had chairs for six, she and Gabe at the ends and the two boys near her, leaving two empty chairs near Gabe. The arrangement was a holdover from when the youngest boys needed more help. She regretted not moving the empty chairs away from the table. Especially since lately he'd only eaten dinner at home a scattering of nights.

"It's good to have you back home," she said, raising her glass of wine in his direction. "How was Denver?"

"It was fine. I came home a little early so I could make it to the chamber of commerce meeting today."

"Oh, I'd forgotten about that." Gabe had been on the local chamber board for years, despite running a global company with offices in Seattle and now, apparently, a lot of business in Denver. She shook the depressing thoughts away.

"Did you happen to see Denny at the meeting? Paula and I talked earlier today about this tacky resort and theme park that some developer wants to build right here in town. Have any of you heard of it?" She glanced around the table and noticed her kids shoveling pizza into their mouths. All the years of teaching them manners, and they still ate like wild animals.

"You mean Worth Winter Wonderland?" Gabe asked. "A representative from Worth Companies presented to the chamber board."

"Oh, my god, you're kidding. Was it horrible?" Sue glued herself to her husband's words, and even the boys looked up from their food.

"Well, it was something. The developer actually wants to control the flow of the Animas River, diverting part of it into a lazy river for inner tubing. They'd channel the rest into a surfing wave and whitewater kayak course."

"That sounds pretty cool," Jaxson said. "Too bad I'll be gone before it opens."

"Well, I hope it doesn't happen at all." Sue jumped in. "There's a hotel, a theme park, all kinds of stuff." She took a breath. She couldn't boss people into thinking a certain way, not even her kids. She needed to approach this like a professional, with prepared arguments. She looked at her husband. "What else did you learn about it?"

"Yeah," Chase said. "That river thing sounds like an environmental catastrophe."

Yay, Chase. Her youngest had her auburn hair and an environmental streak stoked by last year's biology teacher. The boys steamed at each other across the table, but Sue refocused on Gabe.

"On the highway side of the river, they're planning a thousand room resort, along with a shopping corridor, IMAX theater, and restaurants. They'll put the theme park on our side of the river, complete with year-round snowmaking, rides, and an event auditorium."

Sue's stomach clenched at the details, the pizza threatening to come back up. Gabe knew even more than the article, each detail worse than the last.

"This town could use some more action." Jaxson wouldn't let it go.

Sue wondered whether he really believed Durango needed the resort or if he just wanted to torment his brother. The boys couldn't be more different, Jaxson with his dad's dark curls and a self-confidence and popularity all his own. Chase was much more reserved, like Gabe.

"It sounds horrible!" Chase's fury daggered across the table toward his brother, who sloughed it off with a nod of his head.

"Kids, we can do something about this. I am opposed to this development, and I've done a lot of research online and even went down to city hall today to learn more." Sue watched a single eyebrow arch high above one of Gabe's green eyes. She hoped the hint of a smirk at the corner of his lips was positive. She hadn't married the most talkative man, but she could usually read volumes in his expressive face.

"I'm not going to stand by and let this happen without a fight. I want to do something about it." She sounded far more confident than she felt and braced herself for their reactions. No one was used to seeing her stand up for anything but family.

"That's great, Mom. We can get people at school involved, and I can design a website." Chase was the most tech savvy of the four boys. His older brothers taught him everything they knew, and then he learned twice as much on his own. He was forever buying new gadgets for filming, recording, and playing video games. He might come in handy.

"This battle's going to get political," said Gabe. "You'll need people on your side."

Following local politics was like sport fishing for Gabe. Sue never understood why he was so interested in small town intrigue when he ran a global business, but he always had his pulse on politics and the Durango business community. She rarely learned anything through the mom gossip chain that he didn't already know. He might be a secret weapon.

"I'm sure I can mobilize the moms. Maybe I can start a petition." After shepherding four boys through the local schools and volunteering for their classes and sports, she knew most of the moms in town. Perhaps she could make a difference. Sometimes the scope of this task threatened to pull her under, but Sue wanted to swim.

"It's going to take a big cross-section of people to stop this project, probably throughout southern Colorado, especially if the Worth Company pressures the business owners and politicians," Gabe said.

Well, what do you suggest?"

"Mom, you should start a podcast," Chase said.

"Yeah, right." Jaxson snickered.

Sue rolled her eyes. Teenagers. As much as she loved podcasts, she knew petitions. Learning to put on a podcast would be terrifying. And thrilling. "Awesome. Here's my first episode: put your plates in the dishwasher and start your homework."

When the boys had left the kitchen, she caught Gabe grinning. The sexy smile made her wonder what he was thinking.

"Want to help me feed the horses?" she asked.

They headed to the barn together. Sue filled a bucket with oats while Gabe distributed flakes of alfalfa to the animals. They reached the donkey's stall together, and she turned to study him. "Do you support the development?"

"No. It seems like a risky investment, not to mention what it would do to the valley."

"Smart man," she said, happy they were on the same side. They'd been so distant lately. Not like when they'd moved here from Seattle, or when the kids were younger, and their lives revolved around the boys' sports.

Still fit and strong, Gabe moved with purpose from stall to stall. Sue glanced at him as she worked. She still loved him, still wanted him. She just wished she could see inside his mind and make sure they still wanted the same things.

She poured the last of the grain into the donkey's trough and took the now empty oat bucket into the feed room. It surprised her when Gabe followed her into the small room and closed the door. He walked up to her, wrapped an arm around her waist, and pulled her close.

"It's exciting to see you so riled up about this development," he said, leaning in for a kiss.

She felt his excitement, and her eyes widened. What had gotten into him? He kept kissing her, hungrily, sexily, slowly backing her up until she was against the far wall. One hand slid under her shirt and the other started to unbutton her jeans.

"What are we doing?" she asked.

He pulled back and smiled. It was a smile from years past, her favorite smile, the one he saved just for her. What the kissing and touching had started, the smile finished. Desire grew from flame to fire. She smiled back and pulled him close, reveling in his touch.

Later that night, she smiled again as she climbed into bed next to her sleeping husband. They hadn't done it in the feed room in years. With four boys in the house, it had been almost impossible to find a place to be alone, and several times the feed room had been that place. Still, it had been a while.

She sank into the mattress, her muscles heavy and relaxed and her toes still tingling. Like most couples, having kids had put a real damper on their sex life. Even with two of the boys gone, they were almost never alone together. And now with Gabe traveling so much, it was even less.

His phone dinged and lit up on the nightstand. He usually remembered to put it on the charging station in the hallway where it wouldn't interrupt their sleep. She grinned. Their adventure in the feed room must have exhausted him.

She slipped out of bed and grabbed the phone. When she plugged it in at the charging station, the screen lit up. She couldn't miss the text messages from someone named Lucinda.

"Meet me @ Rioja at 8"

Sue remembered the fancy Spanish restaurant from the last time Gabe took her to Denver. Eight o'clock was late for a business meeting.

She read the second text. "Can't wait to learn more about your dynamic interface. I hear it's powerful!" The wink emoji that ended the text seemed unprofessional, even flirtatious.

Sue closed her eyes. It embarrassed her to spy on her husband like some paranoid housewife. But she'd seen Lucinda's photo on the texts. Shiny black hair, red lips, obsidian eyes you could drown in. She exuded competence mixed with beauty.

Sue dropped the phone as if it had bitten her, and it clattered to the table. She made herself take a deep breath. Gabe loved her. He'd just shown that.

Sure, he spent way too much time in Denver these days. He'd promised he'd be able to manage the company from Durango. Now he flew to Denver almost every week.

Perhaps she should have become one of those wives who was involved in her husband's business. She used to be, back when he'd wanted to know whether he should take the company public, and she'd been on the accounting team that gave him the answer.

If she'd stayed involved, she'd know all about Denver. But she'd set the parameters of their relationship, first when she moved to Seattle to be with him, and later when she quit working to stay home with the kids. Those had been the right decisions. They'd led to a wonderful life.

Funny how things turned out. Growing up, she'd never wanted to be a homemaker like her mom. But two decades had gone by since she'd had a job, and with the last kid closer to being gone, the decision had come back to haunt her. Now that the mom gig was almost over, who would she be next?

Chapter 4

Sue rushed through her chores the next morning, eager to get to the important work of saving the valley. First, she emailed Kira Sutton, the attorney who had written the article, and let her know she wanted to oppose the Worth Winter Wonderland Resort. Hopefully the woman who'd written such a powerful article would provide Sue with recommendations on what to do. She didn't expect an immediate answer because the environmental organization was in San Francisco, an hour earlier than Durango. Sue's days started early, and it wasn't even eight yet.

As she got up to refill her coffee cup, the computer chimed. Ms. Sutton's email asked if she was available for a phone call at one Durango time. Now that was her kind of woman! She replied yes and sat down with fresh coffee to continue her list.

Out of curiosity, she looked up 'how to start a podcast.' She certainly liked listening to them. When Jaxson mentioned it, the idea had seemed absurd. But maybe it would be fun. Her favorite podcasts sounded like friends chatting, and people might want to share their views on the development.

Between podcasts, research, and rabbit holes, the hours flew by. Promptly at one, the phone rang.

"Sue, this is Kira Sutton." The voice on the other end was straight out of a seventies radio program. Sultry and low, it perfectly blended calm and control.

Interesting how she just assumed it would be Sue on the phone. She had the odd sensation the woman could see into her living room. "Thanks for calling, Ms. Sutton."

"Call me Kira. Are you serious about wanting to stop the Worth development?"

"Absolutely. It's ridiculous, we've got a natural wonderland here already. We don't need some rich guy to come in from New York and give us snow, kayaking, and a lazy river. We've got all that stuff!" She didn't care if she sounded indignant. The more she learned about the development, the less she liked it.

"Have you talked to the Worth representatives?"

"No, but they made a presentation at the chamber of commerce yesterday. I stopped by the city for information and they're actually considering giving Mr. Worth incentives to build this monstrosity."

"I've worked with communities opposed to Mr. Worth before, and you're going to have quite a battle on your hands. I love your passion. Do you think other people in the community feel the way you do?"

"I'm sure of it. People come to Durango because it's a great place to raise kids or because they're skiers, mountain bikers, or hikers. Everyone loves the mountains and valleys the way they are. It's hard to imagine anyone wanting to put up with something like a fake winter wonderland." The thought made her want to spit.

"That's good news, although I'm sure there are pro-development people too." Kira said. "Activating public opposition is the best way to stop it. You'll be competing with money, slick advertising, and beautiful promises that will never be kept."

"But how do I get people involved?" For all the neat technology she'd researched, her only real expertise was in accounting and bake sales. Kira made it sound like it would take a professional team. "Do people hire your firm to manage things like this?"

"Sometimes, but there has to be a grassroots effort in place first. I'm sure you have enough connections in town to organize that."

Sue sighed. This woman had a lot more faith in her abilities than she did. "I've volunteered at the school and for nonprofits, but nothing on this scale. My kid suggested a podcast."

"That's not a bad idea, if you think people would listen. Whatever vehicles you use in this fight, the goal is to get as many community members as possible on your side. That's the only thing that will move politicians."

"That's what the assistant city manager said."

"You spoke with Amanda Payne? What's she like?"

That Kira had heard of Amanda surprised Sue. She smiled, realizing she'd made a good connection. Maybe she wasn't so bad at this after all.

"She seemed really nice. You could tell she had to be politically correct, but I got the feeling she didn't like the development."

"Really? You should keep talking to her. It could help to have an inside connection."

Sue laughed. "You make it sound like this is something out of a le Carré novel."

"Stopping a development like this takes bold tactics. I'll send you some pointers on how people in other communities successfully fought environmentally questionable projects. Let's talk again once you've looked at that."

A lump in Sue's chest grew. She needed Kira's knowledge and professionalism on this project. Except for one big issue. "I don't have any money to pay you." Attorneys charged hundreds of dollars an hour.

"Don't worry about that right now. My company works with communities across the globe to find and protect environmentally sensitive land. We often start off working pro bono, and many times never end up charging communities. Maybe we can find a nonprofit to fund the work or look for grants. Don't worry about money for now. I have a personal interest in the Worth development."

Personal? That sounded interesting. Sue decided not to ask. Why look a gift horse in the mouth? The conversation wrapped up with the promise to talk again in a few days, once Sue reviewed Kira's information, which arrived in her inbox before they hung up.

Inspired by the call, Sue found the tab on her computer that showed a podcast starter kit. She clicked the "buy now" button, then followed that up by purchasing soundproof batting.

Gabe's study would be the perfect location for her studio. It's not like he used it much. Located on the second floor, its sole window was double paned and faced the mountains. The only noise that might interrupt a podcast would be the donkey braying, which might be good for some comic relief.

Sue took a break and stretched, then decided to spend some time in the garden. She had so much to think about, and gardening helped her focus. The plants looked fine, despite her ignoring them for a day. She clipped Swiss chard and noticed she could probably harvest spaghetti squash soon. The pumpkins still looked good for a change. Usually, they grew to the size of bright orange tennis balls peeking out from their green canopy, then caught a fungus that made them sag and wither. She could never get them to hang on until they were ripe. Maybe this year would be different.

While gardening, she listened to one of her favorite podcasts. The show featured two sisters chatting about happiness and ways to help women enjoy their lives more. While they were experts in their careers, one a psychologist and one a writer, most of the time they just dished. Sue would love to have a podcast like that. When she first started listening, she'd thought about starting one on how to raise four boys, her only current area of expertise.

For years, she'd tried to figure out what to do once the boys left. A podcast would be fun, but she'd need a peppy sidekick. Two completely different voices filled her ears, one sister a cheerleader, the other serious. Their different takes made the show interesting. Sue had never been the peppy type.

She ran through her list of friends, but none seemed right. Plus, she had a hard time imagining bantering with any of them for twenty to thirty minutes every week for years on end. She was an only child, and while she enjoyed being around her friends on occasion, she appreciated her alone time.

She weeded the tomato plants, their sharp scent piercing her thoughts. They had been bountiful this year, but only a few stragglers remained. She could relate.

The end-of-year garden as an analogy for life would be a good subject for a podcast, although people probably wouldn't like the dark humor she saw in the fading beauty. The title could be *The Second Half*, or *The Ending*. She'd already reached her fiftieth birthday, and most people didn't live to one hundred.

If she did live that long, she wondered if it would be with Gabe. Her father had started traveling more for business when she was in high school, then divorced her mom the minute Sue left for college. Maybe her podcast title should be *How to Survive When the Kids Leave and Your Husband Dumps You*. Now that would be a podcast for the ages.

She shook her head. No getting sidetracked. She had things to do.

Sue left to photograph the proposed development site before the sun went down. Documenting the current state of the land had risen to the top of her to do list. Three quarters of the land combined crops with pasture and swept from the river to the base of the mountains.

A trail crossed through the property along the riverbank. On warm days, Sue often brought Samson to that part of the river, where a horseshoe bend had carved a sandy beach. He'd walk in until the water covered his knees, then paw at the river until they both were soaked. Worth would probably block the trail.

She drove to the other side of the valley to photograph the rest of the site. The nearest bridge across the river was two miles toward town. The next closest lay five miles in the other direction, toward the ski area and Silverton. There was no development between this side of the highway and the river, just scrub, trees, and swampland. Without this land, Worth couldn't access the bigger plot across the river without a major detour. The city land was crucial. If she persuaded the mayor and city council to vote against the project, it would die.

She pulled off the highway and walked through the scrub, taking photos. The spongy ground pulled at her boots as she walked. The river must have passed through here before changing course to its present location. The air smelled of sage, and the shadows of birds flitted in the branches of the larger trees. The trees would be cut down if the resort came. The birds would be gone. All of it would change.

The sun had already passed beneath the mountain ridge lining the west side of the river. Days were short in a valley. She zipped her fleece jacket, pulling it tight around her neck before heading back to the car.

A black SUV had parked near her blue one. As she approached, a tall man with silver-blond hair got out of the driver's seat.

Unease washed over Sue. She'd pulled uncomfortably far off the main road, and she hadn't told anyone where she was going.

"Hello, there," the man said, lifting a hand in a half wave and walking toward her.

"Hi. Can I help you?" Sue's automatic response left her flummoxed. The last thing she wanted was a conversation with a stranger at dusk.

"What are you doing out here?" he asked.

"I'm taking pictures, not that it's any of your business." Sue hoped she looked as prickly as she sounded.

"Hey," the man put both hands up as in surrender. "I'm not a threat. I'm just out here looking at a proposed development site."

That changed things. Maybe he'd be on her side. "Me too. This is where they want to build that Worth Winter Wonderland project."

"I've heard that. What do you think about the development?"

"Look how beautiful this place is," Sue swept her arm toward the trees, river, and mountains. "Why would anyone put a theme park here?"

"I've heard it's going to be a luxury development. First-class all the way." Conceit laced his words.

"Are you from here?" Sue asked, wary again now that he seemed pro-development.

"No, just visiting. You?"

"Um, I've got to get back now. It was nice meeting you." She left a wide berth between them as she walked back to her car. Her foot sank into soft mud, and her ankle turned before she pitched onto her knees, flinging her phone into the dirt.

"Let me help you!" The man trotted over to her and grabbed her by the upper arm.

"Stop, please. I'm fine." She glared at him, and he took a step away from her. Sue retrieved her phone from the dirt and slid it in her pocket before clambering to her feet. "I'd appreciate it if you'd leave me alone."

"Lady, maybe you shouldn't be out snooping around other people's property. It could be dangerous."

A sliver of fear ran up her spine. She had to stay angry. It kept the fear away. She gave him a long look with all the fury she could muster, then turned and headed toward the car. The second she slid into the front seat and locked the doors, relief flooded her. That guy was bad news.

Chapter 5

The next morning, Sue woke with a flurry of energy. She wouldn't let some guy in a field intimidate her. She would fight this thing. The excitement in her chest bubbled all the way out to her fingertips the way it used to.

Hunger rumbled her stomach as she cooked, and she decided to join the boys in a big breakfast of bacon, eggs, and thick slices of toast. She needed energy for the day. First, she'd get an appointment with the mayor. Then she needed to build a local team. It was time to activate the mom brigade.

She called the boys for breakfast. Chase stumbled downstairs, then set his laptop next to him on the table.

"No screentime during meals," Sue said.

"Mom, you need to see this."

She set his plate down and leaned over his shoulder. A website came up with an aerial photo of their valley. The colors reflected the greens and blues of the land and sky, and a logo in the top right corner showed two hands like mountains holding a line-drawn valley adorned with pine trees and a twisting, meandering river. The title of the site was Save the Animas Valley.

"What is this?" A knot of tension released in her shoulders. It looked like someone had already started a movement to stop the development, and they'd done a good job. The site evoked the tranquility of home. She pushed down a tinge of disappointment as well. At least she could still participate in someone else's effort.

"I made it for you." He turned and handed her the computer, looking up at her with Gabe's eyes and a half smile all his own. Faint blue shadows ringed his sleepy eyes, and she suspected he'd worked late into the night.

It took her a moment to fully understand what he'd done. Gratitude plunged through her. This wonderful child had created a gift far better than any he could have purchased. He had seen her, seen what she needed, encouragement. His work had turned her ideas and desires into something real.

"You made it for me?" She sat in the chair next to him, so thankful for this child who, without her asking, had made something important just for her.

"It's so you can stop Winter Wonderland. You need a website. You can post your podcasts here and on streaming app. It will keep people updated on what's happening. There's a place for a blog if you want to do that, and we can link it to all your social media."

"When did you do this? How did you do this? I love the logo, it's beautiful." If she had the talent to create her perfect website, this would be it. It was like he'd seen inside her. He wanted her to succeed, and his confidence in her bolstered her own.

"My friend Emily made the logo. She's an amazing artist."

"Is she the one with the long black hair you're always hanging out with?" asked Jaxson as he walked into the kitchen. "She's hot."

"Get a plate." Sue shook her head at her older son. They never stopped tormenting each other. She caught a glimpse of Chase's blush and knew to ignore it. Hormones had raged through their house for years, and she'd learned that asking about girls blew her chance of learning anything.

Jaxson filled a plate with food and joined them. He took the computer from his mom. "This looks really good," he said after a few minutes. It was a rare compliment for his brother. "I'm not sure about the name."

"I like it," Chase said. "It's what she's trying to do."

"What does animas mean?" Jaxson asked while he chewed.

"Don't talk with food in your mouth. It's Spanish. It means soul," Sue answered.

"Save our soul. That's pretty cool, but weird," Jaxson said.

Chase grabbed the computer from his brother and started typing. "The Save the Animas Valley URL is available. Twelve bucks a year. Mom, where's your credit card?"

Where had this helpful boy come from? Getting any of them to do everyday tasks usually took heroic nagging, but now Chase moved so fast she barely kept up.

She didn't want to lose the momentum, this connection between her and her kids. She got up from the table, found her wallet, and handed over her credit card.

"I'm going to get a couple of add-ons, but it won't be over thirty bucks. Anything else we can get later. I'll connect the website to the URL this afternoon, and I'll get you an email address. I can probably have Emily design a business card for you."

Was she really doing this? It had only been a couple of days since she read the article. It was one thing to oppose the project, but a website and business cards signaled a deeper level of commitment. But she only had ninety days, eighty-eight now, until the council vote. She pushed away the lump of doubt. Why not do it?

Chase hadn't stopped typing. "We can get you fifty business cards for twenty dollars, and you can pick them up inside Walmart."

"How do you know that?" she asked.

"I just looked it up."

The child worked miracles. She looked at the two boys, one on the computer, the other shoveling breakfast into his mouth. "Let's do it," she said. "But I'm going to need your help."

Jaxson glanced at her but remained silent. Chase looked up from his computer. "I'll show you how to use the site on Saturday, and I'll ask Emily about designing the cards. We can test the podcast equipment as soon as it gets here. You work on content."

"I will work on content," she said. The world felt a little lighter despite the nagging fear about everything she needed to learn and do.

"I've got a meeting with the mayor set for next week. Are you in?" Sue asked as soon as Paula answered the phone.

"I'm sorry, but I can't make it."

"That's okay," said Sue. "I've got another proposition that's even more exciting. Chase is helping me start a podcast. I'd love for you to be on it with me. Between everyone you know in town and Chase's expertise, I think it could be a great way to get the word out about the development."

"About that," said Paula. "Denny was at the chamber meeting since he's on the board of directors. He thought the presentation went well. A lot of people in town are going to want this development."

"Really?" Sue struggled for words. She couldn't believe Paula might be pro-development. Paula was like her. She had kids and loved Durango because of the quality of life. Was Sue wrong about this?

"Listen, personally, I think the development sounds like, well, like a lot. But Denny thinks it will be good for business. You know, all the new jobs."

"But Paula—"

"Sue, I just can't get involved in this. I'm sorry, but I've got to go."

The phone went dead. Anger and disbelief waged war in Sue. Paula had always been the strongest link in the network of moms. Who the hell let her husband decide what she could get involved in, and all just to sell a few more cars at the dealership?

In addition to her mean thoughts, anger also fueled Sue's determination. She'd have to find people who hated the development as much as she did. People who cared more about the community than making a few more bucks.

That afternoon, Sue called Amanda at the city and suggested they meet for coffee as soon as she got off work. When Sue opened the coffee shop door, the aroma of rich dark roast slammed into her and stopped her in her tracks. That smell! She should quit worrying about the environment and get a job here if she wanted a second career. Even when she bought coffee beans from her favorite store, she couldn't replicate this smell at home. She'd tried. The growing tourism industry had definitely brought better coffee shops to town.

She ordered an almond milk latte from the hip barista, then crossed the glazed concrete floor and sat at reclaimed wood table. She'd had meetings there before, planning school events or travel to hockey tournaments, but today's buzz was new. It reminded her of when she'd worked, always arriving ten minutes early, notebook in hand.

Saving the valley was a front-line endeavor. She'd have to approach people she'd known for years and ask for their support. Where once she'd thought would be this easy, the conversation with Paula had drawn new battle lines. She'd need to recruit people she didn't know, people outside her comfortable circle of moms and middle-aged friends.

Battle lines. War. Worth had invaded her town. She pictured herself as a warrior queen planning strategy and tactics.

She'd considered the project from multiple angles, the way she used to analyze companies. While the website and podcast might influence people, first they had to tune in. That would take marketing and networking, the friendly kind from a Durango mom instead of a New York City developer. Then she needed to motivate people to save the town they loved by writing letters and showing up for government meetings. It wouldn't be easy, but if she broke it down into small steps and tackled them one by one, she'd get there. Talking to the assistant city manager was the next step.

Amanda walked in the door, wearing black skinny jeans instead of burgundy ones this time, along with a boxy cream sweater and gorgeous scarf. Sue bit her lip. She needed to up her clothing game. Frumpy mom clothes wouldn't cut it next to someone so put together.

Amanda's smile lit her entire face. She looked genuinely happy to see her, and Sue half wanted to hug the woman for her enthusiasm. It reminded her of Chase this morning, or of Leslie Knope, her favorite eager, earnest TV city employee.

Sue broadened her smile to match Amanda's, thinking about how this project exposed her to new people, and new sides of people she'd known their entire lives. She'd missed this type of interaction by thinking of herself as just a mom. Moms could do anything.

Amanda got her coffee and sat across from her. Too excited to bother with the normal pleasantries, Sue hurried to explain what Gabe learned at the chamber meeting. An arched eyebrow told Sue some of this was new information.

"How is the project progressing from your end?" Sue asked.

"Right now, it's coming in for a zoning change," said Amanda. "They don't have to give us all the details yet. The developer only needs to let the city know how the property will be used and how the development impacts the existing land and infrastructure. They let us know they wanted to use the river for recreational uses, but they didn't specify a lazy river, kayaking, and surfing."

"Is that really how this is supposed to work?" Sue asked. If the city had to approve the project, how could they know less than the chamber of commerce?

"It sounds like they're using the chamber audience to sell the sizzle of the project. What they gave us is more cut and dried."

"But how can you not know the specifics of what's going to happen there?"

"That comes later. If they get the zoning change, then they submit the project plan to the planning commission for approval."

"Should I wait to rally the troops until the planning commission meeting?"

Amanda shook her head. "The zoning change is actually more important. Once the land use is changed to accommodate a large hotel, theme park, and retail, then those uses will be legally allowed on the land."

"Is it possible for me to get all the information they've given you?" Sue asked.

"Of course. It's all public information. By early next week we'll have a page about the project on the city's website with everything that's been submitted. We will also post the environmental impact study, although the developer has sixty days to turn it in."

Sue leaned forward, suddenly hopeful. "Environmental impact study? Does that mean that if it's going to have a negative effect on the environment, the project won't go forward?"

Amanda sighed. "Unfortunately, it's not that simple. The developer could mitigate the negative effects. For example, if the development would snarl traffic on the highway, they could pay to add a stoplight or turn lanes or some other improvement to address the negative effects."

"Those don't sound like improvements to me." She studied Amanda who seemed so open, even welcoming, and decided they needed to get beyond facts and figures. "How do you personally feel about the development?"

"That's not important. What's important is how you feel about it." Amanda pursed her lips. "I'm here in my official capacity. As a city employee, I have to remain unbiased."

"How long have you lived in Durango?"

"All my life."

Sue's mouth fell open. How could the woman be unbiased? Her success or failure would be something they would have to live with forever. Why didn't Amanda understand this?

Her confusion must have shown on her face, because Amanda hurried to explain. "I understand how strange that must sound. I do have personal feelings, but I have to set them aside for the analysis and be as fair as I can to the project and the community." She paused and looked around her, as if searching for reinforcements, or perhaps enemies. "It's my job to get the facts out there. I provide information to the city council, and they decide what is right for the community. And, of course, the public weighs in. My role is to get the facts right. The city council decides the outcome."

Sue watched Amanda's forehead wrinkle. Were her eyes glistening? Amanda seemed trapped between her rhetoric and her emotions. Sue wanted to delve deeper.

Amanda spoke first. "I prefer to keep my personal feelings to myself. It's not that I don't want to share, but it's just so early in the process."

"I understand. I'm sorry to push you." Sue was sorry. She didn't want to lose whatever relationship they'd developed. Did Amanda like the project and just wouldn't say so, or did she hate it as much as Sue did?

"It must be hard to walk that line between your professional obligations and what you want for the city. I just have a really hard time understanding how a development like this fits our community. We already have the perfect winter wonderland and summer playground."

"I know. I really do."

"Do you have kids?" Sue asked.

"Yes." A smile lit Amanda's face, the worry replaced in an instant. "I have a thirteen-year-old son and a six-year-old daughter."

Sue smiled back. "I've got four boys. Two are in college at CU Boulder. My seventeen-year-old and fifteen-year-old are still at home. Is your son joining them at Durango High next year?"

"He sure is. I can't believe he's going to be in high school already."

"Trust me, it's better than middle school. Usually. You won't believe how independent they become, except when it comes to laundry," Sue remembered the website and her heart swelled a little. "This morning, my son Chase made a website to help me fight the development. He wants to help me create a podcast also. He seems genuinely excited about what I'm doing." She heard pride in her voice as she spoke.

"I think a podcast is a great idea! People can tune in and listen anytime, and the old episodes will always be there for new people to hear. I'd even be willing to come on and talk about the process from the city's point of view."

"You'd do that?" Sue asked, a little surprised.

"Absolutely. Informing the public is part of my job, and I'm always searching for ways to get information out there. It's a struggle to reach people, since most don't log on to the city's website for information. I'm sure the chamber of commerce will ask me to speak about the process and facts of the project. I'd be happy to do the same for you."

"Well, that's one episode. Now I've only got to fill ten or eleven more slots before the council vote." Finding speakers seemed like it would be the most daunting part of the podcast.

Amanda leaned forward, clearly energized by the idea. "I bet you could get the attorney who wrote the article to talk to you, and maybe your sons could pull together an episode focused on high school kids. You could also talk to the local chapter of the Sierra Club. They'll probably take a stance on the issue. You might even get the mayor to come on. He hardly ever turns down an opportunity to talk to the public. I don't think you'll have any trouble getting content."

Sue stared, gaped mouth and flabbergasted. In thirty seconds, Amanda had come up with more podcast topics than Sue generated in two days of brainstorming. Doubt cast a shadow over her confidence. This project needed someone with more community connections, someone who knew all the local players and was used to working with them. Someone more technically savvy. She hated the thought of voicing her doubts to Amanda, but the need for help trumped pride.

"You know so many people. I wish I had your connections."

"I can help with that. I'll put together a list of organizations that might be interested, along with their key contacts."

"That doesn't go against your policy of being unbiased?"

Amanda shook her head. "Not at all. I'd do the same for anyone, and I've given the chamber similar information in the past." She reached across the table and put her hand on Sue's. "I'm happy to do it for you."

The intimate gesture surprised Sue, and she wondered what it meant. Surely Amanda was telling her she was on her side. It felt like the beginning of a new friendship.

On the way home, Sue bought a couple of steaks for Gabe to grill. She foraged for salad ingredients from the garden, then opened a bottle of wine. With the boys gone for the high school football game and a party after, they would have the house to themselves.

She set the table on the back porch. The view of the mountains as the sky darkened and the stars began to sparkle always reminded her of how lucky she was. She lived in a magical place.

As soon as Gabe got home, she told him how happy the boys had made her, glossing over Jaxson's reluctance. "I also plan to take over your office to record podcasts."

He chuckled. "I approve of the office getting a little more use."

"Yeah, about that." Sue wished she'd needed to search harder for an office. Her heart rose to her throat as if trying to block the words she needed to say.

"I know I've been gone a lot. I promise this is a short-term issue."

"Well, that's good." The old Sue wanted to stop there and let the uncomfortable conversation die. The new Sue wanted answers. "What exactly do you mean by short term?"

Gabe rocked back in his seat, looking uncomfortable, maybe even guilty. "I've got some stuff to figure out. We've been coasting along for a while, and I feel like maybe it's time for a change. Like you, with this new project you're working on. How's that going?"

"It's going okay." Sue waivered and reminded herself that Gabe was a good man. "Can I help with anything you're going through? With the company, or anything else?"

"No, believe me, I'd much rather hear about you." He looked weary.

Sue sighed, then followed him to softer ground. "Do you think the chamber will support the development?"

"Probably. At the board meeting, the Worth representative talked about all the jobs they'd create and the retail they'd bring in, including national chains people love. He compared it to the Cherry Creek shopping center in Denver."

That would be a hard argument to combat. Most of Sue's friends loved the upscale shops at Cherry Creek. She'd even bought handbags and home accessories there. Nothing in Durango came close.

"They told us the development would mean more business for everyone. Winter Wonderland will use local print shops, banks, and attorneys. The resort's employees will mean more money for residential real estate companies and apartment owners, while the visitors will fill local restaurants and bars. A lot of people bought into the story."

"Yeah, like Denny Galloway." Sue explained what had happened with Paula. She tempered her earlier frustration with her friend. You never knew what happened in another person's marriage.

"Some people are going to feel that way. Others don't see how the development makes financial sense. A couple are concerned about the environment."

"It seems like the chamber of commerce should have the community's interests at heart."

"A chamber of commerce is an association of local businesses," Gabe said. "Besides, the Worth representative made it sound like a real win-win."

"Are you changing your mind on the project?" It hadn't occurred to her he might decide the business advantages of the development outweighed the disruption it would bring.

He put down his glass of wine and reached out to her, running his fingers along the line of her jaw. His touch sent a jolt of electricity straight through her. "I think what you're doing is great. That development doesn't belong in this valley. I'm sure Harold Worth has never visited Durango, never seen the beauty of this place. All he sees is cheap land and ever-increasing tourism. He sits in a skyscraper in New York City and doesn't understand what's truly valuable in this community. A guy like that doesn't belong here."

God, she loved this man. He might not talk a lot, but when he did, his words were meaningful. He saw inside her like no one else. She didn't want to lose him.

She still needed to understand what was happening in Denver, who Lucinda was, and what he needed to figure out. But not tonight. It had been a good evening. Tonight, she wanted to hold on to her love for her husband, secure on her back porch, staring out at the beautiful place where she lived. For one more night, she could pretend that none of this would ever change.

Chapter 6

The following Monday, Sue prepared to meet with the mayor. Since she'd promised herself to up her clothing game, she chose a pair of black slacks and a lightweight sweater. She thought about the cute scarf Amanda had worn, but nothing in her closet seemed right. A shopping trip needed to be added to her to do list. She'd forgotten how much the right clothes could build confidence.

Carla greeted her by name when she walked into City Hall, a small concession that let her breathe a little more easily. She smiled at the mayor when Carla led her into his office, but that smile quickly faded. So much for dressing up. The mayor's coffee-stained Western shirt pulled at his paunch as he reached out to shake her hand.

"Welcome Sue. How is Gabe doing?" He gave her hand a quick squeeze, then gestured to the chair in front of his desk as he settled into his padded leather seat.

"Gabe's fine, thanks." Sue sank into the low chair. She had several inches on the mayor when standing, but now she looked up at him past a gaudy acrylic award with images of an eagle and an American flag pronouncing Mayor Buddy Travis the Durango Chamber of Commerce *Citizen of the Year*. An oversized gavel sporting the mayor's name flanked the award.

"How are the boys?" he asked.

"Everyone's fine. The older two are at Boulder, and the younger ones are finishing up high school."

"Those are great boys, good hockey players."

Sue only nodded. Time to move past the pleasantries.

"So, what can I do for you today?" he asked.

"I'd like to know your stance on the proposed Worth Winter Wonderland Resort. I've done some research on the developer and his plans, and I'm concerned about the impact to the community." It was fun to be back in this situation, interviewing an executive, or in this case, political leader, about something important. She'd prepared a list of questions, just like the old days.

"Now Sue, city staff is still gathering research on that, and the item doesn't come before city council for months. I'll have a better idea once the numbers are in, but it's expected to have some real benefits for the community."

"If I remember correctly, you've lived in Durango your whole life?"

"Yes, I have. My parents came here in the forties. I built a business here," he pointed to a framed photo of cows grazing in a lush pasture, "raised my kids here, and when my own boys took over, I decided to give back to the community."

"Given that," she said, "I've got a couple of questions for you. I've looked at the city's tourism website. The tag line says, 'Durango is a dozen vacations in one destination' and touts everything from hunting and fishing, to outdoor recreation, to the historic downtown, arts, and culture." She counted off the items one by one on her fingers. The mayor steepled his own fingers but said nothing.

"Given this, and the booming tourism industry, do you really believe a theme park is a good idea? The city is already rich with tourism resources."

"Well, tourism is a much more complicated business than you probably realize. Bad economic times hit it hard, and that affects city finances. We need that money to pay for police officers, to keep our streets clean and paved, and to pay for our parks and the community center. I'm sure your kids love using our great community center."

"They certainly enjoy the pool and climbing wall." His pat political answers didn't address her questions, but she expected this from someone who had to run for office every four years. She needed to dig deeper. "I'm curious about one thing. If tourism income changes with the economy, won't another development cause the city's income to fluctuate even more?"

Sue paused, waiting for an answer. Instead, the mayor shifted in his seat and raised his eyebrows like she'd done something wrong. His glare emitted heat and arrows, and she recognized the look from her own parenting. She'd found a soft spot and kept picking.

"Why wouldn't you look for a development that diversified the city's income?"

The mayor fumbled with a pen as his face grew pink. She had to admit some satisfaction at his discomfort, mostly because of how he'd talked down to her. Now at least he knew she understood economics.

"Sue, it's not that simple." The mayor shook his head. "Harold Worth has come to us. He wants to invest in this community and will spend his own money to do so. This will be good for Durango."

"I'm not sure that's true," Sue countered. "I've done quite a bit of research on Mr. Worth, and he borrows money to build his projects. In fact, most of his developments are so highly leveraged that if they don't make money early, he lets them go bankrupt. Some shut down and stay closed for years while he fights with the banks."

The mayor cleared his throat. "I'm sure you know Mr. Worth has many millions of dollars. Hell, he was on the cover of *Time* magazine last year. He sent me a copy. Gabe's a money man, you should ask him about Mr. Worth."

Sue's eyebrows rose. It took audacity to think she needed to talk to her husband to understand money. Sue had dug deeper into Mr. Worth's finances than the mayor, not to mention Gabe. Buddy still didn't get it.

"You may not know this, but I'm a CPA. I encourage you to look a little more deeply into Mr. Worth's financial background and prior projects." Dead air punctuated her sentence. She hadn't kept up her accounting credential, but he didn't need to know that.

When he didn't respond, she continued. "I have another question for you. Tourists overrun this town summer and winter. How will our small community handle the visitors Winter Wonderland will bring?"

"That's the beauty of our city process. The developer must do an environmental study, and he'll take care of any impacts to the community. If you're just patient, everything will work out." The mayor's patronizing tone returned.

Hackles up, Sue wondered if he knew how infuriating he was. "I understand the developer has to do things like add stoplights and turn lanes at the entrance to the development, but are these really improvements to our community? It sounds like he just has to pay for the infrastructure his resort needs."

"I think you're missing the point of all the dollars this project will bring to town through increased taxes. It will create jobs. There will be a lot of new money circulating in Durango because of the wages he'll pay. This could be a windfall for our city."

"But aren't you considering giving him a break on those taxes? And speaking of employees, where will they come from? We've got low unemployment. Also, the environmental study doesn't cover things like employee housing. It's already hard for teachers and even city employees to find affordable housing in Durango. Won't this make the situation worse?"

The mayor shifted in his chair like he was trying to scratch an itch. "There are certainly things we have to look at. There's a lot of moving parts, but we owe it to the developer to give him fair consideration."

"I think you owe the community fair consideration. I'm starting a community-wide effort to get the truth out about the development." Part of her wanted to keep arguing. She could win point-by-point, and his ever-deepening flush revealed she was getting to him. She softened her tone to keep the doors of communication open. "I hope you will consider joining me on my podcast."

"Sue, have you talked to your husband about this? He's a businessman and understands these things. I think you're getting all heated up and emotional before you need to. There's plenty of time to review the project."

Sue went cold. What an ass. Did he even realize women had the right to vote? She couldn't believe she had voted for him in the past, not realizing what a Neanderthal he was. How dare he treat her like she couldn't understand this development? She wanted to respond but was stunned into silence.

"I'd like to thank you for coming in today." The mayor stood, clearly deciding the meeting was over.

She wished it wasn't ending like this. She hadn't wanted to alienate him, but his demoralizing comments had thrown her off her game. "Thank you for your time, Mayor. I look forward to having you on the podcast."

"Talk to Gabe about what you're doing. This isn't something to worry your head about."

Rage finally loosened her tongue. "Mayor, this is my community. There were enough brain cells in this head to get an MBA and work for a big five accounting firm. I'm good at following the money. Worth Winter Wonderland threatens the year-round wonderland we live in today. I don't think you understand where the pulse of the community is on this one." Squaring her shoulders, she stood, reached across the desk to shake his hand, and left without waiting to be walked out. Worry your bald head about that!

She sailed past Carla's desk. A familiar-looking man held the door open for her as she bustled out. She turned back, trying to place him, and almost fell off the sidewalk curb.

"Careful!"

Sue turned to see Amanda getting out of her car.

"Your mayor is a pig," Sue said.

"Our mayor. You look shell-shocked."

"He thinks I shouldn't worry my little head about such a difficult issue. He also suggested I talk to my husband before I do anything."

"Ouch. I'm sorry about that." A pained look crossed Amanda's face.

Sue took a deep breath. Amanda really did look sorry, and she couldn't imagine how much she had to deal with in her job. If the mayor was condescending with a constituent, how did he treat employees?

"Hey, do you want to get another coffee later this week?" Sue asked.

"Sure."

"Maybe I'll add a shot of brandy to help my pretty little head recover from my meeting with the mayor." Her anger had cleared enough to see the humor. After all, she planned on proving the man wrong.

"I'd join you in that too," Amanda said before heading into city hall.

One good thing had come of today's meeting. It would be nice to talk to Amanda again. Plus, she knew where the mayor stood on the development.

When she got home, she emailed Kira about the meeting. Her response was an exclamation mark and an immediate phone call.

"So, does the mayor support the project?" Kira didn't give Sue a chance to say anything beyond hello. An undercurrent of excitement tinged her gravelly voice.

"He was certainly more interested in talking up the advantages than listening to any potential problems. I invited him to be a guest on the podcast."

"That's a great idea, I'd love to be a part of that one. Sometimes politicians unwittingly expose a project's faults. They tend to give up more information than the developer."

"You'd be willing to co-host the episode with me?" Two women playing off each other would make it better. Given that Kira wanted to go after the mayor to expose the project, Sue could play the good cop, be the softer voice. She wasn't used to that role, but it made sense since she was the local.

"I'd be happy to help when I can. I think the podcast is a great idea, one I haven't tried before. I'd like to see how it works."

"Amanda, the assistant city manager, volunteered to be a guest to explain the development process."

"That's great. People will want to understand how to get involved. Can I be the first guest? I've researched the project and can explain the issues. People need to know why they should care from the very beginning."

It was perfect. Kira's article had introduced Sue to the project and made her care. Having her on the podcast would do the same for others. "That would be amazing. Thank you."

"You'll want to do an introduction to the podcast first, in your own words as a Durango resident. When do you think you'll get started?"

Sue exhaled long and slow. This was becoming real, fast. She didn't even know how to use the equipment. Breathe, she told herself. The equipment would arrive tomorrow. Chase could give her a tutorial Wednesday night since he didn't have hockey. She'd have to learn all she could in the meantime. She could do this.

"I'll record the introduction this week, and we can record your episode early next week." Why was she making these promises? She should tell Kira she wasn't sure when she'd be ready. The fear of things moving too fast chilled her spine like cold water.

"Great, let me look at my calendar. How about Monday at five your time?"

"That works." Chase had hockey practice then, but she'd find a way to make it happen. Maybe Gabe would help. Not that he knew anything about podcasts.

"Great. In the meantime, build your network. Let everyone know about the podcast and when it airs. We need as many people in town listening as possible, and the faster you can grow the audience, the better the chance of success. I'm excited about this. Thanks for involving me."

Dear lord. She not only had to learn about podcasting, but she also had to get people to listen! A spark of excitement lit in the place where she'd expected dread.

She had a lot to think about, but another question kept scratching at her. "Kira, why is this project so important to you?"

Kira's laugh was sultry. "That, my friend, is a question for a long night and a good bottle of wine. Let me know if you run into any issues. I'm here to help."

As she said goodbye, Sue wondered what could be so personal that it would get Kira interested in Durango, Colorado. She needed to do a little more research on this woman, although she wasn't sure when she'd have the time.

Chapter 7

"Hello, and welcome to the Save the Animas Valley podcast. I'm your host, Sue Cleary. This podcast is about the facts, and the feelings, surrounding the Worth Winter Wonderland Resort and Theme Park proposed for the north end of the city in the heart of the Animas Valley." Sue sat at a small table in Gabe's office, headphones on, as she spoke into the mic.

Chase faced her and silently gave her a thumbs up. Her voice sounded calm and natural, even though she buzzed with excitement. Just two weeks ago, she would have been listening to a podcast, not making her own.

Sue couldn't have done it without Chase. He acted like starting a podcast was an everyday occurrence. Each time she spent hours trying to figure something out and wanted to give up in frustration, he'd waltz in and fix everything with a click of the mouse and a comforting smile.

She held on to his tranquility as they set up, tamping down the thrill that threatened to crack her voice. The podcast was a new adventure, a new life even, after so many years of everything being the same.

She'd spent hours writing and rewriting the introduction she now read, trying to sound concerned but balanced, inspirational but realistic. Residents of Durango and the surrounding area cared about this valley. Her job, with the help of her guests, was to draw a picture of how this development would change the regional landscape. The introduction wasn't long, just over four minutes, but it seemed like an eternity as she spoke.

"For those of us who live here, we understand that our home is a wonderland every spring, summer, winter, and fall. This morning I looked across our valley framed by the Rocky Mountains dressed in their fall attire of evergreen and flame with patches of aspens quaking gold. The jade river ran freely, and elk and deer shared pastures with horses and cows. This is my home, unmarred by a thousand-room hotel, fake snow, and a theme park that could never match the beauty that surrounds us now."

She ended the podcast by asking listeners to share it with friends and tune in to future episodes. She encouraged people to share their feelings and photos about the valley and the proposed development and gave the website address and social media accounts. Sue pushed the button to end the podcast and removed her headphones with shaking hands.

"Mom, that was great." Chase got up from his chair and fiddled with the equipment. The unfamiliar admiration in his voice pierced her chest and quickly spread its warmth. She'd worried her poetic words were a step too far. If Chase approved, then perhaps she'd done all right. She hugged the boy in front of her, a boy now larger than she. He gave her a quick hug back, something he hadn't done in a while.

"I'll take it from here," Chase said. "It will take a couple of days before it's up because of the review period. It will be a lot easier for you to load them in the future."

"Thanks, I'd like to watch what you do." While technical programs came naturally to him, she needed to learn the process. He wouldn't always be here, but today, she'd enjoy working with her son.

"Amanda, great to see you again," Sue said when Amanda walked into the coffee shop. Sue had set the appointment hoping for an update on the project. She also wanted to get to know Amanda, and perhaps find out where she really stood on the development.

"I've recorded the first podcast!" Sue couldn't contain her excitement.

"That's amazing! When does it go live?"

"Hopefully today. I'm recording an episode with Kira Sutton, the woman who wrote the *Durango Magazine* article on Monday."

"Did you know her organization helps preserve land all over the world? I looked her up online." Amanda practically bubbled with eagerness, reminding Sue again of a brunette Leslie Knope. She hoped the city realized what an exceptional employee they had.

She thanked Amanda for putting her in touch with the Sierra Club. The director shared Sue's concern about the development. She'd invited him to be a guest on the podcast.

Sue handed Amanda a flyer she'd made. "My boys thought it was ridiculous to have printed flyers, but I know people read the bulletin board in here. I tried to give them a few to post at school, but Chase, my youngest, just took a photo of it and said he'd put on Instagram."

"I'm glad you're doing this," Amanda said, taking the flyer. "Some of my friends are concerned about Winter Wonderland, and I'd be happy to share the information with them. Let me send you my personal email address." Amanda reached for her phone.

"You have separate email addresses?" That would be a pain.

"Yes. Things related to my job at the city are public information. Dozens of issues come before city hall each year, and there are always unhappy people on the losing side. I've got to protect my home and family from that."

"Are your city emails posted online?" Sue asked. That could explain why Amanda was so cagey about the development.

"They're not online, but anyone can ask for them as long as it's related to city business."

"Like the development?"

"Yes. There have already been requests for all communications by staff and elected officials regarding the development."

"You're kidding. If I request the mayor's emails about this, does he have to give them to me?"

Amanda nodded, and Sue tried to suppress her smile. The information might come in handy if the mayor didn't want to work with her. Amanda and Kira were giving her a crash course in local government. Sue thanked Amanda for her help.

"You bet. I spent ten years working for one of the rafting companies, so I've got a lot of friends interested in the Worth development."

"You were a river guide? My oldest son, Blake, spent several summers working for Raft Durango. He'd come home sunburned and exhausted every day, full of never-ending stories about the river and the tourists."

"I did guide some," Amanda said. "But I worked for the company year-round doing marketing, bookkeeping, and whatever else they needed."

"You were a bookkeeper? I used to be a CPA. Back before I had kids and we moved here." She loved these connections, rafting and accounting, that drew her closer to Amanda. Surely Amanda shared her concern about the development, despite her position at the city. "How long have you worked for the city?"

"Twelve years. I started in the parks and recreation department and worked my way up. I left the river guide company when I had my son. I needed a job with more stability."

"It's funny how kids change your life. I thought I'd always work." Sue looked at Amanda, the type of woman she thought she'd be. Instead, she'd turned into her mother, a stay-at-home mom whose life threatened to fall apart as soon as the kids left for college.

"It must have been wonderful to stay home with your kids."

"Yes, I was incredibly fortunate." Sue replied, feeling every inch of her privilege, yet still tasting a touch of regret for her lost career.

"I love my job, but I am a little envious," said Amanda. "You get to give everything to your kids. All I've ever wanted is for my kids to have a stable home environment. I made a lot of mistakes early on, but eventually I found the wonderful guy I'm married to now. He's Sarah's dad."

"When I was young, my career was my only focus. I never thought I'd get married and have kids. It's funny how life turns out sometimes." Sue had spent years focused inward on her family, and now this new door had opened. "It's nice to have this project to make new connections in town."

"I sure appreciate that you're taking the time to get involved in this. Sometimes it seems like the same three people who show up at council meetings are the only ones who care about what's happening in the city."

"It took reading about the development to get me involved, but I'm learning a lot. I'm enjoying this far more than I thought I would."

"Speaking of the article, you mentioned you were interviewing Kira Sutton on Monday. Could I sit in on that and see how it's done? I've never been part of a podcast before."

"Believe me, I'm no expert, and I couldn't do it at all without the help of my son, but I'd love to have you there." Maybe Amanda would participate. If Sue could get Kira and Amanda involved in a discussion about the development, people would love it.

That night at dinner, the entire family was home. Sue filled them in on her campaign against Worth Winter Wonderland. She bragged about how Chase had been the brains behind the podcast introduction and told them she'd lined up the first few interviews.

"Mom, I said I'd help." Chase slumped in disappointment that she'd scheduled the next podcast for when he wouldn't be there.

"I know, but between school and hockey, you're not always going to be around to help. I guess I can get dad to pinch hit for you."

That drew a laugh. For someone who owned a technology company, Gabe adopted new technology surprisingly late. This provided an endless source of amusement for the boys.

"Jaxson, what do you think?" she asked.

"Whatever makes you happy." He shrugged his shoulders.

She tried again, mentioning the Sierra Club and how she expected them to vote against the proposal. She got a nod from Gabe, but the boys didn't even look up from their roast chicken. A quick flash of anger hit her. She'd helped those boys with countless projects and always cared about how they felt. But as she looked at them scarfing down dinner, her frustration dissipated. This was her project. She cared about it, and that was enough.

"You boys do the dishes. I'm going to feed the horses," she said, rising from the table.

Making them clean up had new meaning tonight. She could transfer more of her chores to others, or even leave some undone. This small unwiring of her version of motherhood would give her more time for what came next. She could shed herself of her own expectations, and with that, she'd have to understand that her family might not always want to share in her excitement. She stepped into the barn, not leaving motherhood behind but embracing something new.

She had just fed the donkey a handful of oats when Gabe walked in. He looked tired, probably from all the travel. His dark hair seemed a little grayer at the temples, making the green eyes staring at her even brighter. She wished she could help him shed whatever burdens he carried. She remembered the last time he helped her feed the horses.

"Don't you be getting any ideas," she said but couldn't help smiling. He smiled back, his special smile, the one reserved only for her.

"I think I'm becoming an activist. You okay with that?" she asked.

"Sure, but I don't know anything about podcasts."

"When I talked to the mayor, he suggested I have you explain the project to me. He didn't think I could understand it. The words condescending jerk come to mind."

Gabe laughed. "I'm sure that went over well."

The donkey stuck his nose through the bars on the top half of the stall, looking for treats. Gabe opened the stall door to scratch the animal under his jaw and behind his long ears. The donkey turned his head sideways and leaned in, loving the attention. Just like with the boys, Gabe had the right touch.

"The mayor reminds me of your little friend there," she said. "A real jackass. The attorney who wrote the article on the development wants to cross-examine him during one of our podcasts."

"Chico here is more of a gentleman than the mayor. You should get that attorney to cross-examine the chamber CEO as well." He gave the donkey a final pat before leaving the stall.

"I don't understand why the chamber is even getting involved. It seems like the competition would hurt as many local businesses as it helps. Is there something I'm not seeing?"

"The mayor and Drew go way back. I think it was Drew who got him to run for office after he became chamber director. If the Worth Company joins the chamber at a high investment level, the board members will only hear one side of the story." He stood close to her, one arm slung across the top of a stall, his grin lighting her up inside.

"That's unfortunate," she said, staying on track. "I'd hoped they'd be a little more open-minded instead of just selling out. I still think public sentiment will be against the project." Except for Paula. And the supermarket cashier. Before she walked away, Gabe grabbed her belt loop with one finger and gently tugged her closer.

"Gabe, stop trying to seduce me. I'm talking business here. This is important to me."

"I love it when you talk business." He leaned forward to kiss her.

Had her career originally attracted him to her? She had lost that part of herself. He'd been supportive of her staying home, but a full-time mom might not have the same allure as someone more ambitious. Was that what Denver was about?

Doubts raced through her head, but her lips responded to his. His hand moved from her belt loop to her waist, pulling her close.

He was hers. A touch of jealousy added heat to the kiss. She pressed her long body into his, absorbing the jolt of electricity their closeness produced.

"Jesus! Is this what you guys do in here!" Chase was at the door.

"Mouth," Gabe said, giving him a sharp look.

"Sorry, I just didn't expect to walk in on this. That must be why Jaxson wanted me to come tell you guys."

"Tell us what?" Sue compensated for getting caught making out with her husband by putting on a stern voice.

"We're out of ice cream, so we're going to the store. I'll leave you two to, whatever..." He turned and sped out of the barn.

"You are getting me in trouble Gabe Cleary." She looked into his still smiling eyes.

"We've got at least thirty minutes before they come back." He took her hand and tugged her toward the feed room.

"I've got things to do, and I'm not doing it in the feed room again. Besides, the boys will be back soon."

"Fine." He dropped her hand. "But I want a rain check."

"Well, you know if you were home a little more often, there'd be a lot more opportunity." She'd meant to be playful, but she watched his face fall at the comment.

"I've been wanting to talk to you about that. I'm thinking about getting some office space in Denver. There's this company, MAPTech, and we've got some real potential for collaboration with our software."

"Office space? As in you'd spend even more time there?" The accusation in her voice echoed through the barn.

"It'd just be short-term, while we work things out."

Sue stared at him, the shock of his plan running through her veins like ice. At least her dad had waited until Sue left for college to leave her mom. Gabe had one foot out the door already.

Chapter 8

Sue woke to an empty bed and an email from Kira saying she'd be in Durango for Monday's podcast. She had combined it with a trip to several of her company's projects in northern New Mexico. First Amanda and now Kira, the first episode had quickly evolved from a wade in the pool to a cannonball. She would need Chase's help to turn the converted office into a real studio.

It excited Sue to have Kira show up in person, but it would have been so much easier for her to call in to the podcast. Whatever personal issue Kira had with the development must be big. Perhaps dinner and a bottle of wine would loosen the story.

A plan formed in Sue's head. She quickly emailed Amanda and let her know they'd record the podcast in person and have a celebratory, girls-only dinner afterwards. She didn't know where she'd stash the boys, but she needed them out of the way if she was going to pry secrets out of Kira.

When she told Chase about the in-person interview, he insisted they not just soundproof the room but get a better mic and a microphone sound shield. Happy to delegate, she turned her laptop and credit card over to him. He insisted on going through each purchase with her, and they ended up spending over four hundred dollars on equipment. A small price for quality time with her son.

She helped Chase hang blankets in the office in an attempt at soundproofing and rearranged the furniture to accommodate the podcast. By the time they recorded Monday's session, Gabe might actually need that office space in Denver. An odd satisfaction that she could create her own life out the empty space he no longer used settled in, accompanied by a tinge of loss. She clearly couldn't keep him from spending time in Denver, but she didn't have to sit around pining for him.

Happy with her work, she took a last look at the now transformed studio, then picked up the cleaning supplies. She stepped into the hallway and ran smack into Gabe, guilt jarring her as much as surprise.

"Whoa there," he said, grabbing her shoulders to steady her.

"Hey, sorry. I was just getting the studio ready. I'm afraid you won't be able to use your office for a while. Kira is coming to town on Monday to record the podcast. I invited her and Amanda over for dinner that night. Can you keep the boys busy?"

"Happy to. We can order pizza for everyone if you want. I'll even pick up some wine for you and the ladies."

"That would be great. Thank you." First Chase and now Gabe, if she'd known how much her family would contribute, she'd have tried something like this years ago. She'd created a whirlwind of activity in her life and stood at its center.

Sue parked in front of the tiny airport on Monday afternoon and went inside to wait for Kira. She'd looked up her photo online and was sure she'd recognize her long blonde hair and pretty features. What she didn't expect was how tiny she'd be, even in four-inch heels.

At five feet ten inches, Sue was almost always the tallest woman in the room, but this difference in height was ridiculous. Plus, the woman dressed big city in a formfitting black and cream checked suit, midnight silk blouse, and perfect makeup. It had probably been years since any woman in Durango had looked so fierce.

Kira's outfit wasn't practical, or even reasonable for Durango, but it made Sue want to try harder than jeans and a patterned tee. Kira looked commanding, smart, authoritative. Sue wanted the same. Next week she'd go shopping.

She screwed up her courage and walked toward Kira. "Hi, I'm Sue Cleary. Nice to meet you."

"Sue, it's great to meet you too. Sorry I'm overdressed, I had a meeting this morning and didn't have time to change before catching my flight."

"You look great, and we can add video to the podcast if you'd like." The second the comment left her mouth, she wished it back. Only one of them was camera ready.

"I don't think that's necessary. Thanks for meeting me here. I'm excited to see the site and learn more about you and Durango."

Sue drove Kira through downtown, past the train station and to the nearby Strater Hotel where Kira had reservations. One of Sue's favorite buildings, its American Victorian architecture had resulted in a stately building, like the mountains behind it. Packed with antiques, the lobby smelled like something from a bygone era, a combination of cedar and old silk.

Once Kira had checked in, Sue drove her down Main Street and showed her the town's western architecture, mingled with newer buildings. They passed an old school bus owned by one of the river rafting companies full of tourists returning from an afternoon trip. The crowd looked tired, wet, and happy, and most of them headed straight from the bus into the chocolate shop several feet away. Nothing about the town was slick, and fancy brand names didn't grace the stores, but it seemed to work just fine.

Restaurants, bars, clothing stores, and outdoor equipment companies lined the street in the picturesque heart of town. Sue pointed out a few art galleries and her favorite saloon. The everyday retailers, grocery stores, gas stations, and hardware stores were relegated to less expensive real estate outside the main tourist drag.

"It's gorgeous," said Kira. "Like a fairy tale."

"I always thought it was more like an old-time Western this time of year. The fairy tale comes in the winter when the world turns white. Lights and garlands hang from every building, and even the train wears holiday decorations."

"I'd love to come back then. It sounds wonderful."

"I'm glad you're here now. I can't thank you enough for the interest you've taken in our town and this project."

Sue turned off Main Street and onto the highway. The town fell away quickly, and the river and railroad tracks accompanied the road as they drove north. They rounded a curve, leaving town behind, and the high snow-capped peaks at the far end of the valley popped into view.

Sue pulled off the highway and then onto a dirt road, stopping in the same place she'd parked when she's seen the man here. The land in front of them held broad trees and low scrub from the tracks to the river. Beyond the river, crops decorated patches of land in squares of green, gold, and the matte brown of freshly tilled earth, stopping at the sharp ridge that rose from the valley's edge. This was the hundred acres Worth wanted.

Its beauty pulled at her. She couldn't imagine a huge hotel, fake hills covered in artificial snow, and theme park rides taking the place of this more natural beauty. She wondered what the woman beside her thought, but Kira had pulled out a pad and pen and was writing furiously, occasionally raising her head to stare at the land.

"Do you want to get out and walk around?" Sue asked.

Kira pointed to her stilettos and shook her head. "Next time."

When Kira finished with her notes, Sue turned the car around and headed back toward town until they reached the bridge that crossed the river. Staring at the cropland side of the project, Kira again scribbled in her notebook. Sue's knee jigged as she waited for her to finish writing. She wasn't sure whether to explain things or just keep quiet.

Eventually, Kira nodded, and Sue drove on. "This is a travesty," the woman whispered under her breath. Kira understood.

At the house, Sue led Kira upstairs to the office-cum-studio. They had decided to record the podcast as soon as Kira arrived, in case something went wrong and they needed a second go at it.

Two chairs sat close together in front of the mic, and Sue had placed another chair to the side of the table for Amanda. Close enough to observe, and even close enough to speak, if she chose. Three sets of headphones lay on the table. Sue reviewed the mechanics with Kira, feeling somewhat like an imposter since she had just learned this stuff herself.

Imposter or not, excitement ran through her. Anticipation and terror motivated her in equal measure.

They reviewed the questions she planned to ask one last time. Sue read the list, checking each item, while Kira summarized her answers. When they'd reached the second to last question, the doorbell rang, and they went downstairs to meet Amanda.

Sue invited them into the kitchen. With the podcast closing in, her throat seemed a little scratchy, so she poured them short glasses of water. She chugged hers down.

Almost unknowingly, she pulled a bottle of white wine from the refrigerator and poured an inch into her empty water glass. Seeing her, Kira swigged the last of her water and set her glass out for her own inch of wine. Amanda followed suit with a sly smile. They toasted, a call to arms.

After the wine, they made their way upstairs and took their places. Sue gave Chase's speech about the importance of silence. No rattling papers, tapping the desk or adjusting things. Then they began.

Sue spoke with the slightest tremor in her voice. She closed her eyes and conjured friends on the other end of the airwaves. She explained to them how she was afraid of losing what was best in the valley. The cadence of her words slowed, and she imagined she was talking to her favorite group of moms. Warmth seeped into her voice. The tremor faded.

She told the story of reading an article and riding her horse onto the ridge, where she stared at the valley, unable to imagine the river diverted, a snow hill in summer, a huge resort, and rides. She needed to know more, so she reached out to the city and to the author of that original article.

"Today, I'd like to introduce the author of that article, environmental attorney Kira Sutton, who is in town today to record this podcast."

"Thank you, Sue. For those of you listening today, I want you to know this the first time I've visited Durango, but I know this developer well." Kira's velvet voice shot a warning through the room and out across the airwaves.

Kira went through example after example that shocked Sue, despite her research. There was the golf course development in Spain where environmental promises were trampled, marring the coast. Of the supposedly guaranteed jobs, Worth had only delivered one tenth. An apartment project in New York spawned accusations of racism when the original tenants were evicted and replaced by those with more dollars and whiter skin. Florida properties bought at rock-bottom prices sold for ungodly amounts to Russian oligarchs the same year they raised the Worth name on a hotel in Moscow.

The trail of bankruptcies and bad deals enriched Worth. Incentives the Worth Company received, whether outright payments or tax refunds, took money from schools, roads, and public services to line Worth's pockets. They left communities without the resources to repair the damage of failed projects.

Every example Kira gave raised Sue's temperature a few degrees more. She looked at Amanda, whose large hazel eyes seemed flattened with shock. When Amanda returned her gaze, a spark passed between them. They were mothers and something, someone, threatened their home. There were other mothers out there. Sue would make sure they listened.

By the time Kira finished, she'd dropped a bomb, leaving the future almost too bleak to contemplate. Sue closed her eyes and pictured the lush fields and sparkling river she'd seen just hours earlier. The bomb hadn't dropped yet, not here anyway. Sue would provide hope.

She imagined speaking in every living room in town. "Listeners, that could happen here, but hasn't yet. I used to think it never could. When I first read Kira's article, I didn't think anyone in Durango would take the Worth Winter Wonderland application seriously. Then I learned some at city hall take it seriously indeed."

"Yes," Kira said. "Worth tends to approach city officials and local organizations that will support them first."

"That's right. A Worth Company representative gave a presentation to the chamber of commerce, and many there think it's a good idea." Sue imagined her friends listening and told them she was scared, especially after Kira's presentation.

She looked at Amanda as she explained how the people of Durango could make their voices heard before the city council voted on the project.

Amanda leaned forward, intent on the microphone. Sue sat back, encouraging her. Amanda spoke as if she'd been doing this her whole life. No tremor, just sincerity shining through.

"This is Amanda Payne, assistant city manager. I've lived in Durango my whole life. I know the community cares about the town and the environment, and I want you to learn the facts about this project."

She thanked Kira for her information and assured listeners more data would come when the city published the project documents on their website. Amanda looked at Sue and gave her a wink. "Finally, I would like thank Sue Cleary for creating this podcast to spread information and get people involved."

"Thank you, Amanda. I'd also like to thank Kira Sutton for joining us today. For those of you listening, please share the podcast with others in the community." Sue encouraged listeners to visit the Facebook site and share photos on Instagram. Then it was done.

The moment she clicked the button to end the podcast, a rush of emotion overcame her. It was like when she married Gabe, she was calm through the ceremony but afterwards couldn't stop shaking with an odd combination of relief that it was over and terror that she'd put something in motion that couldn't be undone.

Kira broke into a wide smile. "I think that deserves another glass of wine."

"Oh! My husband got us a bottle of champagne." Sue jumped up, no longer able to control the excitement she'd blanketed with calm while they were recording. She knocked over the microphone in her rush to usher the women downstairs. The public-facing conversation had ended. The private one, where she hoped to uncover the motivations of her partners, was next on the agenda.

Chapter 9

At the table on the back patio, the last of the day's sun highlighted the mountains. Sue struggled to pry the champagne cork from the mouth of the bottle, finally putting it between her knees for leverage.

"No! Let me," Amanda said, reaching for the wine. "I've had plenty of experience waiting tables all over Durango."

Sue sank into her chair and let Amanda battle the cork. The rush of excitement from the podcast drained away as she relaxed and surveyed the women with her. "We did good. It feels like we just started a revolution."

"I'm probably not allowed to be part of a revolution," Amanda said as the cork made a satisfying pop. "But it is part of my job to get the word out."

"You know, you're allowed to voice your opinion on issues as long as you're not doing so in your official capacity as a city employee," Kira said, legalese slipping into her language.

"I know, but in a town as small as this, most people can't see where that line is. I need to stay impartial."

"How do you do that if the city council isn't impartial?" Sue asked. The mayor had seemed one-sided in their meeting, even though he said he wouldn't decide until all the information came in.

"Well, the mayor doesn't have to be impartial," Amanda said. "He was elected to make decisions on behalf of the public, and my job is to provide them factual, unbiased information so their decisions will be impartial."

"And you have to go along with whatever they decide?" Sue asked.

"Yes, that's how it works. The less I reveal my personal feelings, the better, and not just about this issue, about everything, local and national. They need to trust me to give them accurate information. If I'm overly involved in politics, they'll think I have an agenda beyond the public good. Plus, I'd likely get fired."

"If that ever happens," said Kira, "I want to take on your lawsuit."

"They'd be smart enough to find other excuses for firing me." Amanda cocked her head to the side, clearly mulling over her words. "Maybe."

"Is it hard to work there? The mayor didn't seem to be a big follower of the #MeToo movement." His condescending tone still burned Sue's memories.

Kira's eyebrows rose, and Amanda's cheeks turned pink. Sue wished she'd handled the mayor's rudeness better. She'd probably think of the perfect thing she should have said six months from now, but she wasn't that quick in the moment.

It took Amanda a moment to answer. "I have to work with the mayor and council, but I don't work for them. They hire the city manager, and he oversees the city staff. I work for him."

"Mike has to be better than the mayor." Sue said. It surprised her when Amanda didn't immediately respond.

Kira leaned forward in her seat and gazed intently at Amanda. "How long has the city manager been in his position?"

"About six years. There was a different city manager under the last mayor."

"Do you have a split council?" Kira asked.

"Yes, I'd say it's pretty evenly split. Two of our council members are businessmen who side with the mayor. The other two, retired teachers, are more progressive and environmentally friendly."

Sue watched the two women, amazed at how quickly Kira was getting the lay of the land. She already knew things Sue would have never thought to ask on her own. The city had always seemed well-managed. When she had questions about something political, she asked Gabe. He'd probably love to listen in on this conversation.

Kira stayed focused on Amanda. "Would you say the city manager supports the mayor?"

Amanda looked uncomfortable but didn't shy away from the question. "It is his job to support all the council."

"Of course," Kira said. "But the mayor hired him. How was the city different before this mayor and manager?"

"There was plenty of new development in the past, but also less leeway with changing the rules to accommodate it. If you didn't build to Durango's code, you didn't build here."

"Got it," Kira said. "And since then, the focus has been on attracting new development?"

"The mayor prides himself on his job creation skills," Amanda said.

Kira's eyebrows arched appraisingly. "That's interesting, since Durango's economy has tracked pretty steadily with the nation's over the past twenty years, and unemployment rates haven't changed much since the mayor took office."

"How do you know that?" Sue jumped into the conversation. Where was Kira getting this information? How did she know so much more about Durango than she did? The knowledge gave her power.

"Most of it's on census.gov. It helps to understand the economy of a place, especially if you're coming in as an outsider." She looked at Amanda a little sheepishly. "I'm sorry about the interrogation. This case is important to me."

Amanda grinned. "That's okay, I'm used to it. And you're right, the mayor and my boss are good friends."

As Sue followed the twisting conversation, her mind caught an idea. Perhaps the mayor and Mike had more in common than a friendship. "Amanda, is Mike a chauvinist? Like the mayor?" Both women turned to Sue, surprised looks on their faces.

"I don't think he's that bad." Amanda stared at Sue for a long second before dropping her head. "He's more modern than the mayor. That helps."

Sue's stomach turned. She'd thought Mike was one of the nice dads. He greeted everyone with a smile and a pat on the back at hockey games. Looking at how vulnerable Amanda seemed, it hit her that Mike probably didn't treat Amanda any better than the mayor did.

"In some ways, Durango is still pretty much a man's world," Amanda said, sounding resigned. "We do have two women council members, which is nice, but the mayor's a man, all the county commissioners are men, the city manager and most of the department heads are men. This is the West, and as progressive as our community can seem, men still hold the power in town."

"Believe me, it's that way most places," Kira said. "Hell, half the reason I'm here is I'm up for a promotion against a handful of guys in my firm. I'm intrigued by this podcast idea. It's innovative and may help me stand out."

"Is that the reason you wanted to be involved in this project?" Sue asked. The question felt personal, but Sue wanted to understand what had been important enough to bring Kira to Durango.

Kira's face changed. Sue had gotten used to Kira looking fierce and in charge. Now she seemed to withdraw into herself.

"No, that's something else entirely." Kira's voice was soft, but she didn't explain.

Sue sat back, studying the two women. Amanda and Kira seemed entrenched in the same battle she'd left decades earlier. When would being smart and capable be more important than gender? These women could help Sue save the valley. She didn't need to pry into their stories to accept their generosity. The interrogations could happen on the air. Tonight, she wanted to celebrate.

She heard Gabe drive up and poured the last of the champagne into their glasses. Soon, he opened the porch door, a large pizza box in one arm.

"Hello, ladies. I thought you might be hungry." He set the box down in the middle of the table.

"Hi, hon. I'd like you to meet my friends, Kira and Amanda." Sue didn't know if they were friends yet, but she wanted them to be.

Small talk followed the introductions, and Sue went to the kitchen to grab plates, napkins, and a pitcher of water. She overhead Kira asking Gabe what he did for a living as she walked back onto the porch.

"I've got a company that develops software for government agencies."

Sue headed back to the kitchen for the red wine, glasses, and a corkscrew.

Returning to the porch, she heard Amanda tell Gabe they used his company's software at the city.

"It's a great product and provides a technical backbone for many of the country's small cities." Amanda said, explaining the product for Kira.

As Sue sat down, Gabe opened the new bottle of wine. He caught her eye as he twisted the metal opener into the soft cork, and she stiffened. She knew he didn't want to talk about his work.

"How did the podcast go?" he asked, turning the conversation in another direction.

"It went great. It feels like the start of something big." Sue looked at the women who already had big lives and big jobs. "At least to me."

Amanda and Kira agreed, filling Sue with satisfaction. Gabe poured the wine, then gave them a quick wave before escaping.

She watched him head to the barn to feed the horses, a solitary figure walking through deepening shadows. Something in her heart wanted to reach out to him and force him to her so she could forget all her doubts and anger about Denver. Instead, she turned back to her new venture.

The pizza box was open, and Kira and Amanda were deciding between the half with mushrooms and pepperoni and the half that was all veggies. Gabe had probably worried that someone was a vegetarian.

"Gabe's really great," Kira said.

"Yeah, and his company is impressive. It's the best in the industry. The finance department runs so much better now that we use it."

The conversation morphed from business to family. Forever the accountant, Sue's brain did the math while they talked. She had four kids, Amanda two, and Kira none. Married and divorced, Kira now had a long-term boyfriend. Their lives had led them down different paths, yet they had many similarities. Perhaps her connection with these women was a way back to who she'd been before accepting the full-time role of mother.

"Amanda, do you want to be city manager some day?" Sue asked.

Amanda, who'd been laughing at something Kira said, set down her wineglass and turned to Sue. "I don't know. Mike says I'd hate it."

"Why?" Kira asked.

"He says I'm good at operations. His role is more about maintaining positive relationships with the council, which he doesn't think I'm cut out for."

Kira let out a loud guffaw. "You are delightful. I can't imagine you not being able to maintain good relationships with anyone."

Sue opened another bottle of wine. "Yeah, that just sounds like the man trying to hold you down." She laughed at her comment as she poured the garnet liquid into crystal glasses.

"Well, I don't think my boss is going anywhere," Amanda said. "Besides, he shared his thoughts about me with the council, so I doubt they'd think I'm qualified."

"That sounds like a dog pissing on its territory." Sue laughed at herself again. She'd say anything with a little wine in her.

"Once, I actually overheard the city manager telling people I didn't want the top job. He said it was because I needed to spend time with my kids, but I clock more work time than he does. Unless you count having beers with the mayor."

Hearing the sudden edge in Amanda's voice, Sue couldn't help asking the next question. "Why don't you go work somewhere else?"

Amanda looked at her in surprise. "Oh, I'll never work anywhere else. That's why I don't challenge him when I overhear things like that. I have a great job. The absolute best." Her anger had vanished.

Sue looked at Kira, expecting to see the same surprise she felt, but her face was unreadable.

"When I first got to the city," Amanda explained, "I realized that it's not like a regular job where you have to worry about selling enough products or services to cover expenses. People have to pay their taxes, so everything I focus on makes Durango better. I get to work with some wonderful people, and it's stable. I have regular working hours, don't travel much, and have great benefits. Seriously, I think I have the best job in Durango."

"Except for your boss," Sue said. She couldn't help the cutting remark.

"Believe me, there are assholes everywhere," Amanda said.

"Here, here," Kira raised her glass. "But we can beat them and keep them from ruining this valley." They all drank to that.

Sue hadn't realized she'd been lonely. Not lonely exactly but missing something. In the last few days, she'd gained a project that was both exciting and important, and now she'd formed a bond with women she liked, respected, and wanted to spend more time with. She hoped she wasn't imagining this world grown larger.

The following morning, Sue unloaded the dishwasher while trying to figure out the next steps in the podcast. Mostly, she wished she'd had a glass or two fewer of wine, especially when Chase came bounding down the stairs. His loud footsteps and overwhelming energy aggravated her entrenched headache, and she was about to tell him to be quieter when the excitement on his face stopped her.

"Mom, it's really great! That guest you had on was fantastic. I didn't know any of that stuff, and I don't think anyone else does either. There's no way we can let that guy come here. We've got to get this out now! I want to get it edited before I go to school."

The rush of words was as unexpected as the wave of enthusiasm. None of the boys had been that excited about something she'd done since she'd planned a trip to Disney World ten years ago. She wanted to match his happy excitement, but the wine had left her foggy. She took a long draw of coffee, hoping that would help.

"Mom, are you listening?"

"Yes, Chase. I'm just moving a little slow this morning. I'm glad you liked it." She couldn't resist his smiling face and grabbed him in a hug, some of his excitement rubbing off on her.

He pulled away. "It's great. Can I have some breakfast? I want to get started on it right away."

She looked at her son. She wanted to sit on the back porch for a few minutes and drink her coffee, but how could she ask him to make his own breakfast when he'd helped her so much with her project? Before she decided what to do, Gabe came into the kitchen through the back door.

"I fed the horses." He looked from his wife to his son. "I feel like making pancakes this morning. How does that sound to everyone?"

"That's awesome," said Chase. "Can you make bacon too?"

"You bet, why don't you help me? Grab the bacon, eggs, and milk from the fridge."

Gabe had already taken care of the horses, and now he'd make breakfast. She hoped her gratitude showed in her glance and grin. Lucinda's photo flashed through her mind, but she shoved it away. Why had she ever doubted him? He gave her a wink, then took two frying pans from the rack above the kitchen island and got to work.

Sue slipped out of the kitchen and onto the back porch needing to plan her day. Once the podcast was live, she'd post it on Facebook then find ways to market it. The urgent need to start a list for the day pulled at her, but a comfortable chair and brain fog overruled instant action. Instead, she stared out at the mountains and let the cool, pine-scented air seep into her.

It had been late when Gabe volunteered to drive Amanda home and Kira to her hotel. Sue had started to clean the kitchen but ended up back on the porch. The barn and the mountains behind it were lit with starlight. It had been such a fun evening. They all mentioned how rarely they had long, tipsy conversations with other women.

There were still a few wine stains and pizza crumbs on the table, and they made her smile. Even with the dull ache at the back of her head, she sensed a new fullness in her life. Slowly, excitement took hold.

The aroma of bacon wafted out from the kitchen, and her stomach growled. She drank the last sip of coffee and walked into the kitchen for a refill, ready to take the next step into this new venture. Fortunately, she had an army of help. With Gabe picking up the slack, Chase frothing at the bit, and two new friends bringing their expertise to the project like bright lights of knowledge, the momentum felt unstoppable.

Chapter 10

"Decent job, but you need to bone up on the facts—your guests knew far more about the development and city process than you did."

Of the thirty-six people who had commented on the Save the Valley Facebook page, three comments came from the same person. That beauty was followed by a slightly more helpful one. "Your nervousness at the start of the program showed. Try these exercises." The troll had the audacity to link to a website listing fifteen ways to calm your nerves before a big presentation.

The final warned her to present both sides of the development in the future if she wanted to seem legitimate. Her frown deepened into a scowl. Who was this a-hole who called himself The Professor? Total jerk. At least she was doing something about the development, not commenting from the sidelines.

Troll aside, things were going well. The other commenters opposed the development, and Chase had told her that while only forty-two people listened to the introduction, five hundred and twelve had listened to the episode with Kira. He'd also shown her how to advertise the show on social media. She had decided to spend fifty dollars, but when he told her she'd need to spend more to build an audience, she upped it to two hundred. The more people who listened, the faster the word would spread.

The phone interrupted her thoughts. "Ms. Cleary, this is Carla Borelli from the City of Durango. The mayor would like to speak with you. Can you hold while I connect you?"

Well, that was a surprise. She'd been meaning to get back in touch with him to schedule him for the podcast, but she hadn't expected an unprompted call.

Maybe he'd act a little more respectful now that she'd started something people listened to. She agreed to hold.

As she waited, worry replaced confidence, and that sticky fear she'd done something wrong crept through her. He probably wasn't happy about the podcast, and he was the mayor, after all. This would not be a congratulatory call.

After way too long on hold, she heard clicking and then the mayor's voice. "Hello, this is Buddy. How can I help you?"

"Mayor, this is Sue Cleary. Um, you called me?" Weird so far.

"Sue, I listened to your recording, and I have to tell you I'm really disappointed."

She didn't respond. She wasn't a child, and if he was going to treat her like one, he needed to explain himself.

After an awkwardly long pause, he continued. "Now, Sue, I'm not sure why you felt the need to bring an outsider in to talk about our community. What she said was very one-sided, and it's going to give people the wrong impression."

"Mayor Travis, when I met with you, I invited you to speak on the podcast. I do hope you'll accept my invitation. That way you can present your side."

"Sue, right now we're just trying to get people information and not take sides. We have a whole team working on this. What that woman said is just her opinion. Some folks around here aren't going to understand that."

"Well, I think the people in Durango are capable of making up their own minds on this project." She wanted to add that since they decided he should be mayor, he might want to trust them. Besides, he had definitely seemed pro-development last week.

"I don't think you understand that if you start spreading misinformation and being negative, this developer might just go away. Then we wouldn't have any project to consider, and we'd lose jobs and money that could really help our city do great things."

Sue took a deep breath and gathered herself before she spoke. "I'm trying to be fair here, and I again invite you to come on the program and explain the issues as you see them. Later this week, Amanda Payne will be on the podcast to talk about the city process as the project moves forward."

"I'm not sure that's such a good idea. If this thing is going to be one-sided, then I don't think the city should take part. So far, you've just provided a bunch of negative information that people might take to be true."

"Do you think anything in the podcast wasn't true?" Her heart sank as she realized she hadn't actually researched the specifics of Kira's claims.

The mayor echoed her doubts. "Are you sure what that lady said is true? You don't want to disseminate fake news."

"Ms. Sutton is a well-known environmental attorney, and I don't believe she'd risk her reputation by presenting inaccurate information."

"Sue, I'm not sure you understand how tough the world is out there. People will say anything to get you to believe what they want. We don't have to worry about that so much here in Durango, where our politicians are just members of the community. I think your Ms. Sutton has a dog in this fight that you don't know about. Why else would a high-powered attorney spend her time on our little neck of the woods?"

That struck a chord. Kira had admitted she had a personal reason for getting involved but hadn't shared it with Sue. In fact, each time it came up, Kira changed the subject. At first, Sue had thought it wasn't her business, and hoped Kira would tell her when she was ready. But the mayor believed it was her business. At least the mayor's wanting to create jobs and revenue focused on the community. She needed to understand Kira's motives.

"Mayor, I promise I will do all the due diligence I can on this project. That's part of the reason I keep asking you to participate. The community needs to understand this development. Will you agree to speak?"

"You know, I think I'd rather have Drew Polowski from the chamber talk about this. Do you know Drew?"

"I do. So, you want me to have Mr. Polowski speak about your views on the project?" Why bring in another person when the mayor could address this himself?

"Sue, you are new to this sort of thing. Drew can talk to you about the facts of the project, including those your last guest left out. He can tell you about the good things this development will bring Durango. I'll let him know you're going to give him a call."

Again with the condescending language. Sue struggled to hold her tongue. Of course, if she chewed him out, he'd say she was hysterical. He had no trouble treating her like a child but refused to stand in the spotlight himself. Sure, she'd talk to the chamber, but from what her husband had said, they were completely biased. Talk about one-sided, they'd had a presentation from the developer's representative and felt that side of the story was plenty.

"Buddy, I'm happy to call him, although I'd still like you to be on the program." The hell with calling him mayor. If he was going to act like she was beneath him, she'd give him the same respect.

They said their goodbyes, and Sue hung up the phone. Frustration pulsed through her like a heartbeat, and she fought the urge to type a Facebook post chronicling their conversation. She wouldn't let her anger prompt her to do something harmful. Instead, she'd funnel her frustration into a to-do list. She grabbed a pen and the small notebook that was already on the desk.

1. Find out why Kira cares so much about this project.

2. Call Drew Polowski and let him know the mayor wants him to speak about the Worth development on the podcast.

3. Warn Amanda about conversation with the mayor.

She wasn't sure what to write for number four. There were other guests she wanted to invite, including the developers. She'd ask for Mr. Worth but would probably end up with some lackey. There were a million other things she needed to do to keep building momentum, but she really just wanted to scream at someone about how badly the conversation with the mayor had gone.

She couldn't believe she'd voted for him multiple times. He'd seemed like a nice guy, the kind you wanted showing up at business openings and leading the parade. Now that she knew him a little better, she couldn't believe a guy like that represented Durango.

The entire council was white and middle-aged, or older, and mostly male. Durango might be a small town, but it was full of interesting, creative people. Most of the city council didn't represent this. Could she trust them to build a community her children would want to live in?

A new frustration settled into her chest. She wanted more from her town. Durango was a great place to live and raise kids, but it could be better. It could treat its citizens better. After all, the mayor talked to her that way when he knew and respected her husband. How did he treat other people? How would he treat the busboys in the local restaurants or, heaven forbid, their wives and mothers? Durango needed to be a better place than that. The problems expanded beyond Worth Winter Wonderland.

The development would occupy most of her time for the next ninety days, possibly more. But maybe she needed to stay involved in community issues beyond that. Frightening and exciting, she wished she could talk about this new idea with Gabe. But he was back in Denver. She looked at her list but decided not to write *discover the real reason Gabe spends so much time away* for number four.

Instead, she emailed Kira. She let her know about the mayor's call and how he wanted to know why she was so involved in the project. Then she left a message for Amanda, asking for a return call.

The phone rang ten minutes later. Kira.

"Hey, Sue. I'm still in New Mexico. I was going to fly home out of Albuquerque tomorrow, but I've changed my flight. It's just as easy to drive back to Durango and fly home from there. Is that okay with you?" The voice was still sultry and low, but Sue could hear concern as well. What was going on? Kira didn't seem like the vulnerable type.

"I'd love to have you," Sue answered. "If you want to stay through Friday, you might be able to sit in on Amanda's podcast. We're recording it at three."

"Sure, it'd be great to see you again."

It unsettled Sue that Kira wanted to come back to Durango so soon. Perhaps the mayor was right and her personal reason for being involved in the project was a big deal.

"Okay, I'll see if I can get a room in the hotel."

"You're welcome to stay here."

"I'll take you up on that, and I'll bring the wine this time."

Sue crossed out the first item on her list. At the end of number three, she added an ampersand and wrote "see if Amanda can stay for wine after the podcast. Kira needs to tell us something."

Two days later, Sue, Amanda, and Kira crowded around the small table near the microphone. Sue started the podcast by thanking everyone for listening and letting the audience know that, so far, over eight hundred people had listened to the first episode. She didn't tell them she'd now spent four hundred dollars advertising to grow the audience.

Sue worried Amanda would be nervous. She'd let it slip that her boss suggested she not go on the program. Amanda had reached out to the city attorney, who confirmed that she couldn't pick and choose who she showed up for. If outside groups asked for a city representative to speak about the public process, someone needed to respond. Everyone had to have equal access to the information. According to Amanda, Mike still wasn't happy, but the lawyer didn't give him a choice about her participation. Sue hoped Amanda wouldn't face any repercussions.

Amanda performed like a pro as she calmly walked the audience through the process and even took a few questions via the Facebook page. She mentioned how elected officials needed to understand the public's view of the development. She explained how and when people could let their voices be heard and talked them through the city website which now had a special page for Worth Winter Wonderland. All the documents the city had on the project were available online.

Sue couldn't help feeling proud of Amanda. She was far more professional than the mayor, chamber president, or city manager would have been.

"One of the best ways to get involved," Amanda said into the mic, "is to let the city council know how you feel."

"Do phone calls, emails, or social media work best for contacting council members?" Sue asked.

"It depends. For dialogue, in person and phone are usually best. If you're part of a group of people with questions, elected officials often attend local forums. I'm also happy to provide factual information to any group with questions."

That comment had to be aimed at the mayor and city manager. Sue gave Amanda a thumbs up.

Kira joined the conversation, asking Amanda several pointed questions about what the developer had provided so far, the information still to come, and when they should expect it. Using her silky voice to full effect, she thanked Amanda for putting the documents online for community members to review. "That is a refreshingly transparent move by the city."

It was a feel-good way to end the podcast, and Sue hoped Amanda's performance would help the mayor and Drew realize what a great employee they had. In one more nod to the mayor, Sue announced that her next guest would be Mr. Drew Polowski, the president and CEO of the Durango Chamber of Commerce. She'd snagged three important interviews in a row. The podcast was developing into quite the little venture. Satisfied, she clicked the button to end the recording. Only one task left for the day, figure out the personal reason behind Kira's involvement.

Chapter 11

Gabe had volunteered to pick up barbeque for dinner. Sue wondered if guilt made him do it. She'd seen yet another text from Lucinda on his phone. She grabbed the three bottles of wine Kira had brought, clanging them together more violently than she'd planned, and took them to the porch where Kira and Amanda waited.

Sue watched Gabe through the glass door, offset from the crowd of boys who had shown up for dinner before the big high school football game. He looked lonely, like an outsider in his own family. He must have sensed her gaze and glanced her way. The longing she'd seen in his eyes shuttered, and he gave her a crooked little grin before his attention turned to a peal of laughter from the boys. Had she imagined his unease? She turned back to her friends.

The women opened the wine and toasted the second episode, then dug into plates filled with barbeque, coleslaw, potato salad, and cornbread. Sue struggled between asking Kira about her involvement in the project and giving her space to bring it up on her own. She let the conversation wander, content in the circle of budding friendship.

"So, what got you involved in this project?" Amanda asked.

"Sue has asked that question also," Kira's attention beamed onto Sue. "You deserve to know the truth, because while I think this project is important, I'm usually not involved at such a grassroots level."

Kira's voice slowed, as if the words didn't want to come. "This isn't a story I've told many people." She looked at each of them and then turned to her glass again as if searching for courage. She took a long sip. "Can I trust you to keep this information confidential?"

Sue nodded. Instead of agreeing, Amanda stared boldly at Kira with eyebrows raised. Kira noticed and sat up a little straighter.

"I promise it has no legal bearing on the case. It is completely personal," Kira said to Amanda.

"Then I will not betray your secret." Amanda raised her glass.

"I'll drink to that," said Sue. The combination of tension and red wine left her flustered. She didn't want to lose this glimpse of friendship mixed with ambition so different from her ordinary life. "I feel like we've formed some sort of secret society and should take a blood oath of secrecy." Sue regretted the odd, blurted words the second they left her mouth.

Kira laughed. "I'm fine if we just toast and promise to tell each other the truth, although I'm open to something more barbaric if you think it's important."

"I go for wine over blood every time," Amanda said, tilting her already raised glass. "Maybe it's the excitement of the podcast, or maybe it's the booze, but I feel like we're at the beginning of a special friendship."

That was exactly how Sue felt! Why had she mentioned a blood oath? Everything she wanted to say came out strange. Perhaps she'd spent too much time around teenagers, or it had been too long since she'd had a job. She tried again. "Thank you for being a part of this with me. For the first time in a long time, I feel like I'm working on something important."

Sue and Kira smiled at her, but they didn't say anything. Why would they? They both had big jobs and probably did important work all the time. Her thoughts ricocheted between the success she'd achieved so far and concerns she hadn't really done anything yet.

Kira dipped back into her story, relieving Sue of the awkwardness of the moment. At least she couldn't say anything ridiculous while the other woman talked.

"It's been a couple of decades since I was at Brown, but an experience there drives my interest in this development. I thought I'd left it behind, as the mistake of a stupid college girl. Recently, with all the stories in the news about sexual assault, it's been haunting me more and more."

As she began her story, Sue saw the earnest girl she must have been. Kira warned the story mirrored others they'd probably hear. She had felt special after a popular boy asked her on a date. She even had a beer at the frat house that night, despite being straitlaced and afraid of getting kicked out of school. She didn't want to seem out of place. Her date returned to the keg and his friends, leaving her to nurse her beer and watch him from a corner.

"After fifteen minutes alone, I decided to leave. He said he had something to tell me first." Kira swallowed, then shook her head and lowered her eyes. The tension at the table had grown thick, and Sue and Amanda exchanged a wary glare.

"I let him lead me into a bedroom. He told me I was beautiful, and he kissed me. I kissed him back, at first. I'd dated a couple of guys in high school, but college had been lonely. When he started toward the bed, I told him I had to go. Then he picked me up and stumbled there anyway. He crushed me when he fell on me. I told him 'no' over and over until he covered my mouth with his hand. I bit him, and he called me a bitch. He covered my mouth again, more carefully this time. When his other hand moved south, it scared me enough to fight my way out from under him. He told me to relax and came for me again. I slapped him as hard as I could and told him that if he raped me, I'd go the police and ruin his life." She shuddered.

Kira took a long draw of wine, emptying the glass, before continuing. "The threat to his career stopped him. He called me a bitch again and said I wasn't worth it. Then he left the room."

Kira stopped talking. Sue had been in that room with her, and it took a moment to return to the safety of the back porch. She looked at Amanda, who had silent tears rolling down her cheeks. Returning her gaze to Kira, Sue saw how tiny she really was. Her personality, authority, and that silky voice usually filled a room in a way that made her appear far larger than her petite frame. This story left her small.

"I'm so sorry," said Sue.

"I've never been more scared. I was so afraid he'd come back and try again, maybe with one of his friends. You hear those stories. I stood at the door shaking and listening until I thought he had gone. I left the house like a ghost."

Kira said it took days before she left her dorm room and convinced herself to get over it. If she flunked out, he'd really win. Her preoccupation with doing well in school became an obsession.

"Anger is an incredible motivator." Kira sat back, and Sue figured the story had ended. She and Amanda glanced at each other, and Sue took a breath, readying a comment.

Kira spoke first. "He was in almost all of my classes, but I hardly spoke with him for the next two and half years. It was torture, especially when he was the teacher's pet. He could be so charming, but I'd seen what that charm could turn into. I blamed myself for getting into that situation, drinking, going into the bedroom, kissing him."

Kira got up, walked around the table to the bottle of wine and refilled her glass, still talking. "The happy ending is that I got my revenge. He always bragged about going to Yale Law. His father and grandfather had gone there, and with his connections, grades, and internships, he thought it was a sure thing. It wasn't." Kira sat, her lips curling into a smile.

I wrote an essay about my experience with him in my law school application, explaining both the necessity and the shortcomings of harassment laws. I didn't use his name in the essay, but I made it to Yale. He didn't."

Stories like this rarely had a silver lining. Kira might be small, and Sue had noticed her hand tremble as she poured the wine, but she was tough. A heavy sigh turned Sue toward Amanda. She was still crying. Amanda brought her wineglass to her lips with shaking hands. Sue thought the story was terrible, but she was proud of Kira for besting the guy. Amanda seemed stuck in the hurt part.

"Before today," said Kira, "only my ex-husband and my boyfriend knew about this. It's honestly not something I've thought about a lot over the years. Until recently. I was so young then, and today my forty-one-year-old self hurts for that girl. He probably behaved like that over and over, leaving a trail of scared, self-conscious women in his wake."

"Fucking bastards." Amanda's voice shot across the table. "They never pay." The tears had stopped, but her red eyes and blotchy skin remained. "I'm so tired of this disgusting behavior. I swear every woman has a similar story."

Sue didn't, but this didn't seem like a good time to bring that up. She could imagine herself in the same situation, and she worried about her boys and raising them right. Even before #MeToo, she had talked to them about the importance of consent.

"So, here's the part that no one but me knows," said Kira. "This story is connected to Durango. When Brett Kavanaugh made it to the Supreme Court and all the #MeToo stories came out, it triggered something. I started wondering what had happened to the guy back in college who tried something with me. It turns out that he's been at the Worth Company for years."

The words crashed down on Sue, making it hard to breathe. This was way more personal than she had imagined. She struggled with the right and wrong of Kira's decision. It wasn't illegal, and Kira was the one who started this whole thing. Sue probably wouldn't even know about the development without Kira's article in *Durango Magazine.*

Amanda spoke first. "I don't have any problem with why you're involved in this project. I don't even need to know why. It's none of my business, and it's no one else's either. You have no reason to explain your motivations." She paused and refilled her wineglass. "Thank you for sharing your story. I know how hard that can be."

"I can tell," said Kira. "This seems like a safe space for talking."

"Believe me, I've got more stories than we have time for," Amanda said.

"You know," said Sue, breaking into the conversation. "It's none of the mayor's business why you're involved in the Worth development."

"Of course not," said Amanda. "Did he tell you it was?"

"He told me I needed to understand Kira's motivations since she wasn't from here."

"Someone should ask him about his own motivations." Amanda crossed her arms.

"Is that an insinuation?" asked Kira.

"I'm not aware of anything in particular. I'm just surprised by his level of involvement."

"I wish he were a little more involved," said Sue. "He won't even come on the podcast. He had me invite the chamber director instead."

"He's involved. He's just pulling the strings from behind the stage," Amanda said. "There's no way the head of the chamber would do the podcast if the mayor hadn't asked him."

"Doesn't the chamber represent the business community, not the mayor?" Sue asked.

"The mayor and the chamber president have a special relationship. Besides, there are hundreds of businesses here, and less than one-third are chamber members."

Kira jumped into the conversation. "The chamber's board decides whether the chamber supports the development, not the mayor. Let's find out if the board has voted on it yet. The president wouldn't be able to take a position on it, on air, without board approval."

"Gabe is on the board. I'll ask him about it."

"That might be useful," said Kira.

Using her husband to influence the chamber board hadn't occurred to Sue. Would he be willing? It was one thing to agree with her over dinner, and yes, the development was close to their home and would ruin their peaceful life. But she'd never asked him to intervene like this before. He'd sponsored the boys' sports teams and donated to school fundraisers, but using his influence instead of his money might be different.

Denver. Would he be around even if he agreed to help? He was leaving again in the morning. She looked at her companions. "I'm sure he'll help when he can. He travels a lot for work."

The conversation lulled. Sue's mind sped a hundred directions at once, flipping from Gabe and his travels to the mayor's over-involvement in the project, to Kira's revelation about harassment. She could have been raped. It happened so many years ago, yet clearly it still affected her. And Amanda's tears. She must have been through something similar.

Kira rescued Sue from her thoughts. "Amanda, has the mayor met with Worth Company?"

"Yes. When the developer's rep was in town to meet with the chamber board, he also met with the council members." Her face reddened before she added, "and I've overheard Mr. Worth himself calling the mayor."

"That's probably worth investigating," Kira said.

Sue watched realization dawn on Amanda's face, followed by indignation as she straightened in her chair. "I will not spy on the mayor. We have a public process that I need to follow. I am a city employee."

"I'm so sorry, that's not what I meant," said Kira. "I never want to put you in a position that makes you uncomfortable. I meant it was something I need to look into."

The trust in the room had stretched. Sue wouldn't let it break. "We've shared so much tonight. I wish I could explain how much this means to me. Kira, thank you for telling your story and for being involved. I shouldn't have doubted you."

Kira thanked her. "I've had this rage building inside me. Sharing the story turned down the fire a little bit."

"Hopefully not enough that you'll stop helping!" Sue said.

"Not a chance." Determination laced her smile. "I have a dog in this fight, and I'll be here until the end. Besides, when I think of plopping a fake outdoor experience into this beautiful valley, it makes me furious."

"Me too," said Sue. "I hate what this guy wants to do to our valley."

"Agreed," said Amanda, raising her glass once again. "And like Kira's confession, my opinion on the project needs to stay at this table."

They clinked glasses and drank, and Sue stood to open another bottle of wine. The awkwardness had retreated.

"I grew up here and stayed here because I can't imagine a better place to raise kids," Amanda said. "Given Mr. Worth's track record, I'm worried about the development going into bankruptcy. We don't need a broken down, decaying behemoth haunting our valley for the rest of our lives. I need you to stop him. That's my secret confession."

Kira laughed. Sue loved how the throaty sound brightened the dark night. The bonds of trust and friendship strengthened again.

"Okay, your turn," said Kira, looking at Sue. "What confession are you going to share with us tonight?"

"I don't really have any stories. My life has been pretty boring compared to you two."

The moment the words left her lips, she cringed. What bigger confession was there? Her life was small, boring. She had never wanted it to turn out that way. She'd had so much ambition as a young woman and wanted more than anything to make something of herself.

Now here she was, fifty-one years old, sitting on her comfortable back porch with two women who'd made different choices. They shaped the world for their communities every single day. She had missed that part of life. Her chest closed in on the nothingness. She panicked when the first tears came, but she couldn't stop them. Damn it, she had nothing to cry about, but the tears came anyway, ugly and making her gasp for air.

Kira and Amanda jumped out of their chairs and hurried to her. Kira kneeled beside her while Amanda stood above her, rubbing her back.

"Hey, it's okay," said Kira. "You can tell us what's wrong. We're here for you."

"Nothing's wrong," Sue forced the words out between sobs. "There's absolutely nothing wrong." She dragged herself back together, using her napkin to wipe the tears from her face. "Please, sit. I'm fine."

They returned to their seats, but concern remained on their faces. She had to say something, but it embarrassed her to explain her tears. "I'm sorry," she finally said. "I've put a damper on the evening."

"That's no problem," said Kira. She got out of her chair again and reached for the wine. Once everyone's glasses were filled, she sat back down and looked at Sue expectantly.

"I'm sorry, there's really no reason for my outburst. I don't have anything deep to share. You both have these big jobs and do important work every day. I don't have that." Sue's voice faded. "I always thought I would."

"Sue, you are raising four boys. You have a loving husband and a beautiful home. You have done important work every day of your life. Now you've volunteered to put much of that aside to lead a project you're passionate about. Don't sell yourself short." Amanda's compassion tore a new sob from Sue.

"You've started a podcast," Kira said. "You've already got lots of listeners. You confronted the mayor. I think you're amazing."

Their words were a balm, even if they didn't reach the fears too deep to mention. She was proud of raising her boys, but worry about the future still battered her. When the boys were gone, would she lose everything the way her mom had? She shook the thoughts from her head. She needed to concentrate on the women in front of her. She'd throw herself into these new friendships and shoulder the responsibility of stopping the Worth Winter Wonderland. She'd leave her worries about tomorrow for another day.

Just then, Gabe opened the door to check on them and her heart broke all over again. She had to talk to him tonight.

Chapter 12

After Amanda's husband picked her up and Kira went upstairs to bed, Sue attacked the mess she and her friends had made and the one the boys had left behind. Everyone always expected her to clean up. By the time she finished cleaning, her anger had reached the boiling point.

She sank into a chair, and wine-fueled emotions swirled around her. Was Gabe having an affair? Confronting him tonight would start a war in her marriage, yet somehow that prospect enticed her. She could make something happen instead of passively waiting.

She rose, buoyed by a night of too much alcohol and overpowering emotions. Armed with those unfortunate weapons, she climbed the stairs.

Curious and not accusing, she'd start by asking him about the work taking him to Denver. She'd let him know she was interested in the business and ask the questions she'd come up with over the past weeks and months as his trips became more frequent and longer.

Gabe looked up the moment she entered the room. His benign gaze turned questioning when she banged the door she'd meant to close quietly. The planned, logical questions deserted her.

"Are you having an affair?" The accusation in her voice made her want to throw up, especially when she saw the instant shock on his face. She hadn't meant to start this way.

"Of course not. Why would you ask that?" he said, his voice a harsh whisper.

She could have responded with the truth, told him she loved him, and didn't want to lose him. She could have told him the time he spent away from home scared her. "You've been gone so much lately that I can't figure out if it's business or your dick keeping you away!" Where had that come from? She didn't talk like that, yet the words had spewed from her mouth.

"Shh. Be quiet, you're drunk." He jumped out of bed and stepped toward her, then stopped and stared like he wondered what to do next. "I'm not having an affair. I wouldn't do that."

He looked so uncomfortable. Maybe that's what guilt looked like. "Liar. It's been proven that most men have affairs." she said in her ugliest voice. Calling her husband a liar was like stabbing herself in the heart.

Regret tasted like metal on her tongue. She'd seen his face turn from shock to anger. At any point, she could have stopped. But she didn't. "I always knew this was going to happen. You're like every other guy out there, who uses his partner until it's time to upgrade to something better."

"I'm not going to put up with this, and I'm not going to have you wake up the whole house with baseless accusations." He walked into the closet and pulled on sweatpants and slippers.

She should have admitted she was drunk and gone to bed. Instead, her arsenal of words almost empty, she called him an asshole, accused him of turning her in for a newer model, and repeated that she'd always known this was going to happen.

"What the hell is going on?" He looked at her for a minute, but she had no answer. Then he slid past her and into the hallway, closing the door almost silently.

Hours later, a shaft of morning sun assaulted her pounding head through the window. It hurt to get out of bed, but she made her way to the bathroom and splashed water on her face. She was sick with regret, but the kids and the horses needed breakfast. And she had to figure out if an apology was going to be enough.

She pulled on clothes and went to the kitchen where the kids were already wolfing down cereal. She found a note on the kitchen counter from Gabe. He'd left for Denver and wouldn't be back for two days. Not that after last night he'd want to come back at all. She tried to keep her face blank and started the coffee, then kissed each boy on the top of the head before leaving for the barn. She told herself they didn't notice anything was wrong. They didn't notice she was shattered and afraid of the things she'd said.

The horses wouldn't sense anything either, and better, couldn't ask questions or engage in conversation. Talking just might be that final glass straw that fractured her into a breakdown.

She threw hay into the stalls and poured grain into buckets. The animals nudged her out of the way as soon as she finished. She didn't know why her eyes were leaking. They did that in the morning sometimes, now that she was older, especially when it was windy. The air in the barn was still.

She leaned back against one of the stalls and slid down until she sat in the cool dirt. Last night she'd said everything that she always wished her mother had said to her father. She'd fought her mother's battle against the wrong man.

But Gabe was gone too much. She tried to reconcile her justification with the hurt and anger on his face. By the end, he'd looked at her with pity, and she understood she broke something in him, in how he saw her. She had felt self-righteous then. She'd hurt him the way he'd unknowingly hurt her. It was a short-sighted win.

Had last night started the demise of their relationship or just sped it up? A quarter of a century was a long time to be married these days, and it felt like there were more than statistics against them.

As a girl, she'd been weaned on romance novels and fairy tales, believing in happily ever after. She'd sat on the landing above the foyer, legs between the banister spindles, when her mother's book club met. They couldn't see her from the formal living room, but the acoustics were perfect for hearing every word and giggle.

It was there she'd learned about love and romance, listening to the women talk after reading *The Far Pavilions* and *Bloodline*, epic romances where love triumphed. She couldn't wait to sneak the books from her mother once they'd been read and discussed at the monthly meetings.

She had learned about sex as well, not just between the pages of a beloved book, but from the personal stories she overhead from her hiding place. Mousy Mrs. Brown talked about sex in the kitchen, or once in the car after parents' night. She had spared her friend Janie this revelation about her mother, but she'd never looked at Mrs. Brown again without blushing.

Her last summer of listening, she was twelve and had already been given the talk, but that didn't compare to the book club education. One month, the last month for Sue, they read *The World Is Full of Divorced Women*, a title impossible to forget.

The meeting started with the women talking about the sex in the book, and the many affairs the main character enjoyed. It had shocked Sue to hear Mrs. Anderson say she was jealous of the main character's sex life. She'd said she'd only had sex with her husband, so how did she know if it was good or not? That question fell far outside the ideal of love and marriage that twelve-year-old Sue believed in. Then the conversation turned to divorce.

Sue had known two kids in her class with divorced parents, but the book club ladies talked about lots of couples with troubled marriages. The dad of a boy in her math class who had left home and gotten an apartment. A mom who hid her bruises but wouldn't leave. A husband having an affair with a waitress at Applebee's whose wife had thrown all his clothes onto the lawn. Sue heard her mother's voice say the couple was trying to work it out.

Sue hadn't wanted to listen anymore. This wasn't what love was supposed to be like. She left her perch and crawled toward her room but stopped before she was out of hearing range. She sat with her back against the wall, stories about the families of her friends falling apart assaulting her. It seemed wrong to listen, but the sad stories had an uncanny pull.

She had convinced herself to head to bed when the ladies started saying their goodbyes. Then she heard Mrs. Holly ask her mother if she could stay a few minutes. Mrs. Holly was the most glamourous mom Sue knew. Sue babysat for them at least once a month and knew Mrs. Holly better than most of the book club moms. She still looked like the cheerleader she once was, with long blonde hair, big blue eyes, and Barbie's body. Her husband had, of course, played football and had the dark, swept back hair and chiseled jaw of a Hollywood actor. Mrs. Holly had always talked more about romance than sex at book club meetings, of walks along the beach in Malibu and the night of her school prom when she had first promised to become Mr. Holly's wife.

As soon as her mom had shut the door on the other ladies, Sue heard Mrs. Holly crying. Sue crept back to the landing. Her mom made the same cooing noises she made when Sue scraped her knee or came home from school crying because of one thing or another. Sue heard Mrs. Holly say she was getting a divorce. It seemed impossible. They were the storybook couple.

That was the first time Sue had understood the difference between books and life. Mr. Holly was having an affair with his secretary, and he had fallen in love with her. Mrs. Holly said the secretary was pregnant. The fairy-book love story had ended, but what came next was worse.

Mrs. Holly told her mom that she didn't know what she was going to do because she had never worked and didn't have any skills. Sue's mom told her to hire a good attorney to make sure she got child support and alimony. How did her mom know about stuff like that? All she had ever done was stay home and be a wife and mother. Sue panicked before remembering Aunt Linda had gotten a divorce. That explained it. That's when Sue went to bed. She didn't want to learn anything else.

It had taken hours to fall asleep that night. The shift in perspective was too much to process. She wished she'd never listened in on book club, hadn't learned the one marriage she and her friends aspired to was mortally flawed. This wasn't the way things were supposed to go. In fairy tales and books, a woman found the man she would love forever, who would love her back, without worrying about alimony or how to afford the kids. She certainly shouldn't have to worry about the love of her life having sex with someone else, making a baby, and leaving.

The fading hope for the future that swept through that twelve-year-old girl hit Sue again on the floor of the barn. At fifty-one, she hadn't learned anything. Once upon a time, Sue's story had been the fairy tale. She met her prince charming when she wasn't looking for him and lived happily ever after, with a loving family and a wonderful home. But happily ever after ends. The kids leave, the flame fades. Whatever was next wouldn't be pretty.

Once the Hollys divorced, it had seemed like marriages fell apart everywhere she looked. The dads remarried more often than the moms, often to younger, prettier women. Sue left her fantasies of romance behind and began toughening her skin. She forged her own way instead of waiting for a man to sweep her off her feet and take care of her forever.

After that night at book club, she had watched her parents more closely. Her dad worked hard and made business trips. She felt a pang as she thought about her last few years of high school when her father started traveling more and more, a familiar scenario. By the time her parents' marriage ended in divorce, Sue had decided to never rely on a man.

She got up from the floor, head aching and hips stiff from sitting so long, but anger pushed aside regret. How had she repeated her mother's life? It was the one thing she had promised herself not to do. At least she had built up enough of a nest egg from when she worked so she wouldn't end up with nothing. The way her mother had.

Her dad had waited until she left for college to divorce her mom, so if history was repeating itself, she still had a few years left. She'd use them well, starting by stopping that goddamn development.

Chapter 13

When Sue returned to the house, Kira stood in the kitchen with a cup of coffee. Her packed bags lay on the floor. They spoke for a few minutes, both a little worse from the wine. Last night Sue might have shared her turmoil hoping to straighten it out, but the morning light focused her on more practical things.

Once Kira left, Sue postponed working on her list until she'd taken care of the garden and put in a load of laundry. The penance for her bad behavior gave the aspirin time to kick in. Surely, the alcohol caused her upset stomach and not the shame of attacking Gabe. That, she pushed down each time it wanted to erupt.

When she finally sat at her desk, she called the head of the chamber first. Although he'd agreed to the interview, he hadn't scheduled it. They set the date for Monday afternoon, but he told her he wanted the interview conducted in his office. Sue spent fifteen minutes trying to convince him that the sound quality wouldn't be good enough. She compromised by agreeing to visit his office that afternoon with her audio engineer. If he okayed it, they'd record in Drew's office, if not, Drew would come to her house. She texted Chase after the call to see if he was available to meet her at the chamber that afternoon.

She spent several hours editing the prior night's recording, then uploaded it. Chase had taught her the basics of sound editing, but it probably took her five times as long as it would have taken him. Not that she was moving at normal speed.

The day finally improved when she heard the recording. It was good. Despite the mayor's fears, the tone was factual and informative. Amanda's explanation gave people a way to get involved. While Kira's comments leaned anti-development, interviewing the chamber president would provide balance.

She sent the podcast link to her email list and uploaded it to social media. The second she'd pushed the buttons, she panicked, afraid it wasn't ready, wasn't good enough, or that she'd made some mistake. It was too late to pull the information back.

She'd done so many things wrong over the past twenty-four hours. She wished she was smoother and more natural with Kira and Amanda. Her part of the conversation had been awkward, like she was trying too hard. Not to mention the blowup with Gabe. As frightening as it was, the podcast made up for that, at least a little. It was her chance to make a difference.

She took two more aspirin and a hot shower. With no other tasks left to think about, the argument with Gabe played repeatedly in her head. They'd have to talk. She had some things to apologize for, but she also needed to have honest conversations with him about the state of his business and the state of their marriage. And he had to quit running away to Denver. She remembered the text she'd seen from Lucinda, saying she couldn't wait to see him again. Naming a time and yet another fancy restaurant. Using the wink emoji. The real question was whether he was running away from Sue or running toward someone else.

Her phone rang as she stepped out of the shower. When she answered it, it surprised her to hear the mayor's voice.

"Well, you've really done it now. I tried to warn you about this."

Despite the rude start to the conversation, a lump of fear hit her stomach instead of indignation. She hoped Amanda hadn't gotten in trouble for being on the podcast. "What are you talking about?" she asked.

"It was a really bad idea to have a city employee on your little show. I want you to know that her boss is angry about her performance. We call that insubordination."

"But she got his permission to be on the podcast." Amanda had told her that, even though she'd said he wasn't happy.

"Sue, it is my job to protect the reputation of this city, and we can't have city employees getting out in front of an issue that is coming to city council."

"Mayor, did you actually listen to the episode?" Sue asked. "Ms. Payne did not take sides. She just explained the process the project will go through."

"It is not your role to decide what city employees should do. Did you even try to contact Drew at the chamber like I asked you to?"

Finally, her anger kicked in. Being mayor didn't give him the right to treat her that way, or to threaten Amanda. "Mayor, of course I followed up with him and we are recording his episode soon. I don't appreciate your micromanaging this process. As a resident and voter in Durango, I have the right to voice my opinion. We do still have free speech in this country."

"Well, I've got one more thing to tell you. This is going to cost you personally if you keep stirring things up."

Was he threatening her? What the hell? What leverage did he think he had? "Mayor, if you have something to tell me, please say it."

"Did you know that our city uses your husband's software? You might want to remind him of that when you tell him what you've been up to. We are, after all, helping to pay for that nice house you live in."

The audacity of his comment sucked the air out of her. Sue gripped the phone hard, wanting to rage. That's what he wanted—an irate woman screaming into the phone. She took a breath, forcing calm. She wouldn't yell. It didn't work with three-year-olds, and it wouldn't work with the mayor.

"Buddy, the way you are speaking to me is inappropriate. I started the podcast to get the facts to the public, and it's working. And by the way, my husband knows exactly what I'm doing." Of course, now she'd have to tell Gabe about this along with apologizing for last night. Her marriage was in enough trouble without the mayor getting involved.

"Sue, you are hurting the people around you. You might not care about that, but I care about the people in this community. Think about that before you let this thing get out of hand. You have a nice day now."

Click. He didn't give her the opportunity to respond or even say goodbye. Good riddance. What had gotten him so upset? The podcast hadn't been that bad.

Concerned about Amanda, she picked up the phone again and called her. "It's Sue, I just talked to the mayor," she said after the initial hello. "Are you doing okay?"

"Uh, yeah. What exactly did he say?"

Sue heard the caution in Amanda's voice. "He said you got in trouble with Mike."

"Oh. Well, you knew he wasn't too excited about me being on the podcast, but he had given me the approval to go ahead. I guess the mayor didn't know it was happening and didn't find out until someone from Worth called him. The mayor yelled at Mike for not telling him. That stuff just kind of rolls downhill."

"I'm so sorry. And I thought I was the only one having a crappy day."

"Not you too! What happened?" Amanda asked.

"I managed to get into a fight with Gabe last night. Then I woke up with a headache, argued with the chamber president, and got a call from the nasty old man who runs the city, who happened to threaten me and tell me I didn't care about people."

"Oh god, I'm so sorry. I encouraged you to get involved in this."

"Are you kidding? You gave me the facts, just like you did on the podcast. Have you heard it? I thought it was great."

"Oh, yeah, I heard it. I had to listen to it in Mike's office. But you're right, it was good, and I don't think I appeared biased."

"Drew Polowski will be on Monday's podcast. You're welcome to come over."

"No thanks. I'm going to keep my head low for a while. I can't risk my job for this. You should have Kira on. She can cross-examine him."

"I don't know if the head of the local Podunk chamber of commerce is ready for the velvet-voiced attorney. I think I'll give her a call." It was a fantastic idea, and Sue wished she'd thought of it.

After Sue hung up, she felt almost as bad as she had earlier in the day. Amanda had been her usual warm self, but worry laced her voice. It couldn't have been fun getting chastised for being on the podcast, and the mayor had made it sound even more serious, like her job was in jeopardy.

Enough of these fucking men! Where did they get off pushing around competent women? Amanda shouldn't have had to listen to the interview with her boss like a child getting in trouble. Drew Polowski shouldn't dictate where they recorded her show. The mayor sure shouldn't call and threaten her under the guise of getting her in trouble with her husband. And Gabe, running off to Denver instead of sticking around and working things out.

She'd had enough. She never used to let people walk all over her. Rage-fueled energy raced through her. No more. No more waiting to see what others would do. It was time for action, time to resolve her problems once and for all.

Sue looked at the clock, almost one. She pulled on a jacket, got in the car, and drove to the airport, anger feeding her actions. She'd wrestle control of her life, her future, the way she had with the podcast. Before she knew it, she sat in the departure lounge of the airport, a ticket to Denver in her hand. Under the anger, relief trickled into tense shoulders, relaxing them and allowing her to hold her head a little higher.

She would not end up like her mother, not without a fight. Gabe had a date with Lucinda tonight, she'd seen it on his phone. She wasn't sure if she'd confront him. She'd decide that later. If he was having an affair, well, they'd end things. Her marriage wasn't worth her pride.

She was also better off than her mother financially. From her first job, she'd saved money. Even after she'd married Gabe, she'd kept her savings separate from their joint account. She'd made some good investments over the years and had watched that pot of money grow. She definitely had drawn down the balance lately, paying for advertising for the podcast and now buying a last-minute, round-trip ticket to Denver. Some things were worth the money.

When she landed in Denver, there were several texts from Chase who waited for her at the chamber. She'd completely forgotten their appointment. Not only that, but she hadn't told the boys she wasn't home. She called Chase and explained that she couldn't make it and wouldn't be home until late. Before he had a chance to ask where she was, she told him she'd gone to New Mexico with Kira. The lie came easily. Who was she becoming?

Chase didn't question her and told her he could see from the lobby that the chamber office wouldn't work because of floor to ceiling glass panels along one wall. She asked Chase if the chamber president was there and overheard him talking to someone.

Soon, Chase was back in her ear. "No, the lady here said he couldn't make it today. She told me to go in, but I really don't need to."

"That's fine, Chase. Thanks for being there, and I'm sorry I couldn't make it. Just thank the lady and tell her I'll be in touch with Drew. You and your brother pick something up for dinner, okay? I'll be home after you're in bed."

Chase hung up with nothing more than a "bye, Mom," unfazed at her being gone. She stood in the massive Denver airport, tiny beneath its soaring roof. She'd lied to her kids, missed an appointment, and was about to either spy on or confront her husband. For once, she had important work to accomplish, but she'd ignored that to follow an impulse.

She took one step forward, and then another. Her marriage was important work as well. Step by step, she moved through the airport and to the train into town.

Forty minutes later, Sue walked into the bright afternoon air. She loved what they'd done with this part of Denver. The ballpark rose to her right, and restaurants and bars packed the streets between Union Station and Coors Field. The restaurant where Gabe would meet Lucinda was a couple of blocks away, but she had two hours to kill. Sue wandered the streets, peering into the restaurants and shops that had opened since her last visit.

Glimpsing herself in a plate-glass window, she decided to go shopping. Once again, she was in jeans, a tee shirt, and a fleece jacket. She wandered down the street, paying a little more attention to the clothing in some of the windows. A mannequin wearing a teal turtleneck sweater with multiple diagonal layers topped by a black leather-look jacket caught her eye. The modern style wouldn't have appealed to Sue two weeks ago, but today it looked polished and hip, like something Amanda would wear. She took a deep breath and walked into the store.

Fifteen minutes later, she held a shopping bag with her new purchase. In addition to the sweater and jacket, she had a new pair of black skinny jeans. She'd tried on the leggings the girl in the store suggested, but she just couldn't do it. She no longer had the ass of a young woman, and the denim held everything in place.

A little farther down the street, she came to a blow dry bar. The women on her favorite podcast had talked about these. She opened the door and asked for an appointment.

She hardly recognized herself when she left the salon. Her wild auburn hair now lay shiny and straight, and she kept running her hands through the silky strands. She regretted having her makeup done. She looked ready for a night on the town, not a confrontation with her possibly cheating husband.

With less than an hour left before Gabe's dinner date, Sue staked out the restaurant. Directly across the street was a large brew pub with seats along the front window providing a perfect view. Sue walked into the brewery and went straight to the restroom to change into her new clothes. While there, she scrubbed off a little of the makeup and replaced the lipstick with a moisturizing gloss. Good enough.

She found the perfect seat at the window and ordered a pilsner. A few sips in, her shoulders sank, and she leaned into the back of the seat. The long day and late night caught up with her body, but her mind bounced justifications for her trip to Denver back and forth like a ping pong ball. She didn't want to be the kind of woman who spied on her husband. Of course, she didn't want to have to worry about her husband having an affair.

The amber liquid cooled her throat. She would not cry over this. Tonight, she would have the facts, and she would deal with whatever she learned.

A server stopped by to ask if she wanted another beer. Sue looked at the glass in front of her surprised it was empty. She nodded at the woman.

Instead of getting lost in her thoughts again, she checked her phone. Twenty more minutes. An email from Chase contained the latest podcast numbers. Geez, over two hundred people had already listened to the latest broadcast. At least she was doing one thing right.

People came and left the restaurant across the street. Eventually, a sharp-dressed woman with shiny black hair and full red lips sauntered down the street and opened the door. Perhaps that was Lucinda. If so, Sue had a battle on her hands. The woman was young, beautiful, and obviously a professional—all the things Sue had let slip away.

A few minutes later she saw Gabe walking toward the restaurant with purpose, at ease in this world away from home. Without thinking, she rushed outside. Across the street, the woman with the red lips hung out the restaurant door and beckoned to Gabe.

Any practical feelings about letting things play out vanished. She was halfway across the street before she even thought to look for traffic.

"Gabe!" she called, before having to stop mid-street to let a delivery truck go by. Of course, the driver honked as he passed.

The truck rolled on, leaving Sue standing in the middle of the street. Gabe stared, open-mouthed and clearly confused. She'd have given just about anything to be anywhere else at that moment. She finished crossing the street, her legs heavier with each step. The woman who must be Lucinda stood outside the restaurant, staring at her with crossed arms.

Gabe was the first to talk. "What are you doing here? You look different."

"I, I needed to find out what was going on. With us." A wave of nausea ran up her body. Why was she here?

"Jesus Christ, Sue." Gabe said.

The next thing Sue heard was a voice yelling behind her. She turned to see the server from the brew pub skittering across the street waiving a white piece of paper. "Ma'am, you forgot to pay your bill."

"Have you been drinking?" Gabe asked.

She wanted to die, right then and there. Disappear in a puff of smoke, never to be heard from again. Instead, she started rummaging through her purse for her credit card.

Gabe took two twenties out of his wallet and handed them to the waitress. "Will this take care of it?"

"Yes sir!" she answered, before turning to recross the street.

"Oh, Sue." The disappointment in his voice threatened to undo her.

"I'm sorry," she muttered. Her cheeks burned with embarrassment, and her feet stuck to the sidewalk, keeping her from fleeing the horrible situation she'd created. She looked straight at Gabe's chest, unable to meet his eyes. The click of high heels approached.

"Sue, I'd like you to meet Lucinda Vargas, CEO of MAPTech. Lucinda, my wife Sue."

Sue looked at the woman and managed to get out a hi. Dark eyes stared back at Sue. A smile lit the bright lips.

"It's nice to finally meet you." The woman extended her hand as if nothing in the world were wrong.

Lucinda's nonchalance offered an escape. "It's nice to meet you too. I was just in town to do a little shopping, but I've got to head back home now." Sue briefly grabbed the woman's hand, then turned toward the train station.

"Sue." Gabe reached for her elbow, stopping her. "Would you like to join us?"

"No, no. Everything's fine. I'll see you when you're back in Durango."

"I can't leave you like this." His desperate voice added one more layer of guilt.

Sue turned to Lucinda. "Do you mind giving us a moment?" Her flat voice had an undercurrent of anger.

Lucinda's eyes went big, and she backed away, telling them she'd be inside.

"That was rude," said Gabe once Lucinda was out of earshot. "What the hell is going on?"

She couldn't decide between apologizing and asking what indeed was going on. The silence grew awkward.

"Let me cancel this meeting," Gabe said.

"You don't need to do that. I'll just go home."

"I can't leave you like this. I don't know what's wrong, but . . ."

Sue looked at the man who used to act like the world revolved around her. "You don't know what's wrong? You're in Denver more than you're home with your family, and you don't know what's wrong? Your behavior is what's wrong. Your absence is what's wrong." She watched the pain cross his features, surprised at how little it moved her. He was just like her father.

"I'm trying to change things."

"Whatever that means. I'll be at home with our sons." She turned away and marched toward the train station. She'd had enough. He called her name once but didn't come after her. That hurt more than anything.

Chapter 14

S he made it through breakfast the next morning without the boys suspecting anything. What would they think if they knew how she'd acted, what she'd done?

Gabe hadn't come after her yesterday. He hadn't called. Embarrassment and fear kept her from making the first move, the wrong move. What wrong moves had her mother made?

She knew she needed to own up to her mistakes, but after the argument and the trip to Denver, she didn't trust herself to make good decisions. Just thinking about it made her hands tremble. So, she wouldn't think about it.

She needed something big, something to keep her busy and focused away from the troubles with Gabe. At least for today. Thank god for the podcast. It expanded her world, made her learn new things, and she loved doing something important.

She needed to grab this opportunity make it bigger, do more. After so many years in Durango, she thought she'd known almost everyone, but that wasn't remotely true. Who were these people posting on Twitter and Facebook? She wanted to meet them, have them join her crusade. Well, everyone except The Professor, who continued with his unwanted tips.

The idea of meeting the people listening to the podcast stayed with her through the morning chores. She could plan a small event, maybe here at the house. If the weather held, they could have a barbeque between the house and the barn. They'd done that once before on the fourth of July, when the kids were young. A pang of regret slid through her when she realized she needed to fix things for there to be a *they* this time around. She promised she'd call Gabe before noon.

When she opened her calendar, she noticed the gold star sticker. She'd forgotten lunch crew day. Years ago, she'd tried to start a book club with some of her friends, but the books never got read, with talk of families and gossip taking precedence. By popular vote, the group of eight friends decided to get rid of the reading, and just have lunch together once a month. They took turns hosting, and each brought a dish. Today, they'd meet at Paula's house.

Sue gathered fresh tomatoes and basil from the garden and made them into the base of a chopped caprese salad. She didn't have mozzarella but could grab a container at the gourmet market on the way to Paula's.

She broke her promise to call Gabe, telling herself she didn't want to disturb him during the workday. The pull to apologize for her accusations seemed to grow with each passing hour, but it never overcame the difficulty of actually picking up the phone. She didn't know what to say. Sue considered calling her mom. It would be nice to talk to someone who'd been through this, but not now.

Before leaving for lunch, Sue placed more ads for the podcast, not just online but in the local paper. She spent her own money. Gabe wouldn't have minded her spending their money, but this made the project hers. It put a little more risk on the line.

Sue settled onto Paula's floral sofa, a plate of food on her knees. She'd hatched a plan to run her event idea by her friends and maybe recruit some help.

"I can't believe you've started a podcast. That's amazing," Colleen said. "I've heard every episode."

"Thanks. I've been surprised at how many people have tuned in, and I don't know most of them. People seem to be as worried as I am about this development."

Colleen plunked herself into a chair next to Sue. "I certainly don't want it in the valley. It's less than a mile from my house."

"I thought we weren't going to talk about this here," Paula said. "You know Denny supports the development."

"How can he?" asked Colleen. "This Worth guy sounds really bad."

"It's going to bring a lot of money to town. All of our businesses will do better." Paula sounded like she'd stolen the chamber president's list of development attributes.

"They're also supposed to bring upscale shopping and dining to town." Becca plumped her bottom lip and whined. "We could really use that. I'm tired of having to go to Denver for quality shopping."

The rest of the women looked around the room, apparently deciding which side to take. Sue didn't want it turning into a brawl. After all, some of those against it might come around with a little more information. Paula stared at her defiantly.

"I'm thinking about hosting an event where I can meet the people who listen to the podcast."

"That's a great idea." Colleen jumped back into the conversation. "You could have a community event down at the fairgrounds, like the school carnival but bigger."

"Oooh! That could be fun!" Maggie, always excited for a party, joined the conversation. "You could have bands, and a cocktail bar, and pageants for the kids. And food trucks! That's the latest trend. You have to have food trucks."

"I was thinking more along the lines of a barbeque at the house."

"Oh, no. You've got to go big with this," Colleen said.

"Well, I think this is ridiculous." Paula shook her head and stared at Sue.

"Are you kidding?" Colleen gave Paula a sharp glance before turning to Sue. "This is going to be great! I bet we could have some kind of fair. You could bring in the organizations who are against the development. Maybe it could be a state-wide thing. There's lots of environmental organizations in Colorado."

Colleen's excitement fueled Sue's anxiety. She had wanted to do something, but something small and friendly. Now, some of her friends had latched on to a giant event, one that would require renting the fairgrounds and planning activities.

By the time they finished eating, the event had grown into a nonprofit fair with bands and food trucks, along with a tent for podcast supporters. Meanwhile, Paula stewed in her chair, her lunch co-opted. Sue didn't know whether to feel guilty or betrayed by Paula's obstinance.

Sue committed to the huge event, even though it made her nauseous. It might mean putting off family responsibilities and getting a lot less sleep, but if it made a difference, it would be worth it. At least she had gotten a few volunteers out of the lunch. They formed a committee and decided to hold their first meeting after the next podcast. Sue promised to call the fairgrounds and see when it was available. They had to act soon and hope the snow stayed away.

When she got home, she called Jim Beam with the Sierra Club. Besides having her favorite name in the universe, Amanda had said he was an expert fundraiser. He'd know how to help.

"Ms. Cleary, I was hoping you'd call. Amanda told me what you're trying to do."

Sue fell into his thick cowboy accent, picturing Sam Elliot on the other end of the line. "My friends think I should hold a community event to rally people around our cause. I haven't really done anything on this scale and was hoping you could help." She crossed her fingers and prayed he was as nice as he sounded. She'd never joined the Sierra Club, and now she needed a favor.

"If it will stop this development, I'm happy to help, and I bet I can get a few of the other nonprofits on board. What did you have in mind?"

Sue relaxed into her chair. She'd found an ally. There didn't seem to be a lot of middle ground with this project. People lined up against the development or for it. Like Paula. That one still stung, but it prompted her to try even harder to expose Worth Winter Wonderland's problems.

The second after she hung up with Jim, Sue emailed Kira about the new event and the interview with the chamber president. She also mentioned the call from the mayor and how Amanda had gotten into trouble for doing the show.

Kira called back almost immediately, and Sue had never heard her so keyed up. The smooth voice was clipped and gravelly with a new energy. She was furious about Amanda getting in trouble.

Sue agreed. Amanda had done nothing wrong, and the mayor and her boss shouldn't have threatened her. Kira tied it back to her suspicions about the mayor's role in the project. She promised to research it.

Sue didn't want the details. As much as she hated the way the mayor treated her, she wasn't looking for a scandal. It might further jeopardize Amanda's job or get in the way of their stopping the development.

Kira asked if she could call in to the podcast with the chamber head before Sue had a chance to ask her, and Sue immediately said yes. Having Kira on the call would be a relief. Kira and Amanda had come prepared for their episodes, and she wasn't sure Drew would be so easy. It would help to tag-team him with questions, and it wouldn't hurt that Kira knew so much about the Worth Company.

Before they ended the call, Kira asked Sue to wish her luck. "Tomorrow, I have my last interview for the promotion I told you about. I'm pretty sure I'll get the job since I've done more land protection deals in the past five years than anyone else in the office. I'm even going to include the podcast interview as an example of a fresh approach for raising public awareness for land conservation."

Kira's anticipation of the promotion crackled through the phone and entered Sue's ear like a nudge to do more, to feel excitement about the future. Maybe once this project ended, she'd work for an organization like the Sierra Club.

She hung up, not telling Kira about the mayor's threat to Gabe's business. She needed to talk to him first and find out what he wanted to do about it. It was one of many things they needed to discuss.

She picked up her phone again and stared at it. Maybe she'd eat something before she called him. She probably had a day's worth of excuses not to call. Why was this so hard? As if her anxiety shot straight across the mountain tops, the phone in her hand buzzed. Gabe.

"Hi, Gabe." Great start. "I'm sorry I haven't called. I know we need to talk."

"How are you?"

"I'm okay." Tell him you're sorry. Tell him you're sorry. But the words stuck in her throat as a wash of embarrassment and regret flowed through her.

"We need to talk when I get home." He sounded so far away.

"Yes. We really do."

Gabe was silent, probably waiting for her to go on. She'd give almost anything to know his thoughts. Whatever happened between them, he was one of the good guys. Unlike the mayor. Oh, shit. The mayor's threat about Gabe's business slammed into her.

"I had a talk with the mayor, and there's something I need to tell you. He said the city uses your software, and he threated to cancel the contract if I didn't, well, if I didn't behave and not say things he didn't like about the development." That wasn't exactly what he'd said, but he hadn't been super specific, just super threatening. "I don't want to hurt the company. That's not why I started this."

"You won't hurt the company. Cities can only break our contract if the software isn't performing, and it is. Besides, we have over twelve thousand customers, just in the United States. If Durango doesn't want to do business with us, we'll hardly notice. Don't worry about it."

Well, that, at least, was a relief. The mayor would have to find a new way to get under her skin. Something he was probably already planning. On to more important things.

"How are things going in Denver?" She tried to make the loaded question sound innocent.

"Things are fine. I'm more concerned about you."

Not for the first time, she wished she had a husband who would scream and yell, or even quietly put his feelings out there. Caught in a trap, she had to guess them instead. She used to beg him to tell her what he was thinking, what he wanted, or what was wrong.

And he should be concerned about her. She'd gone half-wild, afraid he was having an affair. She wanted to know if he was going to leave her like her dad had left her mom. She didn't know what words would unlock the truth, much less help her deal with it. But the way she'd acted was unforgivable. "Gabe, are you mad at me?"

The pause was long. "No, I'm not mad."

"What are you thinking? Please tell me."

"Sue, I am not having an affair."

Did she have to spell out every fear? "Then why are you in Denver so often? You always said you could manage the business from Durango. And most of the employees are still in Seattle, not Denver." Why was she whining?

"I've been meeting with the folks from MAPTech."

"Lucinda." The beautiful woman from the restaurant, and his phone. "Isn't MAPTech a competitor?"

"Only in some sectors. Many of our products are complementary or can be if we can get them to work together better."

"When are you coming home?" she asked, the question a stand in for everything she really wanted to know.

"I need to stay another couple of days."

Sue didn't say anything. What was there to say? He could be staying because he needed to work. He could also be staying because of Lucinda. Or because of the way Sue had treated him.

"I know the timing's not good," Gabe said, eventually.

"It's fine." It wasn't fine. She wanted to reach out to him, grab him, and never let him go. But he chose Denver, and she was here.

"I love you, Sue."

"Love you too," she said, hoping the cheer she forced into her voice came across as real. She ended the call.

Nothing made sense. Why would he need to be in Denver so often for one company? Why was he having dinner with her? During the call, Gabe's answers seemed to make sense, but now questions chipped away at her heart. If she could only see the truth, either way, she could deal with it. Not knowing her future kept the danger fresh.

Chapter 15

"It's not very professional that you do this in your home."

Sue stared at Drew Polowski's smug face, hoping hers portrayed her offense at the comment. What a jerk. What had happened to this guy? He'd been fine, nice even, when she'd seen him at kids' events over the years. She opened the door wider and let him into the house.

"My son has worked hard to create a studio with decent sound quality. By the way, he'll be here today to help with the technical aspects of the podcast."

"Which son? Did one of your boys come home from college to help you with this?"

"No, it's Chase."

"Is he even in high school yet?"

"Yes, he's a sophomore, and he's brilliant with technology. If you're concerned, we can cancel the interview, but the mayor was certain you wanted to participate."

"No, no, I'll do it. I was just curious about the setup."

Her discomfort grew as she led him upstairs. She wouldn't have followed him upstairs in his house. But what was she supposed to do? This wasn't a business. She didn't have an office or a studio in a professional building. Still, given her conversations about respect lately, it seemed like a double standard.

Things didn't get more comfortable in the converted office. The small table they'd set up for the podcast had chairs crammed together so they'd both have access to the good microphone. He gave her a skeptical look as he sat down. She had no choice but to snuggle in next to him. At least that's how it felt, now that he'd made it seem smarmy.

She told him to get comfortable, then asked if he had any questions. He didn't. Then she told him Kira would join them from San Francisco.

"Now Sue, that's not right. I didn't agree to be interviewed by her. You should have told me that before I came over."

"She's part of the team. She's been on every podcast so far."

"I feel like you're setting me up."

"Really? I'm not. We have a podcast. The two hosts who've been there from the beginning are participating today. We've invited you here as a guest." She should have told him. She felt kind of bad about it, and about the awkwardness of the studio, but she couldn't let him know. After all, he ran the chamber of commerce. He should be able to handle this. "With all of your experience, I'm sure you'll be great."

Chase, half-hidden behind computer equipment, patched in Kira and Sue introduced Drew.

"Thank you for being on the show today. How did the chamber get involved in the Worth project?

"Well, the chamber of commerce is the voice of the business community in Durango. They contacted us as soon as they identified Durango as a preferred location for Winter Wonderland. Recently, a vice president from Worth Company visited the chamber and explained it to the board in detail. It's important that the business leaders in the community understand and support the project."

What a blowhard. And why did chamber members get special treatment? "Do you know if Worth Company plans to talk to anyone else in the community about the development?" Sue tried to keep the annoyance out of her voice.

"I know they've given a presentation to city council members."

"They made a presentation to the mayor and city council privately and not in a public meeting?" Kira asked.

"Um. I don't know the particulars."

Sue caught the stammer in his voice and noticed his cheeks getting red. Bird dog Kira had flushed him out. Sue's cheeks tightened into a genuine smile. This was going to be fun.

"That's interesting," Kira said. "If that's true, then they are providing the city council, who votes on this issue on behalf of the public, information the public doesn't have access to."

"That doesn't sound fair." Sue slid the comment in as she watched Drew's face redden.

"The city has put everything on its website," he said. "I heard it on the podcast a few days ago."

Sue tried to cover her grin with a hand, but she could tell it went all the way to her eyes. He listened to the podcast! The mayor listened. Her friends listened. Amazing. She started this thing, and people listened. She forced down her glee and concentrated on the conversation.

"Everything they've given the city staff is on the website," Kira said. "We don't know if they distributed additional information to elected officials. Do you know if city staff were in the meetings?"

"They weren't in the one I was in, but that was just with the mayor," he said.

"You met with the mayor and the developer about the project? What did you discuss?" Kira had weaponized her silky voice.

Drew shifted in his seat, and Sue swore the heat coming off him increased by a few degrees. He turned as far as he could in the small space to look at Sue. "I thought you brought me in here to discuss the project."

"Yes, we did. We are interested in what you learned from the developer," Sue said. "Would you share that with our audience?"

"This is a really good project. You guys shouldn't dismiss it without learning the details."

"Well, that's why you're here," Sue said. "Please, tell us what is good about the proposed Winter Wonderland Resort and Theme Park."

"Well, it's going to create lots of jobs. Hundreds of jobs. High paying ones."

Kira broke in before Sue could respond. "Typically, the vast majority of jobs associated with this type of development are low-level service jobs. Why do you think this project is different?"

"The vice president of Worth Company promised high-paying jobs. He said that at the chamber meeting and again with the mayor."

"Well, I'm sure there will be a few." Kira said. "Did they talk about how they usually bring in executives from other parts of the company for those high-paying jobs? Regarding the rest of the jobs, doesn't Durango already have an unemployment rate below five percent? Where will those employees come from? Do you think they'll use imported labor they way they do in other Worth developments?"

"Um. That's a lot of questions. I can tell you they assured us this development will be good for the community. It will create jobs that are important for our economy. But it does more than that. Worth Company will also pay area taxes and support local businesses."

He pivoted back to his comfort zone, the confidence returning to his voice. Sue could have warned him he would not best Kira, but it was more fun to watch the coming train wreck.

"Local businesses are the backbone of Durango," he continued. "When a big company like this comes in, it benefits us in many ways. The employees live in local housing and shop at the local grocery. They get their hair done at Durango salons and go to local gyms. And that's only part of the picture. The resort's visitors will eat at our restaurants and shop on Main Street and in our galleries. They'll ride the train, ski the mountain, and drink in our bars. This is going to be a boon to the economy."

"Thank you for telling us that," Kira said. "I have a few more questions. First, if most of the jobs are low income, which I expect they are, employees will have trouble finding housing. Isn't affordable housing already an issue in Durango? Also, they won't have much disposable income. Where do you suggest people earning minimum wage shop and eat?" Kira paused briefly and Drew stiffened.

"Regarding the resort's guests," she continued, "isn't the point of having a ski hill, lazy river, and other amenities to make sure people don't leave the resort? I imagine Worth Company provides their guests with plenty of shopping and dining opportunities. This is how resorts work, even without a theme park. With one, well, how many times have you gone to Disneyland and ended up shopping in Anaheim?"

"I am sure people at the resort will shop and eat in Durango."

"Well, perhaps you're right. It's possible Winter Wonderland will be different from every other Worth property," Kira said. "I'd like to move on to something else you mentioned, taxes. You said that the development will pay a lot in taxes, but isn't it true that they're asking for tax concessions from both the city and the county?"

"Only in the beginning," Drew said. "That's just a little seed money to sweeten the pot. It's nothing compared to the huge investment they'll make. If this resort goes to some other city, Durango would lose out on the project's benefits. The city needs to make a few concessions."

Sue wasn't sure whether it was anger or desperation that had crept into Drew's voice. He sighed heavily when he heard Kira speak.

"According to the documents they've submitted, Worth has asked the city to abate their business, property, and sales taxes for fifteen years. That's longer than it takes a kid to go through the school system. In addition, they want the city to pay for their infrastructure improvements. Plus, there will be ongoing costs to local government. With that many new people, Durango will need more police officers and have to provide other services. Basically, the demand on city services will increase. If Worth Company doesn't pay any taxes, then the rest of the community will have to foot the bill."

There was a long silence. Kira's diatribe had sucked the air out of the room. Sue didn't think Drew could possibly respond.

"Ma'am, I think you are taking some of this out of context. When you take an overall look at the project, it is very good for our community." Drew's voice started soft, then strengthened. "And we're not even talking about the intangibles. This will boost Durango's reputation among international travelers, and they spend more than domestic ones. Our local businesses will prosper as they benefit from the money this project brings to the community."

It was a good recovery. The debate was like a professional tennis match, with volleys crossing back and forth. Drew told stories about business leaders at the chamber meeting excited by the project's potential benefits. Once, he even mentioned Gabe. "Sue, your husband was there, and he seemed supportive. I'm not sure we heard any objections."

What an ass. He had to make this personal. "My husband's company is a member of the chamber. But the board hasn't voted on this, have they?"

"No. We expect to at our next meeting. I believe the project will have broad support. I mean, you should see the artwork. It looks beautiful and will fit right into our valley."

"You've seen pictures of it?" Kira broke in.

"Not pictures, um, like paintings." Drew's voice slowed, as if he realized his mistake as he spoke.

"Artist's renderings," said Kira. "There aren't any depictions of the project on the city site. Do you have copies of them?"

"No, they belong to the developer. But I'm sure they'd be happy to provide them to the city. I don't think anyone would be against the project if they saw what it was going to look like."

"Would you ask them for copies on our behalf?" Honey poured from Kira's voice. "I'm sure the people in Durango would love to see what this project will look like."

"Why don't you just call and ask them?" Drew stiffened even more and leaned away from the microphone as if it might bite.

"But you have such a strong relationship with them. After all, the vice president came to visit you," Kira said.

Sue barely heard the "oh shit" under Drew's breath. She glanced at Chase where he'd been sitting quietly on the other side of the room. He grinned and nodded.

"We'll reach out to the company," Drew said, backing his chair away from the table. "Sue, I'd like to thank you for having me on the program today." He got up and left, quickly but not quietly. It would take some serious editing to get the scraping chair and slamming door out of the recording. Unless they decided to leave them in.

Sue wrapped up by telling listeners the community event in Durango for podcast listeners, and she'd post the details on social media. She announced her next guest, Jim Beam with the Sierra Club, and told listeners she had reached out to Worth Company but had yet to receive a response. Finally, she thanked Kira and Drew for being on the podcast, although Drew was probably halfway back to his office by then.

The second she clicked the button and ended the recording. Chase started howling with laughter. "You really got him, Mom."

Kira had been the one to get him, but it was her program. She was proud and appalled at the same time. Drew Polowski had been a jerk, and he tried to sell something he didn't totally understand. But humiliating him didn't feel good. It wasn't something she wanted to teach her kids. If that was the price for stopping the development, was it worth it? She feared she'd have more opportunities to test this question.

The next day, Sue attempted to bury herself in her work. Gabe had texted that he needed one more day in Denver before coming home. He'd said he was sorry, but he hadn't called.

She wished they had another podcast to record. It had become a great distraction from her marriage woes. Instead, she busied herself planning the biggest event she thought she could handle. She had just put down a deposit to rent the fairgrounds when Amanda called.

"You won't believe what you've done!" Amanda barely waited for Sue to say hello. "People have been calling here all day. I don't know how many people listened to the podcast with Polowski, but I swear every single one has called demanding the pictures of the development."

"Do you have them?"

"No, they weren't required to turn in any visuals with their application. Believe me, they turned in the bare minimum. But the incredible thing is that so many people called the mayor that he ended up on the phone with Worth. We should have electronic copies of the renderings by the end of the day."

"No way! The podcast is actually making a difference." The electric excitement Sue got when her kids won a hard-fought hockey game flowed through her.

"It really is! You wouldn't believe how pissed off the mayor is. He's been yelling all day."

"Oh no. Is he mad at you?" Amanda's job seemed at risk every day with this project.

"I've been lying low. Seriously, I've had my door closed most of the day, and I'm outside in the parking lot now. I think he's mostly mad at Drew, but the city manager caught some flack too."

Maybe that's what Drew's "oh shit" moment had been about. The audio had picked up the comment, and she and Chase had argued about whether to keep it in. She finally demanded he take it out and was glad she had. She could picture herself making the same mistake, and mercy had seemed the higher road.

"So, the mayor didn't think he did a good job?" Sue asked.

"It wasn't his sales job that was the problem. It was the private meeting between him, the mayor, and Worth. They're not supposed to do that. Well, they can, but they have to follow rules like registering as lobbyists. The public process is supposed to happen in the public."

"Then why did the mayor take the meeting?"

"He and all the other council members like knowing what's going on, and it can be a fine line between what's legal and what isn't. The city attorney is meeting with all of them right now to explain that they shouldn't be anywhere near that line." Amanda paused, and Sue heard a sharp intake of breath. "Oh, my god! I just got a text from Carla. The renderings are here. I'll call you back later."

Sue went to bed without hearing back from Amanda and missing Gabe. Her days used to stretch long with chores and plenty of time to fill. She'd been busy with the kids, but never like this. Things moved at a hundred miles an hour now.

From the moment she got up to when she crawled into bed, there was a whirlwind of kids, horses, podcasts, events, the city, Kira, Facebook. It was exhilarating and exhausting.

Today she was glad for the activity that half buried her. It kept her from thinking about Gabe. She didn't want to lose him but didn't know how to keep him. She didn't even know if her worries were real or in her head. But tonight, in bed waiting for sleep, she longed for him. What she wouldn't give for another few minutes in the feed room, or here in their luxurious bed.

But if he did appear right now, would she love him or argue with him? Could she trust herself to choose love?

Chapter 16

Sue checked her email as soon as she woke. One had arrived at eleven o'clock the previous night. The renderings had been uploaded. She took her iPad into Chase's room and woke him by sitting on the bed beside him.

A pillow line running down one cheek, Chase howled as he looked at each of the six pictures. The cries woke Jaxson and lured him from his bedroom.

While the boys' responses were loud, the images stunned Sue to silence. Captions accompanied each depiction. The hotel caption read, "In a beautiful reflection of the lofty peaks of the San Gabriel Mountains, the resort village architecture recreates a mountain wonderland."

It was horrific. A massive triangle rose out of a three-story rectangular platform, dwarfing all around it. The hotel was a child's drawing of a mountain with a flag flying from the top. Hundreds of rooms would be crammed in there. The artist had redrawn the ridge Sue climbed with Samson into a series of triangular mountains, trying to make the surroundings fit the man-made abomination. Despite the teenage laughter and pointing fingers, Sue didn't see the hilarity. This could happen, this thing that might change her valley forever. She wouldn't stay here if that happened, and she didn't want to lose her home.

The other pictures were equally absurd, if not as frightening. The Winter Wonderland Snow Train Rollercoaster tried hard to look like the beautiful narrow-gauge train that already graced the valley. Instead of making its way through forty-five miles of valley, canyon, and mountain the way the real train did, the rollercoaster swooped and swirled through skies currently dominated by soaring hawks.

The climate-controlled, enclosed, year-round ski experience looked like the business end of the world's largest shop vac. They had a real ski mountain here already. Yes, you had to depend on the weather, but indoor skiing?

Then she saw the river. This one divided her sons. Chase was furious, but she saw the struggle in Jaxson. As the river entered the resort, the meandering curves split three ways to offer three different experiences within a few hundred yards. The lazy river diverted from the actual river like a pig's tail, with happy families on inner tubes relaxing in the water, the mom with an umbrella'd cocktail in her hand.

One swath of water led to a rectangular pool, where a teenager who looked disturbingly like Jaxson rode a manmade wave on a red surfboard. Below the pool, the the river flowed into channelized rapids bedecked with boulders, around which happy athletes performed Olympic level kayaking maneuvers. Of course, today's river already hosted rafting and kayaking, just not all within the same few feet.

Another picture showed a street, a near copy of Durango's own Main Street. Instead of the local shops and restaurants, the signs looked like they belonged to Tiffany, Apple, Louis Vuitton, and other swank, recognizable brands.

The remaining color drawings showed the entire development from several viewpoints. Sue noticed a climbing wall decorated in neon lights. Farther on, a Ferris wheel spun like an ornate mechanical spider. Finally, in the last rendering, she saw what could only be described as a skyscraper, at least as compared with the resort and Ferris wheel. Atop the building, in neon lights, was one word, casino.

In Colorado, casinos only existed on native peoples' lands. She assumed it was illegal to have them anywhere else. Surely Worth wasn't ostentatious enough to think he could change Colorado law? Sue emailed Kira the links to the pictures.

The boys wandered off, texting their friends. Sue wanted to go back to bed and pretend the day hadn't started. More than anything, she wished Gabe were here. If she shared her disgust for what the New York real estate mogul planned to do to her valley, perhaps she could process it.

She went downstairs and made coffee instead of returning to bed. The angry tremor in her hands caused coffee beans to scatter across the counter instead of landing neatly in the grinder. Screw this guy. The photos cemented her commitment. She'd spend every ounce of energy and every dollar she had to beat this New York goliath.

By late afternoon, the online community had lit up, and by the following day it had become an uproar. Besides making wicked fun of the renderings, online comments encouraged people to call the city council. Even her troll, The Professor, congratulated her for getting the drawings online, after he pointed out that she needed to better manage the podcast's discussions instead of letting the guests take over.

Sue turned her thoughts away from the troll. Amanda had to be in the thick of the crossfire at city hall, and Sue wanted to hear about it. Midmorning, she finally texted and asked Amanda to call when she got a chance. The anticipation was too much. She needed to hear from her friend.

****

Gabe walked in the house when she and the boys were halfway through dinner. He should have been back by four, but clearly, he'd taken a later flight without letting her know. That and not hearing back from Amanda had Sue so keyed up she could hardly eat.

She stayed out of the conversation as Gabe prodded the boys for information about school, and they made plans for the weekend hockey tournament in Albuquerque. When the boys finally went upstairs to study, Sue asked Gabe to join her on the back deck.

She led the way, determined to have the conversation she'd been avoiding. Sinking heavily into the chair at the head of the table, she motioned Gabe to sit beside her. She took a deep breath, then stumbled over whether to apologize first or explain that she needed to understand why he spent so much time in Denver.

"Sue, I think you have a drinking problem."

She looked at her husband in shock. This was not about her. "Oh, for fuck's sake. I have a marriage problem not a drinking problem." Sue slapped her hand over her mouth. How did those words spill out? She thought back to dinner. No, she hadn't had anything to drink, not since Denver.

"I do not understand what's going on with you." Gabe said. "How do I always end up the bad guy in these conversations? I am working in Denver. Nothing else. I don't know how to prove that to you. I don't know why I have to." The slow burn of his anger turned on, and he clenched his jaw.

Sue watched his hands tighten into fists, a sign of frustration, not danger. Long years together had taught them the ins and outs of each other's personalities. They'd learned exactly how to hurt each other.

"I'm sorry." Her words bounced off him as he stood and walked away.

By the time Sue went to bed, Gabe was already asleep. She wanted to reach out to him for comfort, snuggle into his warmth, and have him tell her it would all be okay. The tips of her fingers pulled toward him, needing him to forgive her. But if she touched him, she'd have to talk about the things she'd done wrong. All the things she was afraid of. Talking would bring tears, and she might make things worse. Better to keep her hands to herself for one more night.

The next morning, Gabe left a note that he'd spend the day in the chamber's coworking space. After school let out, he'd drive the boys to the hockey tournament in Albuquerque, leaving Sue alone for the weekend. Putting off the conversation they needed to have a little longer brought a sad relief.

Fortunately, Amanda's call took her mind off Gabe. "I've never seen the mayor so angry."

"Well, I think the community is pretty angry."

"Oh, they're enraged! Calls and emails have been coming in thick and hot. Not only that, but a vice president from Worth Company called the mayor and said that Harold Worth was furious. The mayor had convinced someone in the company to send him the renderings, but Mr. Worth hadn't planned on releasing them until he had approval for the land use change. The mayor always takes his calls on speakerphone, and when Mr. Worth called, he yelled so loud the whole office heard."

"No!"

"Oh yes. Mr. Worth said releasing the photos threw the entire project into jeopardy. He's not only considering pulling out of Durango, but they fired the person who emailed the images to the mayor."

Sue couldn't believe Worth Company would fire someone for giving the mayor images they'd shown at city hall just weeks earlier. Evidently, that was how things worked at Worth Company. They were ruthless.

"How are you doing? Are they still threatening your job?"

"I'm lying low. I promise. So far, the mayor has taken out most of his anger and embarrassment on the city manager. He was furious when he realized the drawings didn't need to be released yet according to the city's timeline. But once the public wanted to see them, it left him with little choice. Some of that anger made it to me, especially I since approved putting the photos online. But the lawyers would have made us do it. We can't keep documents like that from the public."

The mayor needed to look in the mirror on this one. Sue understood why Worth Company didn't want the public to know what they were planning. The development was hideous. The mayor, however, should want the public to see how it would transform their town. Maybe Kira was right. Perhaps he was too close to this one. Surprised she hadn't yet heard from the lawyer, she sent her another missive, wanting to share the community reaction and Amanda's update.

Sunday afternoon, Sue interviewed Jim Beam for the podcast. That was when she learned about land options. Jim found out Worth Company had optioned the seventy-five acres on the east side of the river. It had been farmland since they moved to Durango, and Sue remembered the sweet older lady she'd met once when riding along the river.

"Unfortunately, Mrs. Walker passed away several years ago," Jim said. "Her relatives have been fighting over the land ever since, some wanting to sell and others wanting to hold it for the future. I've heard Mr. Worth made them an offer double the asking price."

"So, he owns the land now?" Sue asked, dread creeping into her voice. It made the project more real. He was already part of the valley.

"He hasn't actually bought it yet. From what one of the Walker kids told me, he's put up a little money for a contract that guarantees him the right to buy the land if the city allows him to build the resort."

"Don't the kids want to live there?" Sue asked. "It's a beautiful piece of land."

"Nope, they all left Durango. The one I talked to lives in Los Angeles. Kids don't really see a lot of opportunity here."

Sue knew this issue well. "How can we make Durango a better place for kids to return to once they've left home?"

"Well, I believe the town needs to use its natural beauty to attract jobs that will sustain the people and the environment."

By the end of the interview, Sue was proud of how she'd handled this important conversation. They'd talked about the project and about the long-term prospects for Durango. Not even The Professor could complain about this one.

Immediately after they finished the podcast, the first community event meeting happened in Sue's kitchen. The fireworks started quickly. Everyone but Sue thought the event should be a fundraiser. Fundraiser for what? She didn't mind bearing the expenses of the podcast and social media. That hadn't been too bad so far.

"You have to think bigger," Jim said.

His cowboy hat and a big silver western belt buckle matched his drawl, making Sue swoon. Colleen had actually raised an eyebrow and licked her lips when he walked in the door. "Wranglers," she'd whispered in Sue's ear.

Colleen vehemently agreed with the cowboy environmentalist. "We don't know how much it will cost to fight the development, and people want ways to participate."

"But then we'd have to have a bank account and actually start a business." Sue, an accountant at heart, didn't want to grow the effort into something more complex.

"If you're really going to fight this thing, it's going to take some money. There's a couple of ways to do it," Jim said. "You can start a political action committee or register as a nonprofit corporation."

"But I don't want to do any of those things," Sue argued. "Things seem fine. We just need more people listening to the podcast. I can spend a little more on advertising." Her heart beat fast against her chest. She could handle a short-term effort, but a formal organization meant something more permanent.

Arguing was useless. Everyone else at the table demanded a fundraiser. Fortunately, Jim offered to have the Sierra Club create a separate bank account within their existing foundation. He told her this was only a short-term solution. They needed a long-term plan.

The others meant well, but shouldn't they wait to make these decisions? The vote on the development would happen in just over a month.

Unfortunately, it seemed like she had started a movement. Her friends wanted to save the valley forever, not save it from one project. Sue hadn't signed on for any of that. An ache started at the base of her neck and ran across her shoulders. She made them promise not to mention other projects until the council voted on the Worth development.

She had to figure out what to do with the rest of her life. Was this it? She was passionate about stopping Winter Wonderland, but as much as she loved the valley, she wasn't sure she wanted to run an environmental organization. Yet that's what had landed in her lap.

Chapter 17

When Sue came in from feeding the horses the next morning, the cold in her aching fingers sent shivers of ice up her arms. She wrapped her hands around a mug of coffee, relaxing into the warmth before sitting down to oatmeal and the newspaper.

She giggled at the local paper's headline, "Worth Says Premature Release of Drawings Regrettable." Unfortunately, the headline didn't match the article. The paper claimed the drawings released by the city did not represent the development's final appearance.

Instead, the paper quoted Harold Worth. "The renderings exist solely to help us understand what types of buildings and amenities fit on the site." According to Worth, the company wanted to partner with the community to build the best development for Durango.

As horrifying as the drawings were, a talented artist had done them, and they had to have been expensive. Worth's excuses reminded Sue of when her kids tried to lie their way out of something they did wrong. The excuses might be plausible, but given the personalities involved, they weren't believable.

Sue wished the questions had been tougher instead of the article sounding like a Worth Company press release. The editorial board hadn't taken a stand on the development but probably would. She hoped the editors would deal with the hard questions absent from the front-page article. She should probably contact the editor. She could add it to the growing list of burdens she'd never considered when she started this project.

She found the article online and emailed it to Kira. It had been a couple of days since she'd heard from her, and Sue wanted to update her on the fallout from the drawings and planning the event. If Kira lost interest in the project, Sue's job would become much more difficult. She added a line asking if everything was okay before hitting send.

Minutes later, her phone rang. Kira sounded exhausted. Instead of velvet, her voice was rocky, like she'd just woken up or smoked an entire pack of Camels, or both.

"Kira, are you okay?"

"I didn't get the promotion."

"Oh no, I'm so sorry to hear that."

"Honestly, it reminds me of that day back in college. They took advantage of me. I did everything they asked. I protected far more acres of land over the past five years than anyone in the firm. They said to take a leadership position in the industry, and I did. I wrote dozens of articles and spoke at industry conferences. And do you know what they did?"

Kira's shame rolled through Sue's body as if it were her own. When she'd worked, her identity had been completely tied up in her job. Being told she wasn't good enough to take the next step would have devastated her. She struggled to think of something to say to help Kira feel better, but Kira spoke first.

"They chose a loaf. Sure, he's a nice guy, but he hasn't done half of what I've done. He's not out there looking for parcels of land that protect a species or a microclimate. He's never connected two disparate pieces of green space or found a hidden parcel of nature so people in urban areas have the chance to get outside. He just sits in the office and works on whatever project someone brings him. He almost never attends conferences, much less leads them. He didn't even meet the written criteria for the position, yet they chose him anyway. Over me."

"Why?" Sue had seen Kira's ambition in the way she walked in her high heels, how her silky voice threaded its way through a conversation until you thought she knew everything. As a man, she'd probably be CEO by now, but as a woman, well....

"Part of why they said I didn't get it was the podcast. They listened to the last episode with the chamber of commerce. They said I was too aggressive. I don't believe it. I think they were just looking for excuses."

"But you weren't even that hard on him. I mean, you were, but you just took advantage of his comments." Sue went cold. Her project had hurt Kira's career, not Amanda's. At least not yet.

"They said I should build relationships with community members, not alienate them. I told them I had helped get the truth out, but they didn't want to hear it. They told me I might be ready for the position in a couple of years, but the guy they gave it to is younger than me, and he's not going anywhere."

"That is so unfair!" The mother bear in Sue came out. Mother bear with hints of the woman she'd been so long ago, when she'd had a job and ambition and wanted to reach her goals more than anything in the world. She needed to make this right.

"So, I quit."

Holy shit. Kira was so brave. Sue would have analyzed quitting one hundred ways before doing anything. "What are you going to do?"

"I've already got a job. I quit the moment they told me. I didn't even give them notice. If they didn't think I was the right person to lead the legal department, then they definitely weren't right for me. I was so goddam furious, I went on a bender of activity. In two weeks, I start working for a nonprofit focused on protecting marine areas. I'm moving to Palm Beach."

"Oh, my god, tell me you're kidding. How can you move that fast?" It would take Sue weeks, maybe months, to do what Kira had done in a weekend. Hell, she'd been thinking about what would happen to her after the kids left since they were born, and she still hadn't figured it out. Kira was a force of nature.

"I got your messages, and it sounds really exciting there right now. I figured I'd drive through on my way to Florida."

"That's great. I don't want to lose you on the project. Stay at the house." Sue had to offer. Kira didn't have a job, and they had plenty of empty rooms.

"I will, thanks," said Kira. "I'll probably be there in a couple of days. In the meantime, tell me what's happening."

Sue filled her in, still wondering how a person could just pick up their life and leave with two days' notice. It didn't seem normal. Maybe Kira had it together more than anyone Sue had ever met, but it seemed panicky to act so fast. She'd have to talk with Kira while she was here and figure out if she was really okay.

As soon as she hung up, she thought she heard Gabe's truck pull up to the house. He and the kids must be back from Albuquerque. Sue had made no headway on her own problems. And one of them had just arrived home.

She racked her brain trying to figure out the best time and place to talk to Gabe, then realized it was useless. Even if she found the perfect location, Gabe wouldn't say anything. Why plan an outing when he wouldn't even talk to her? She headed for the podcast studio, a place where she could hide from her problems instead of confronting them.

She sat at the small table and examined her guilt. She should just sit down with Gabe and work through their issues. She needed to give him a chance.

Something more than guilt gnawed at her. Fear. Fear that he would talk, that he would tell her the one thing she didn't want to hear. Fear that whatever was in Denver was more important than their marriage. Or worse, fear that there wasn't anyone or anything else, but he would leave anyway. That's what her dad had done. He'd never remarried, he'd never even dated much. He just didn't want to be with her mother.

As far as Sue knew, her mother had never dated either. She hadn't done much of anything since Sue helped her move into the tiny house in downtown Phoenix the spring break of her freshman year.

Sue had hated the neighborhood, which smelled like a mixture of diesel exhaust and dry air. She had hated sleeping on the pull-out couch because there wasn't room for a proper bed in what passed as the second bedroom. She hated that her mom's closet no longer held the colorful clothes she once wore for book club and parties. A few drab boxy dresses and black pants with elastic waists instead of proper buttons and zippers had replaced them. Her mom's old car gathered dust in the driveway while her mom walked to work and the neighborhood store, her world gone small. Sue hated that it smelled like failure.

Nothing would be worse than ending up like that. Why the hell hadn't her mom even tried? Her dad made good money. Her mom could have lived, if not in luxury, then not in poverty either. And her mom didn't even seem to mind. Every time Sue offered to help, her mom turned her down. The pride that had been absent when her father left returned for Sue's visits. Not that she visited often, preferring to bring her mother to Durango to see the kids during the summer and at Christmas.

Sue would never live like that, in poverty with nothing to do but spend decades waiting to die. What would her children think of her? That was the worst of it. She never wanted her children to pity her the way she pitied her mother. That's why she'd built her nest egg, growing her savings and investing wisely over the years. Gabe could go fuck whoever he wanted. She was prepared.

A knock sounded on the office door, then Gabe opened it and stared in. He stayed near the door, as if a physical obstacle kept them apart.

"I ordered pizza for dinner. Is that okay with you?"

Her cheeks burned from her earlier thoughts. "That sounds good."

He smiled and looked at her. She tried to read his face. The smile looked forced instead of happy. It didn't reach his eyes and was void of the usual invitation it held. He nodded, then closed the door. She shuddered, afraid everything she held dear would fall away, was already falling. Sue had watched one woman live that life. She didn't want to be the second.

Chapter 18

Three days later, Kira showed up in Durango. Sue watched the two-seater convertible Lexus pull into the gravel driveway. Thankfully, snow hadn't come early. It was an impractical car for winter in Durango, but Sue pictured Kira in the swank streets of San Francisco, gracefully sliding out of the car in a power suit and stilettos.

Sue had invited Amanda for dinner and looked forward to sharing another long and rambling conversation, especially with Gabe back in Denver. The boys had hockey practice and would grab dinner at a fast-food joint in town, unable to make the drive from the rink to home without stopping for food. This gave Sue the freedom to make grilled salmon, one of her favorite dinners, and one the boys would complain was too skimpy without spending a fortune on fish.

The chilly night made the back patio unfeasible, so the women sat at the kitchen table. Amanda arrived with a bottle of Sauvignon Blanc, which she opened the minute she stepped in the door. Amanda's cheeks looked red and splotchy, perhaps from the temperature dropping outside.

The women settled around the table, and the room glowed with the warmth of friendship. Sue had so much to share.

"Is the community still up in arms about the Worth images?" Kira asked.

"Most of the podcast comments skew negative, but I swear, half my friends believe the paper and think we'll have input into the final design," Sue said.

Kira rolled her eyes and started explaining why that would never happen. Then they heard the first sob. Sue and Kira turned to Amanda. She had one hand at her mouth, perhaps to stifle the next sob, while the other clasped her wine glass. Tears waterfalled down her face.

"What's wrong?" Sue asked.

"I'm going to lose my job." Amanda could hardly get the words out through the crying. Sue's stomach dropped, making room for the guilt that rushed in.

"Tell me exactly what happened." There was steel in Kira's voice. Sue watched as she geared up for battle.

"Everyone's mad at me. Well, everyone's mad at everyone. The mayor is furious at the city manager, and the city manager is taking it out on everyone around him. Both of them were in my office yesterday, telling me this was all my fault. None of it is my fault. They both met with the developer before I knew anything about the project. But they needed someone to blame, so they found me."

"Is it because of the podcast?" Sue asked. Ever since she found out what a jerk the mayor was, she'd worried about this. Of course they'd take it out on Amanda. It's not like those guys were going to take responsibility for their actions. But Sue had dragged Amanda into this the first time she went to city hall.

"It wasn't the podcast. At least not most of it. The developer keeps calling the mayor, threatening to pull out of the project. Residents are contacting us nonstop, most of them wanting the project canceled, and now we've got one city council member asking for a public vote on the project instead of letting the council decide." Amanda calmed as she talked about the facts of the project. Then she paused, unable to go on.

"I really need this job." She was crying again, this time ugly crying with her head in her hands. Sue reached out and rubbed her upper arm. She had to find some way to comfort her.

"You haven't done anything wrong," said Kira. "They can't fire you over this. It wouldn't be legal. They—"

"You don't understand. I need this job. I have a family to support. I have people who depend on me."

Kira quit talking. Sue didn't say anything either. She just kept rubbing Amanda's arm. Kira didn't have kids or a husband, although she had mentioned a boyfriend. Sue had a family but no financial responsibility for them. Even so, Amanda's pain reminded her of her own. The wrecking ball of destruction had swung and was impossible to stop.

Amanda's crying slowed. She apologized, excused herself, and went into the bathroom. Sue and Kira looked at each other in silence.

There seemed to be trouble in every direction. Despite Kira's quick response to losing the promotion, Sue was certain it had stung. Amanda worried about getting fired. Sue bore some responsibility for what had happened to her friends, and her own marriage careened dangerously.

They should be celebrating. Over fifteen hundred people had downloaded the podcast, and the Facebook traffic had been astronomical since they'd published the renderings. Instead, the air hung thick with worry. Amanda returned and apologized again when she sat down.

"There is absolutely nothing to apologize for," Kira said. "It is scary to think about losing your job. Believe me, I just went through it, and even though I'm the one who quit, it scares me out of my mind. That's probably why I'm driving across the country less than a week after resigning."

"What happened?" Amanda asked. "I was surprised you were in town tonight."

"I think I told you I was up for a big promotion. Well, I didn't get it, even though I deserved it." She paused and took a sip of wine. Sue watched Kira's eyes go glassy, not with tears, but anger.

"There was no way I was going to stay at a place that didn't appreciate me. Especially since I've done so much for them over the years. I was furious. I am furious."

Amanda's emotion receded, but Kira's took its place, swirling about the room. Looking at the petite blonde, Sue wondered if she was going to cry the way Amanda had. She couldn't imagine it, but something dark raged in her. In the end, it wasn't tears.

"Those fucking bastards!" Kira inhaled deeply and seemed to grow larger. "I'm so mad! I can't figure out if I'm running toward something or away from what happened, but I couldn't stay there. They betrayed me. I jumped through every hoop, and they hired someone who doesn't have half my experience. I haven't been this pissed off since I caught my first husband fucking his paralegal in the back seat of my car."

Kira looked at them for a reaction, then started laughing. The comment wasn't exactly funny, but it shocked Sue into laughing as well. She looked at Amanda and saw her giggling silently, before letting loose in a guffaw that shook her entire body. The laughter rolled over them, sweeping the anxiety away. Eventually, Kira caught her breath and raised her wineglass. "Here's to us and screw the bastards."

"I'll drink to that," seconded Amanda.

Sue took a long drink. She wanted to tell them she was struggling as well, but sharing felt like jumping off a cliff, or maybe just jumping off the high dive for the first time. She put her wine down. "Why is it that just when things seem like they're going well, like with the podcast, everything else falls apart? My husband has spent more days away from home than here the past couple of months, and I don't know whether I should be pissed off, start crying, or just accept it."

The moment the words left her lips, the room deflated. She'd thrown out an awkward comment once again.

"Now that's completely depressing," said Kira. "I honestly thought you had the perfect life. Gorgeous husband, strapping sons, beautiful home." Kira looked around the house, and Sue followed her eyes.

They sat at a big wooden table surrounded by matching cabinets and soapstone counters. The kitchen opened to a large den with soaring windows and mountain views. Sue saw the house through their eyes, an outsider's view she hadn't experienced in many years. Her home fit perfectly into the magnificent mountains and felt grand yet warm and livable. It was the perfect family home. Sue had always felt that way, she'd just forgotten it lately.

Amanda's voice brought her attention back to the table. "I'm with Kira. You can't have problems. You're our fearless leader. Let me get your husband on the phone right now, and I'll tell him to come home and stay home."

"Seriously, we need you focused on this fight," said Kira. "Look what you've done so far. It's amazing how much attention the podcast has brought to this issue in just a few weeks. Tell us how we can help."

They needed her? That wasn't how this worked. She needed them. They had the expertise she lacked. Sue's emotions swung again. Their need was a gift, something to cherish. And not only that, they cared about her. Emotion buffeted her heart.

"You two." She couldn't think of what to say, how to acknowledge the warmth and connectedness. "You are both wonderful. Thank you." Her voice cracked, and love welled to the surface until it overflowed as tears.

"Sue," said Amanda, reaching out to touch her arm, her voice filled with caring. "How bad is it?"

"I don't know." When she thought about losing Gabe, she froze with a loneliness worse than the coldest winter day. It scared her so badly she'd rather hide than face it. "We've been married a long time. The last kid will be gone soon. Maybe things have just run their course. That's what happened with my parents."

"That doesn't mean it's going to happen to you!" The force of Amanda's voice split the room. "I vowed I would never repeat my mother's mistakes. I haven't so far, and I never will."

Sue tilted her head at the familiar mother story and found a way to avoid talking about Gabe. "What's your mom like?"

Amanda looked from one woman to the other. "She'd dead now. But when she was alive, she was a drunk. She cleaned houses and tended bar. I grew up sharing a single bedroom with her in a shared house over on Front Street. Plenty of drug addicts and other people down on their luck lived there over the years. We were the only ones who stayed very long."

"That must have been rough." Sue had driven by Front Street. It hadn't benefited from the revitalization of most of Durango's neighborhoods over the past couple of decades. Once she'd seen a homeless man throwing up in the bushes there in the middle of the day. Two of the kids had been in the car. That sight might have been common in Seattle, but not in idyllic Durango. That's why they'd moved here. Perhaps it made her kids a little soft for the hard world, but hearing this story made Sue glad she had protected them. She wished she could have protected Amanda.

"It was rough," Amanda responded. "Mom wasn't a great parent. She came home with different guys all the time, and I spent almost as much time sleeping on the couch in the common room as I did in the double bed we shared."

Amanda looked around the table and must have seen the shock on the other women's faces. Her tone softened. "It wasn't all bad. The woman who owned the house was wonderful. She was more of a mom to me than my real mom. But the best thing about the way I grew up was that it taught me how not to raise a kid."

"Wow," Kira said, her eyebrows raising a notch.

"That's why my job is so important to me. I started working for the city before Toby was born. I needed to find a secure job with regular hours and enough money for a small apartment, no roommates."

Suddenly, Amanda's face brightened. "I didn't learn about the benefits that came with the position until the first day of work. Health care, retirement, paid leave, I thought I'd won the lottery."

Amanda shook her head, seemingly still amazed at her good fortune. "I'd been working since I was sixteen, but jobs on the river and waiting tables never had benefits. After that day, I vowed I'd never leave the city. In fact, I'm so grateful for my job that I've always outworked everyone else and tried to be the perfect employee. I think that's why they promoted me over the years."

Amanda looked startled as the words left her mouth, her eyes darting toward Kira. Kira didn't get her promotion.

"I feel like a lot of your problems are my fault," Sue said. "None of this would have happened if I hadn't stopped by city hall that day. You were nice enough to talk to me, and I dragged you into trouble."

"You didn't drag me. I came willingly. I thought it was the right thing to do. I still think it's the right thing to do, but sometimes being right isn't enough."

"Amanda," Kira said. "The city attorney gave you approval to speak on the podcast, and you had nothing to do with the renderings getting published. They can't fire you for this stuff."

"I'm in charge of the project, and it's not going well. I went on the podcast even though I knew my boss wasn't happy about it. Besides, I'm an at-will employee. They don't need a reason to fire me."

"Listen to me. I'm an attorney. They can't fire you for this stuff. I promise you'd win in court, not that it would ever get that far. You were carrying out your duties."

"But I'm sitting here with you guys now. This isn't part of my duties. I am so conflicted." Her shoulders sagged. Sue hated seeing her dragged down.

"You are allowed to have private opinions on issues," Kira said. "You aren't working right now. You're having dinner with friends. You don't have to toe the city line twenty-four-seven. You have rights, and this is one of them. Promise me that if they threaten to fire you, you will call me before you say or do anything."

Conflicting emotions crossed Amanda's face. Sue wished she had something to offer, some type of assurance. "You need this job," she finally said. "Let Kira help you."

Sue watched the change in Amanda as she slowly sat back and looked across the table at Kira. When she smiled, Sue could almost see the weight lifting. "Thanks. Your support means a lot to me. I'll let you know what happens."

"Well, aren't we a mess," said Sue. "Kira doesn't have a job, you're worried about losing yours, and I'm worried about losing my husband."

"As true as all that is," said Kira, "we are also saving Durango from a particularly unsuitable development."

"Yeah, well, I feel like you saved me too," said Amanda. "I can't tell you how worried I've been the last few days. I'm not going to let them scare me anymore."

"You'd better not. I'm here for you." Kira said to Amanda before turning to Sue. "Okay, one problem down. Now, how can we help you?"

"You already have. You two keep fighting despite everyone dragging you down. Sometimes I think I create most of my own demons. This project turns my focus outward, toward saving our valley and making new friends. Maybe sometimes by helping others, we end up saving ourselves. Seriously, I'm fine," Sue said.

Kira stared at her for a long time. "When you need us, we're here for you."

"Thank you." Like a warm blanket of comfort, their support reminded her of how her mom used to comfort her when the world seemed harsh or lonely. She missed that feeling. Maybe some things you never outgrew.

As the conversation rambled on, Sue learned a little more about her companions. Kira had a boyfriend she'd left in San Francisco. A shadow of melancholy crossed her face when she mentioned him, and Sue wondered if, in her urgency to hit back at her old company, she'd left something important behind.

"When it's the right guy, you just know it," Amanda said. "Toby's dad was the typical Durango ski bum, just like my dad had been. When he decided to move to Aspen, I cut the cord to make sure I didn't relive my mom's life."

The comment hit Sue in the gut. What decision could she make to veer off her mother's path?

Amanda's face lost every trace of worry as she talked about the guy she'd eventually married. "I really believe the perfect guy is out there for everyone. I found someone who cares about family as much as I do. He's a better dad to Toby than his own dad will ever be."

The conversation left Sue wondering about the scars they wore. They each carried experiences from their youth into the present, a constant influence on their decisions. Her thoughts returned to her mother. She'd spent so many years blaming her mom for being weak, but her mother was a saint compared to Amanda's.

What scars did her mom carry that made her give up instead of fighting for alimony and a better life? Perhaps it was time to learn a little more about her decisions.

Chapter 19

The next morning, Sue got a call from Carla Borelli, the receptionist at City Hall. The mayor wanted to talk. She waited on hold while Carla connected her. "Sue, I'd like to come on your podcast," he said before Sue even said hello. "Some of the information out there has gotten out of hand," he continued. "I need to set the record straight."

Sue let the combative comments slide. "I'd love to have you on. When are you available?"

"As soon as possible. I can do it today."

"Okay, how about four o'clock? Can you come to my house?"

"I'll be there. Are you going to be the only one on with me?"

Sue couldn't help smiling as she responded. "Actually, Kira Sutton is in town and staying with me right now. She'll be on as co-host. You're welcome to bring someone else from the city."

"No. I'm best off doing this on my own. I'll see you this afternoon."

Sue went downstairs to look for Kira and found her in the kitchen. She couldn't wait to share the news.

"Did you ask why he suddenly wants to be on the program?" Kira asked.

"No, I was afraid if I questioned him too much, he'd change his mind."

Kira laughed. "This is going to be fun."

Sue had a boatload of chores to do, but none of them seemed as rewarding as spending more time with Kira. "Hey, do you ride horses? I usually go for a ride in the mornings."

"I'm not scared of much, but I am terrified of horses."

They decided to go for a hike instead. Sue drove to a trailhead on the other side of the river. They hiked in silence. The cool air and excitement about the upcoming interview propelled Sue up the mountain. She only stopped when she heard Kira's labored breathing.

"I can't tell you how many spin classes I've been to, and they're obviously not worth crap." Kira panted heavily with her hands on her knees.

"It's the elevation. San Francisco's at sea level, you're over a mile high in downtown Durango. Higher here on the mountain. Have some water."

Once Kira caught her breath, they continued climbing. Thirty-five minutes later, the trees opened at the edge of a cliff, the Animas Valley spreading below them. Beyond that, snow-capped Rocky Mountains lumbered into the distance as far as the eye could see.

"Oh, my god!" Kira walked past Sue, her arms spread as if to embrace the view.

Sue said nothing. Majestic wasn't a big enough word to describe this world. They saw tiny horses in the fields below, where the sparkling river wound its way down the valley. A tractor that looked like a toy turned yellow stalks of grain under the dark earth. And the mountains. Their white-capped peaks flowed one into the other like a vast ocean, stopped only by the far horizon.

For Sue, not only the visible world but her internal life came into sharper focus when she could see so far. She became a tiny part of the landscape, barely noticeable, her problems equally small. This was where she understood she was less than a blip in time, less than a blade of grass in the lawn of the world. In the universe beyond, did she even exist?

If she was so unimportant, why was she here? She had been given a chance, a life to live. To honor this gift, she had to live the best life possible. She had mostly done that. She loved her children and raised them as best she could. Gabe was also a gift, and she had loved him fully. She would always love him, but she would also let their relationship run its course and be grateful to have had it at all.

As she stared out into the world, her thoughts kept returning to her mother. She hadn't done her best there. Maybe her mother had made different decisions than Sue would have. But Sue had no reason to hold that against her. She had always known she was loved. Her mother made sure of that. Her mother allowed her to choose her own path in life. Perhaps she should give her mother the same consideration.

She'd start by trying to understand why her mom had made the decisions she had. She could also give her the same unconditional love that she'd been given, and that her kids gave her. That would be a good start.

She noticed Kira standing still as a rock in front of her, her arms now wrapped around her body. "What do you think?" Sue asked.

"I'm really not sure I'm doing the right thing."

Sue waited. The view up here had a way of working on one's feelings.

Eventually Kira spoke. "I'm afraid I might have been a little rash about leaving San Francisco so quickly. I might not even like Florida. And I'm leaving a lot behind."

"Your boyfriend?"

"My loft, my friends, my masseuse. And yes, Sam." She turned away from the view and looked at Sue. "But you can't live your life for someone else."

"I used to think that. But deciding to share my life, change my life for someone else, ended up being the best decision I ever made." Sue hoped the words weren't harsh.

Kira turned away from her again. "I don't think I can do that. I mean, I did once, with my first marriage. That didn't work out. I'm done trusting men. I know I won't let myself down."

"That sounds lonely." For so many years, Sue wondered what her life would have been like if she'd stayed on her original course. She'd have a big career, no marriage, no chance of repeating her mom's mistakes. She didn't doubt she'd have been successful. Eventually, she'd have become a partner in the accounting firm.

But, oh, what she would have given up! She hadn't once been lonely since she'd made that decision. She'd sat on a floor surrounded by babies and toddlers, wondering if she could handle it. Many times, she'd worked so hard during the day that she fell asleep reading to them in their beds at night. She'd driven more miles of carpool than she'd ever believed possible, but she got to see her wonderful boys grow and learn. Their love had filled her life with joy.

Even today, when one of them called from college, she lit up inside, her heart pulsing through the phone line. And the way Chase had helped her with the podcast. She was so proud of him, so filled with love. And Gabe, who'd been a part of her life for so long, the way he smiled at her, touched her, filled her in a different way. She looked at Kira. She didn't want to be a lonely woman on a mountaintop.

Why had she only considered what she'd given up by marrying and staying home with the kids? She finally understood what she'd gained. What a wonderful life it had been. And tomorrow? She didn't have a solution, but she had a driving desire to talk to her mom. As usual, the mountain had given her perspective, and hope.

"It feels lonely up here," said Kira. She unwrapped her arms. "But imagine, soon I'll be meeting new people in a new place. The work will be exciting. The rest of it will just have to work itself out."

Back home, they prepared for the mayor's interview. He drove up at exactly two o'clock, complimented Sue on her home, and greeted Kira by welcoming her to the community. With his scuffed boots and hometown manner, he was the epitome of a small-town mayor. Sue wondered where he hid his claws.

Once upstairs, he had no trouble snuggling in close to Sue. Kira took the opposite chair and stared intently at the mayor. Sue started the podcast and welcomed him.

"Sue, thank you for your hospitality. I'm happy to be here today to talk about the Worth Winter Wonderland development. I'm afraid the project hasn't been presented to the public in the best possible way, and some of that might be my fault."

He sounded like Amanda when he talked about how public input was an important part of any development decision. He said they kept track of people's opinions when they contacted the city about the project.

To Sue's surprise, he seemed humble, and it sounded like he meant it when he said he had the community's best interests at heart. He apologized, then made a comment about how he wished city staff had kept him better informed.

He had to be talking about Amanda. Something cold lodged in Sue's gut.

"I need the audience to know that there is going to be plenty of time for the public to comment on this issue. I'll make sure of it. After all, there are plenty of people here on both sides of the issue. You've entrusted the city council to vote in your best interest, and I promise you we will do what's right for this city."

Sue was about to ask him what people should do if they were afraid the city council wouldn't vote the way they wanted. Kira got there first.

"Mayor Travis, there has been a public outcry against this project, but many people in the community believe you are supporting it. Would you like to go on the record opposing the project?"

"This project won't come up for a vote for a while yet. I am going to keep an open mind about it until then. I encourage everyone in the community to do the same." He sounded like everyone's grandpa.

"You know, I've lived here all my life," he said. "I've seen a lot of changes in this town. Nothing ever stays the same, and the question is, are we moving forward? When I, as mayor, have to make a decision like this, I ask myself, is the project more good than bad? Is this going to help the community long-term? From what I've seen, there is a lot of good in this one. It will create jobs, bring more tourists, and support our local businesses." He paused, and Kira started to break in with a question. He held up his hand to stop her.

"Now those drawings that we've got up on the city website," he said. "The people from Worth Company have assured me those are just so they understand what fits on the property. That won't be what they actually build. They'll come back here for community input. They're good people. They want to build something everyone will be proud of."

This time he couldn't stop Kira's question. "Mayor, those renderings didn't mention square footage or acreage. They were professional paintings of the project."

"I think they were just trying to get ideas. They don't have to turn drawings in yet. The city council is only looking at land use on this first decision, not design. That comes later. So, the real question is, do we want the jobs and money this project will bring?"

"Mayor, let me stop you there," Kira broke in. "You've brought up several points that need to be addressed. First, I don't think you can state that the project is 'more good' for the community than bad, to use your words. Isn't it true that we won't have the real numbers until they complete the environmental impact statement? Isn't everything else just marketing?"

"Now, they're working on the environmental statement as we speak. But I don't think it's fair to say that everything else they've given us is marketing." The mayor's testiness came through in his voice.

"Well, I'm not sure what else you'd call it, but I'd like to go on to another point. You said the city council looks at land use now and design later, implying the project will come to you for another vote, but that's not exactly true, is it? Doesn't the design go before the planning commission, not the full city council?"

When he didn't respond, she kept up the attack. "And aren't the planning commissioners appointed by the city council, not elected by the people? Finally, once council approves the land use, doesn't that give the developer the right to build everything in those drawings?" Kira's questions came fast, landing blows on the mayor.

At last, she stopped. Sue glanced at the mayor, red and fidgety beside her. Kira had been tough on him, not letting him respond while the questions piled up. She saw the mayor's face deepen in color as he seemed to search for a response.

"The council can always ask to see, and vote on, the project design," he finally said.

"Actually, doesn't the planning commission get to decide whether to refer the item to city council?"

"Well, they'll do what we tell them to."

"That's not how it's supposed to work," said Kira. "It's called undue influence."

"Mayor, what about the housing issue?" Sue didn't like the way the interview was turning into a courtroom drama. Kira might know the city process better than the mayor seemed to, but he was the mayor, and she needed to give him an opportunity to explain the merits of the project.

"Now, Sue, I'm glad you brought that up. I spoke with the developer earlier this week, and I want you to know they're planning on building condos as well as hotel rooms at the resort. That should help with the housing problem."

"But won't that make the development even bigger?" Sue couldn't keep the shock out of her voice.

"The details are still to come, but like I promised before, there will be lots of time for public comment."

Every time Sue turned around, the podcast led them to discover some new aspect of the project. What issues would they uncover?

"Mayor, I'm quite familiar with this developer," Kira said. "They've been sued in other jurisdictions for bribing elected officials. In one case they gave condos to local politicians who voted on their project."

The mayor pounded the table with closed fists. "How dare you insinuate something like that?" The veneer of kindly grandpa disappeared. "You're not even from here. You come into this town acting like you know everything, and now you're making accusations. And you," he said, turning to Sue. "I can't believe you are a part of this. I always thought your husband was a fine, upstanding citizen, but this is a disgrace. I love this community, and I won't be a part of what you are doing here."

With that, he stood up, knocking over the mic and his chair, and left. He tromped down the stairs and then the front door slammed. The diesel engine in his truck roared like an angry animal, and the wheels crunched on the gravel drive as he drove away. Neither Sue nor Kira said a word until the sound of the truck had faded.

They were still recording, so Sue thanked the mayor and Kira for contributing and hit the button to end the session. This was going to take some editing. "Well, that's not what I expected."

"Did I go too far?" asked Kira.

"I'm not sure. I'm really not sure what to think at all."

Combat couldn't be the best way to handle the podcast. National politics were so divisive right now. She'd never expected to find the same thing here in Durango. But the mayor's reaction brought up the specter of hidden things doled out slowly, first the drawings and now the condo units.

She didn't want this horrible development, but the discourse had to be civil. She didn't want to lose the hometown feel of being able to talk to her neighbors about anything, especially when it came to the good of the community.

Kira interrupted her thoughts. "Could I make a recorded statement for the podcast? You can decide whether to include it."

Sue thought about it. Kira had gone for the jugular, but she had brought up truths that needed to be heard. "Sure," she said, before pushing the button to start the recording and nodding.

Kira leaned in close to the mic. "The mayor is correct that I'm an outsider. I am in Durango for only my second time, and I never visited before. I care about what happens here, and I can explain why I feel this way."

Sue's stomach clamped as she stared at her friend. Was Kira going to talk about her assault?

"I have been an environmental attorney for almost twenty years. For all of that time, I have dealt with land preservation issues, often stopping or minimizing the impacts of developments like this one. I have been incredibly fortunate to spend my life defending wilderness areas that have no voice of their own. Earlier today I hiked to the top of a peak and saw the Animas Valley spread below, surrounded by a sea of Rocky Mountains. This land is stunning and irreplaceable." Kira paused, and Sue felt the emotion rolling off the other woman.

"This is a lot of development for such an incredible natural area," Kira continued. "Professionally, I am concerned about the social, environmental, and economic impacts of this project. Ultimately, it will be up to the mayor and council, and the people of this community, to decide what happens here. My only job is to make sure you have the facts so you can make the best decision possible. I commit to continuing to work on this project, pro bono, as I transition to my new position with the Blue Sea Law Firm. Thank you."

She nodded at Sue that she was done, and Sue stopped recording. It had been the shortest podcast they'd had yet, and the most exhausting.

Thirty minutes after they wrapped, Sue got a call from an unknown local number. It was the mayor.

"I want to apologize for the way I stormed out of there, but that lady just went too far," he said.

"I'm sorry you felt that way," Sue said, torn that Kira had pushed him, but the mayor's reaction didn't seem innocent.

"You need to know that I first heard about this project several months ago from Congressman Cory Smythe. He told me Worth Company was looking for a location for a Colorado resort and thought Durango might fit the bill. I knew right away how important it was."

"Why?" Sue asked. She would have told the senator to look somewhere else. Durango didn't need this type of development.

"Sue, I've been mayor for many years, and I've done a lot to help this town. But before I leave, I want to make sure the community is set for the future. This project will do that. It will bring in jobs and revenue that will help future generations when I'm gone."

Sue searched for what to say. "But what if keeping Durango authentic and environmentally sound is more important to people than jobs and money?" The question didn't come out the way she wanted.

"Oh honey," the familiar condescending tone returned. "That's just not the way the world works. Don't you want your boys to be able to have jobs in town?

Have you talked to Gabe the way I asked you to? He'll explain. There are things we want and things we need. Durango needs this project. And you need to get rid of that little lady friend of yours and focus on what's important here."

This time Sue hung up on him. She'd probably be angry when she looked back on the conversation, but right now she was too tired to be anything but sad. Each conversation was worse than the last. How could a phone call that started out with a friendly apology have gone so wrong?

At least now she knew this was a legacy project for the mayor. She understood that kind of drive, wanting to leave things better than when you started. But he was wrong. The costs of the Worth development were too high.

The mayor didn't understand that you didn't choose the path with the most money if it wasn't a good fit. Her years looking at corporate balance sheets had taught her that. Investing in shiny, expensive things rarely worked out unless you'd done a lot of research. Taking the job with the highest salary wouldn't work if you hated the job. You'd either be fired or be miserable. She could have chosen money and kept working after she'd had kids but staying home had been her calling. She'd stayed true to herself.

Worth Winter Wonderland didn't have this kind of authenticity. It was a rich man's play for even more wealth. Harold Worth didn't care about Durango. He only cared about extracting as much as possible from the city. Even in the best-case scenario, the project's jobs would be bought by changing what was best about the area. The worst case would be that the project would fail and go bankrupt. Durango would be left with the carcass of a failed development, losing both money and character. It was too high a price to pay.

Chase interrupted her thoughts, bursting through the front door with a pale-skinned girl with dark curly hair in tow. He introduced her as Emily, and her cheeks turned bright red when she said hello. Sue couldn't help smiling, and Chase shot her with a look of warning. She ignored him.

Unlike her other boys, Chase hadn't had a girlfriend yet, at least not one she knew about. This girl was almost Sue's height and had dark eyes and a smattering of freckles. She dressed like most of the girls, skinny jeans, white sneakers, and a bomber jacket, but wore minimal makeup.

She introduced herself, excited Chase was finally becoming more social. She learned Emily volunteered with the Sierra Club. Evidently, she and Chase had been working on the community event and were adding a donate button to the website. When Sue told them she'd interviewed the mayor, Chase said they'd edit and upload the podcast along with their other tasks.

As she watched them walk up the stairs whispering to each other, she hoped something would develop between them. The two older boys had had steady girlfriends during high school, and she'd loved having the girls around. With girlfriends, the boys studied more and were better behaved. Around their hockey friends, they acted like knuckleheads. Jaxson rarely brought girls home, and she'd given up trying to talk to him about the revolving door of young women he dated. She'd love for Chase to have a girlfriend and spend a little less time with computers. A grin tugged at the corners of her mouth.

Later that night, Sue headed for her bedroom, planning to go to bed early. So much had happened, not just on the podcast but the things she thought about on the mountain. She'd looked into airline flights to Phoenix earlier in the day. It suddenly seemed urgent to see her mom. She'd spent thirty years avoiding her, and she needed to make up for that.

She knocked on Kira's door to check on her. Kira had missed dinner because she wasn't feeling well. "Can I get you anything?"

"A bottle of wine."

The floor creaked as Kira walked across it. When the door opened, Sue saw she'd been crying.

"Can we share the wine? I need a friend." Kira looked tiny, and lost.

Sue led her downstairs, glad the boys had retreated to their bedrooms to do homework. She grabbed a good bottle of Spanish Garnacha from the wine rack, and they settled into the deserted den. "What happened?"

Barefoot and wearing jeans under a long black sweater, Kira hugged herself as if she were cold. Sue wondered if she needed socks. Before she could ask, Kira started talking.

"My new firm called and rescinded their job offer. They heard the podcast and thought I was unreasonably hard on the mayor. They said they didn't want someone who treated people like that to work for them. They were furious I'd mentioned the firm's name."

Her quavering voice shot right through Sue. How had they heard about the podcast? Chase only uploaded it a few hours ago.

As if reading her mind, Kira said, "I sent them the link when I applied, so they must have signed up for the notices. I have no idea what I'm going to do now."

"Stay here until you figure it out." Sue remembered the lonely woman on top of the mountain. This was something she could do, keep a friend from suffering alone.

"That's very generous of you." Kira cupped her wine in both hands. "I don't want to be a burden, but a day or two might help me out."

"Kira, I want you to stay." She did. She shared a connection with Kira and Amanda beyond the development. They were all women struggling to make sense of their lives, and Sue had a feeling they should stick together through the approaching storms.

Chapter 20

The next morning dawned cold and gray. Fall would soon give way to winter. After Sue fed the horses, she put blankets on them before opening the gates to the pasture. She didn't worry about the donkey. His coat had grown long and thick, and he looked like a fat ball of fur with spindly legs and long ears. She jogged back to the house rubbing her arms. It was time for a heavier coat and double socks.

In the kitchen, Gabe and Kira enjoyed the coffee she'd started. She poured herself a cup and stood there a minute, warmed her hands on the mug and dropped her icy face toward the steam.

Kira looked like she'd slept all right, despite the news about her job. Dark shadows lightly tainted her pale skin. Sue saw a trace of the girl she used to be. Her face was rounder and softer without makeup and her eyes not so bold. That must be some great makeup to change a woman into something fierce when she looked so friendly here in the kitchen.

Sue joined them at the table. Gabe listened silently as Kira explained what had happened with the job in Florida. He'd been asleep by the time Kira and Sue finished talking last night and hadn't been up yet when she went to feed the horses. Sue didn't have the chance to tell him she'd invited Kira to stay.

Gabe reached over and set his hand on Kira's forearm. "You're welcome to stay here."

"Thanks, that's what Sue said last night. I may take you up on that for a couple of days."

"Stay as long as you like," Sue said. They talked, made another pot of coffee, and then Gabe offered to make them his special pancakes.

"I'd be happy to take everyone to breakfast," Kira offered.

Gabe looked at Sue in that familiar way, a smile at his lips and friendly crinkles in the corners of his eyes. She smiled back then turned to Kira. "It's too cold to go out. Besides, Gabe makes the world's best whole grain pancakes."

"It will take a while. I've got to make enough to fuel two teenage boys." He pulled a large frying pan from the rack above the island, then turned to the stove.

Kira and Sue sat side-by-side, sharing the paper and coffee but not talking. The smell of brown butter and dough wafted through the house, and Sue relaxed as if someone had hit the pause button on the chaos swirling through her life.

The pancakes were delicious, fluffy and filled with New Mexico pecans. Gabe topped them with fresh bananas, then heated the syrup in a small gravy boat. The smell drew one boy and then the other down the stairs and to the table, their need for food besting their need for sleep. Once they'd eaten, the boys became talkative. Sue looked around the warm room. It had been a while since the kitchen was this full in the morning.

"Emily and I set up a donation page on the website," Chase said. "You should run some more ads and let people know they can donate now. I've already posted it on social media."

As soon as they'd finished breakfast, Kira pulled Sue into the laundry room. "Can I talk to you a minute? I didn't want to say this in front of everyone, but Chase is right. There's a lot to be said for increasing your followers, and I think you can do that on a much bigger scale."

"How? Let's do it."

"Well, there's a catch. It would require an investment. However, if you hire a publicist, I think you will hugely increase your audience."

"How much of an investment?" Sue didn't really want to know the answer to the question. She had built the audience by spending fifty dollars here and two hundred there, but she'd seen the numbers. They needed a lot more followers to influence the vote. Not to mention all the other stuff the committee had thought of.

"It would be four thousand dollars a month." Kira winced as she said the number. "But I think you'd be able to raise more than double or triple that in donations if you hired a publicist."

Sue did the math, the figure a blow to her chest. They'd have to spend eight thousand dollars, maybe twelve. She had the money. She'd squirreled away far more in her private investment fund. This might not be the type of rainy day she'd planned for, but it was pouring, nonetheless.

"Okay, let's do it." Sue tried to shake off the shock as she walked back into the kitchen. She hadn't spent a penny of her savings before this month.

"Hey mom, what's the deal with your troll?" Chase said, drying a platter and putting it away. "He's commenting again. It's like he's grading you for a class. Maybe it's one of the high school teachers."

There was a commotion as Gabe dropped a coffee cup in the sink and Kira simultaneously asked if there had been any donations yet.

"I don't know," Chase answered. "I'll have to call Emily."

Sue noticed that he left the room before making the call. Within thirty minutes, they heard Emily's car in the driveway, and soon she and Chase sat bent over the kitchen table, working on laptops. The kids came up with a plan to spend five hundred dollars on ads, and Sue handed them her personal credit card. The family didn't need to know about the other money she'd committed.

"I'm adding one-thousand- and ten-thousand-dollar donation categories," Emily said. "Although people can also choose to donate any amount."

"Who on earth would donate ten thousand dollars? And what would we do with the money if they did?" asked Sue.

"We've told people we'll use the money to stop unsuitable development in the Animas Valley and preserve the character and feel of the natural environment," Chase said.

"Add a one hundred-thousand-dollar category," Kira said.

"You guys are nuts!" Sue shook her head. The peaceful morning had returned to chaos.

"It can't hurt," Kira said. "If this goes viral, you might raise enough money to start a nonprofit to protect the valley into perpetuity."

The nonprofit again. It would be great to have an organization to protect the valley and make it better. Maybe it could also be a way to keep the community involved. But as much good as it might bring, Sue wasn't sure that was what she wanted to do with her life. It kind of reminded her of her mom, doing good in the local library but having no greater calling. Sue wanted to stop one development. As much as she needed a purpose, she couldn't quite gin up excitement about running an environmental nonprofit.

The doorbell chimed and brought her out of her thoughts. Jaxson bounded out of the kitchen and toward the front door. Perhaps he had friends coming over. She didn't recognize the voice that said hello, but out of the corner of her eye, Sue saw Kira sit up sharply. She heard the name Sam Russell as he introduced himself. He said he was looking for Kira.

Shame and hope crossed Kira's face in equal measure, then Sam walked into the room half hidden behind Jaxson. As he came into view, she saw a handsome Black man with thick hair and eyes so dark they seemed black as well. At least until he saw Kira, then they flashed with light, and relief crossed his face. He said her name, ragged love in his voice. Then he ran to Kira and lifted her in a hug.

Sue watched her friend cling to him like an animal. She buried her face in his neck, her blonde hair splayed across his shoulder. They were oblivious to anyone else in the room. Sue glanced at Jaxson, who stared gape-mouthed at the couple. Sue recognized the expression and shut her own mouth. Even when Kira had told Sue her most painful secret, she had been stoic, the way she was on the mountain. She'd been fierce with the mayor and later angry at her job loss. But the way she held onto this man was something entirely different. It was as if she was being saved. He held her as if he'd never let go.

Finally, he pulled his head away from her to look into her face. "Why did you leave?"

She slid down his body until her feet were on the floor, her eyes fixed on his face. It was a long time before she answered him. Sue wondered if she had an answer.

"I'm sorry," she said. More time passed. "I didn't know what to do. I was so hurt. I was embarrassed, and I had to get away." Her deep and velvety voice slowed, as if molasses coated her emotions and blocked the words.

Sam said nothing. He just looked at her. Finally, she asked how he found her.

"The podcast. As soon as I got the notice there was a new one, I listened. Sue said you were in the studio. I flew out this morning. I just got here."

"The podcast," she said. "You know how I told you I had gotten a job in Florida? Well, I was on my way there when they heard the podcast. They rescinded their offer."

"You accepted the Florida position? We didn't even talk about it."

"But I left you a message about the offer. I said we needed to talk."

Sue couldn't believe her ears. Did Kira really leave her boyfriend without even talking to him? What kind of relationship did they have? Maybe Sam was like Gabe, not a big talker. Or perhaps Kira was like her, afraid to reveal her deepest emotions, knowing rage and blame would show up as well.

Neither Kira nor Sam had acknowledged anyone else in the room. Jaxson got antsy and slipped away. Sue just stared, the raw emotions triggering comparisons to her marriage. Kira's life had changed suddenly, while Sue's meandered toward the horizon.

Sam's voice broke into her thoughts. "You were incredible on the podcast. I've never heard you so passionate or forceful."

"Yeah, I was great." Anger laced Kira's words. "It was enough to get me fired from a job I hadn't even started yet."

Sam took her face gently in his hands, the intimacy making Sue uncomfortable. His voice softened. "That podcast was the first time I realized you weren't perfect. You are always so polished, but on the podcast, you were angry and let your emotions show through."

"We've been dating for five years. You know I'm not perfect."

"We have had a perfect, wonderful relationship. We're good at our jobs, have nice cars, go to nice restaurants. I have always enjoyed being with you. But what I heard yesterday was different. It was raw. That's what life is really about, not just the perfect part but the meaningful part. I want that in my life. I flew halfway across the country this morning because I want you in my life."

"I don't have a job in San Francisco anymore. I actually don't have a job anywhere right now."

"I don't care if you don't have a job. I don't even care where you live. I'll quit my job and join you. San Francisco, Florida, right here, let's do something new and amazing together."

Sue stood unmoving, watching them in silence. His words pierced her to her core. They were perfect words, those spoken by romantic leads in the best books and movies, words of love. Kira took a step back, putting a small space between them.

"But you have a job, a good job, in San Francisco. And I'll never go back to my old firm." Sadness tinted Kira's voice.

"You and I are great attorneys. We can work anywhere. We can get new jobs. We can start our own firm. The whole world is open to us."

"But that's so risky."

"I know!" He threw his arms wide. "Let's take some risks. You took a risk by quitting when those bastards didn't give you the promotion you earned. It's not like we won't be able to support ourselves. We can do whatever we want. I'll quit my job today and follow you wherever you want to go."

"You're crazy. What's gotten into you?" She backed further away from him and for the first time seemed to notice Sue watching them. Kira's eyes grew big, and Sue could see that she'd forgotten where she was for a few minutes.

Flustered, Kira turned to Sue. "I'm sorry. Sue, this is Sam. Sam Russell."

Sue walked over and shook Sam's hand. "I think I should leave you two alone for a while."

"No, this is your house. You know what? I want to take Sam on that hike you took me on yesterday."

It was cold, but Sue found jackets, hats, and gloves that fit them. Fortunately, Sam had the same size feet as Chase and borrowed his hiking boots. Sue enjoyed watching the two of them together. Sam was clearly all in on the relationship, while Kira seemed almost shy about it. Sue wondered if this reflected how much her life had changed over the past few days, or perhaps related to her first marriage, or her experience in college. Trust wouldn't come easily after things like that.

Plus, she had just lost her job. That had knocked her down hard. Sue would never have quit her job the day she didn't get promoted and then leave town without even talking to her boyfriend of five years. It seemed opposite of what someone as put together as Kira would do.

If she had nurtured her career all those years instead of raising four boys, perhaps she'd have made rash decisions when others impeded her progress. But she had chosen differently. She closed her eyes and returned to when she'd made that decision, the baby at her breast staring at her with dark blue eyes full of need and trust. It hadn't been a choice. It was love, and it became the most important thing in her life. Consequences be damned.

She opened her eyes and saw Jaxson heading for the front door. "Hey, come give your mom a hug."

"Rain check, mom. I've got to go." A blast of cold air struck her as he left.

Sue wandered upstairs to see what Chase and Emily were up to but caught them on their way down. They both carried laptops, and she backed down the stairs to let them pass.

"Where are you two off to?" she asked.

"Dad needs his office, so we're going over to the Sierra Club," Chase said.

"I'll see you over there in a couple hours for the event planning meeting," Sue said.

"We'll probably be gone by then" Chase turned to smile at Emily. The girl smiled back and blushed before dropping her eyes. There was definitely something going on there.

Sue wandered up the stairs and heard Gabe on the phone in his converted office. She had nothing to do. No, she had a hundred things to do, a thousand, she just didn't want to do them. The way Sam looked at Kira like she was his world, that was what she wanted. It had been a long time since that had happened. She should probably get used to it.

Chapter 21

Sue had to text Amanda several times from the event committee meeting, first about permitting and then about where to print high-quality, enlarged images of the development. Amanda stopped by the Sierra Club offices with her son Toby after his soccer game. He seemed like a nice kid, gangly at thirteen the way her boys had been, trapped between childhood and becoming a man. Amanda asked the group not to tell anyone she'd stopped by, then jumped in, making suggestions and providing information about the community. She could have easily run the whole event, and Sue half wished she had.

Back home that night, Kira asked if she and Sam could take Sue and Gabe to dinner. They ended up at Sue's favorite restaurant, one of the fancier ones on Main Street. It was a warm respite from the chilly night. The small tables crammed the room, and the magnificent smell of roasting duck, truffles, and just a hint of green chile greeted them as they walked in the door. Chatter bounced around the crowded room, but their small table kept the conversation intimate. They ordered filling meals, a green chile burger for Gabe, steak frites for Sam, seared salmon for Kira, and ragout for Sue.

By the time the wine came, it seemed like they were old friends. Sam regaled them with stories of trips to South America and Alaska to find land to preserve and protect. He explained how his job was similar to Kira's, but he was more on the finance end of things.

While his work didn't require him to visit the places he preserved, he believed he should. If he saw a place, came to understand and love it, he knew he'd be willing to do whatever it took to save it. If he hadn't been a high-priced attorney, Sue would have recommended him to run their organization.

Kira was oddly quiet, but Sue made up for it, questioning Sam about his travels. An equal opportunity conversationalist, Sam tried to engage everyone at the table and asked Gabe about his company. Twenty minutes later, they were deep in conversation about whether the software Gabe had developed to help cities manage their resources could be modified to improve the management of natural areas.

Sue listened but also watched Kira, whose eyes rarely strayed from Sam. Kira's emotions, usually hidden by a cool exterior, played across her face. Sometimes she looked hopeful, even loving. Other times, doubt and trouble crossed her brow.

Sue leaned toward the corner of the table she and Kira shared. "Are you okay?"

"More than okay. We've been talking all day about the future. I'm looking at things I've never seriously considered before."

"With Sam? He seems really nice."

Kira blushed. The corners of her lips turned up in a small, encouraging smile. The expression only lasted a moment before the more serious, more professional Kira returned.

"With him, but also with my career. He got a blank piece of paper, put it in front of me, and told me I could create any career I wanted. I had never looked at it like that, at least not in twenty years. My career track always followed a straight line. I never thought about whether I was happy. It's been fun brainstorming what I really want to do with the rest of my life."

"That's wonderful!" The joy of the other woman's process rocketed through her. Kira was starting over, blank slate. It had to be so freeing and exciting to look at your life as if you were at the beginning instead of halfway through. "Will you stay here while why you work things out?"

"If it's okay with you, I'd like to. Staying here would give me the time and space to figure out what I really want to do next." Kira and Sam would stay at the hotel that night, but Sam had fly out the next day to return to work.

"I'd love to help you with the community event," Kira continued. "Sam might even come back for it."

"Well, I'd love to have you, and we are really going to need help. It's grown far beyond what I originally imagined." She shared the new plans, a stage with different acts and nonprofit booths. Colleen had even contacted a promotion company that wanted to bring in a craft fair. If Amanda hadn't stopped by to help, Sue didn't think she'd have figured out how to organize the thing.

"You should make it as big and boisterous as possible." Kira's voice grew loud, and the men looked over.

It was the first time Sue realized she and Kira had almost been whispering. "That's what everyone is telling me," Sue said in her normal voice. "This type of thing is really not my forte. I've always been more of a behind-the-scenes type of person."

"Not anymore. You've created something people want to be a part of." Kira paused and looked Sue up and down, then glanced at Gabe before turning back to her. "Start thinking of yourself differently. You are so much more than you give yourself credit for. You're more than an ex-accountant. More than a mom and a wife. You're bringing people together to make a difference in Durango."

Sue held her breath to keep her face from crumbling. Kira had seen how hard she'd tried and announced it to the table. Tears filled Sue's eyes and tickled her bottom lashes, threatening to drop. She used her napkin to blot the corner of one eye, while her chest expanded with pride.

Pride. It had been a long time since that rusty emotion had visited. She'd been proud of others, like when she realized what wonderful young men her sons were becoming, but years had passed since her own achievements had filled her with pride.

She glanced at Gabe with this recovered piece of herself. Back when she'd worked, every day she accomplished something. Turning in the smallest report at work had been an achievement, a small step forward in a day. Enough of those days strung together made for a promising career. There was always the next task, a next step on the ladder.

With motherhood, you did your best every day and hoped your kids grew into decent human beings and then left home. Then what? Why did something as important as motherhood make her feel so inconsequential?

She leaned toward the corner again as the guys continued their conversation. "Kira, I need to figure out what to do with the rest of my life."

"Me too." Kira laughed.

"I need to figure out the rest of my life," Sue told Gabe on the drive home that night. It took all the courage she had, but buoyed by her earlier conversation, she got the words out He took his eyes off the road for a moment to look at her. He didn't say anything, but she thought she saw a question there.

"The kids will be gone soon. I need to do something important with my life," she said. They drove in silence for a minute.

"What do you have in mind?"

She told him about Kira and the blank sheet of paper. "I'm working hard to build something valuable for this community, and it makes me feel important." Why did it always sound so bad when she said that, as if she didn't think raising her kids was important? Surely there was room for both, especially now.

"It's time for me to do something more with my life. Maybe not today, but soon."

He didn't respond, but she saw his hands tighten on the steering wheel, his jaw set. He stared straight ahead at the road. Was he mad? Did he expect family to always be enough for her?

She needed more. Not just because the kids were leaving and because she worried that their marriage would fall apart the way her parents had, but because she was smart and strong and could make something of herself. She was already making a difference.

She looked at him, at this man she had loved for so long, with whom she'd spent half her life. He'd always had his own journey separate from the family. He had his company. The company had preceded her and would likely far outlast her. It took most of his days and seemed to take more of his nights. She hoped that was what took his nights.

"What are you thinking?" she asked.

"I want to help you do whatever you want to do."

What did that mean? Perhaps it meant nothing would change once the kids left home. Instead of Gabe having his company and sharing responsibility for raising the kids, they'd be together but each on their separate journeys. Would that be enough for him? Would it be enough for her?

The question hit her like a punch in the gut. She had worried for years whether she would be enough for him once the kids were gone. She had never asked herself the right question.

The question stayed with her as she fed the horses the following morning. It made her think about her mom. Had her dad been enough for her mom after Sue left home? Did she have it wrong all those years? She poured the last of the grain into Samson's trough. He gently nudged her out of the way to get to his breakfast. She stepped aside, then put the bucket down and reached for the phone in her pocket.

Her mom picked up on the third ring and sounded sleepy. "Hello?"

"Mom, it's Sue. You sound tired."

"Thanks, honey," she said with exasperation. "How are you today?"

"I'm good, but I want you to come visit. I'm working on a lot of new things." She told her about the development and the podcast and asked if she'd help with the community event. Sue didn't mention her parents' divorce or the trouble in her own marriage.

"I'd love to see you, but I'm working this week. I've also got plans for the weekend, but I can try to get out of them if you need me."

"Please." Sue heard her voice crack. How could she be fifty-one years old and need her mother so much? She sure hadn't seemed to need her over the past twenty-five years. Hopefully, her mom would forgive her.

"Oh, honey. Let me see what I can do. Flights will be expensive this late."

"Mom, it doesn't matter," Sue said, her voice recovering. "Let me know when you can travel, and I'll get you the tickets. I'd really like to have you here."

Thirty minutes later, her mom phoned back. By then, Sue was in the kitchen making breakfast. She had recovered from her earlier emotional moment and was a little embarrassed at the memory. But when her mom told her she'd taken the day off work and found a flight on Friday morning, her emotions surged back. Now, if Sue could only get past the years of blaming her mother for choices she disagreed with, perhaps she could learn about, and from, her mom's situation.

Chapter 22

A few days later, Sue had just come in from the barn when Colleen called and told her to turn on the TV. She did, but they were talking about a snowstorm on the East Coast. Minutes later, Chase bounded down the stairs, yelling "CNN! CNN!" He shoved his phone in Sue's face.

The Headline News anchor reported that real estate magnate Harold Worth was attempting to build the Worth Winter Wonderland development in the middle of the existing winter wonderland of Durango, Colorado. They showed photos of the bucolic valley, the ski slopes at Purgatory, and the shops of Main Street, then contrasted those images with the painting of Worth's huge triangle resort theme park.

"A local group, Save the Animas Valley, has organized to stop the development," the anchor said before breaking for commercial. The entire story lasted less than a minute, but it got the point across.

Jaxson thumped down the stairs next, still in his pajama pants, hair disheveled and a sleepy look on his face. "What's going on?"

Chase shouted, "It's on CNN!" Then, "I've got to call Emily." He rushed back upstairs.

Apparently, he couldn't call Emily while in the same room as them. He almost knocked down Kira as she came down the stairs, likely drawn by the commotion.

"Jaxson," Sue said, tossing him her phone. "Headline News is doing a story on the Worth development. Find it and show Kira." Sue turned to get another coffee mug.

CNN was huge! Would they want to talk to her? She wouldn't know what to say. By the time she poured Kira's coffee and turned back around, Kira and Jaxson were watching the video.

"Mom, you're going to be famous. That's awesome." Jaxson handed the phone to Kira and came over and gave her a double high five.

Sue lit up like a kid on Christmas. She wanted to hug him, but that would probably ruin the moment. The days when her kids fought each other just to hold her hand or sit on her lap had long passed. "Why don't you go put some clothes on, since we have a guest," she said instead.

Well-built, Jaxson's hockey-hard chest and ripped stomach were on full display above his pajama pants. Dear god, he was going to be a lady killer. Probably already was.

Seeing him as a man instead of a boy shifted the world slightly. Her kids were closer to starting their own lives and families than they were to being children. It was a happier thought than her tired perspective of waiting for them to leave her.

Kira's words whisked away the thought, but not the feeling. "This is fantastic! I hoped this would happen."

"What are we going to do? Do you know how to deal with it? I'm totally out of my element."

"Get ready. This story will launch a lot more publicity."

"Is this what the four thousand a month bought us?"

"This is only the beginning. If we're lucky, the publicity will scare the politicians into voting against the project. We need to meet with the publicist."

"The great thing about having money," Kira said two hours later when they'd hung up with the publicist, "is that you can hire someone like her instead of having to rely on favors."

Sue agreed. The publicist had given her strategies for speaking to the media and tried to prepare her for the negative comments that were sure to come their way.

Evidentially, Worth had hired a nationally known public relations firm for the Durango project.

It didn't take long for the publicist's predictions to come true. The ABC news station called Sue for an interview first. She agreed, and by early afternoon they posted the interview on the website. That prompted an updated round of coverage by CNN, and then other networks picked up the story. Sue rattled off her list of bullet points in a slate of interviews and was sure to mention the community event and where people could donate to save the Animas Valley.

By early evening, things had calmed down, and Sue and Kira were enjoying a glass of wine at the kitchen table when they heard a car on the gravel driveway. Almost immediately, Chase and Emily ran through the front door.

"Donations are going wild!" Chase shouted.

Emily booted up her laptop and showed them they had raised just over thirty thousand dollars in online donations. Sue texted Amanda and asked her to come over. She had to share the news.

By the time Amanda arrived, Chase was showing them how news outlets in Colorado, New Mexico, and Arizona had picked up the story. The CNN footage spread virally across social media. The excitement was like surfing a tidal wave out of control, but so far it was a great ride.

Amanda seemed the most excited of all of them. She started talking about what they could do with even a couple of hundred thousand dollars a year in funding. She proposed creating bike and walking trails, and perhaps even establishing a preserve and parks out of some of the land intended for the resort.

Kira agreed, suggesting they get protected area easements for the paths and create green corridors for both animals and people in the valley. Sue didn't always understand the terms, but it was a language of hope.

She savored her wine in the warmth of the kitchen, excited people spinning around her. She had turned on the switch that brought them together. Their ideas to help the community far surpassed her original vision, but that didn't lessen the pride of what she'd achieved. It was a feeling to bask in, one she wanted in her life. Instead of dreaming of trails and natural areas, her thoughts swam to what other challenges were out there, waiting for someone to make a difference.

It didn't take long until the first negative story aired on CNN. Cory Smythe, the federal congressional representative for Durango and a staunch Republican, backed the Worth development. The second she saw him, Sue realized he was the man she'd seen on her way out of city hall the day she'd met with the mayor. He talked about how the development was good for the community and how a local group had unfairly pressured the company to release pictures of the development before they had gone through the proper public process. He also mentioned how farmland had been misrepresented as pristine.

After the interview, the mood at the table visibly sobered. Kira cautioned that Smythe had done some damage. He had painted them as a group of wacky, unsophisticated do-gooders. He had made a good point about how much of Durango's existing tourism industry relied on manmade attractions, such as the ski resort and the train.

Sue thought people who cared about the environment would now have even more reason to support them. If politicians, especially national ones, opposed the development, it might be a real positive. Most people didn't like politicians.

Jaxson broke the mood by walking in the door with pizzas. They'd eaten more pizza in the past few weeks than in the past year, but Sue quickly let go of the guilt that plucked at her. She tossed yet another bagged salad, choosing to concentrate on bringing her family together in this new way rather than worrying about familiar guilt. She only wished Gabe were here to share the moment and excitement about her project gaining national media attention. Instead, he was in Denver, again.

The night ended on a high note. Donations topped fifty thousand dollars before Sue went upstairs to bed. Kira speculated that some were anti-Worth donations, a monetary vote against the flashy New Yorker who'd been talking about running for governor.

A bigger question for Sue was what the organization would do with all that money. Then she remembered that Amanda and Kira knew exactly what to do with it. First, use it to make sure Worth Winter Wonderland didn't happen, then ensure the Animas Valley remained a beautiful and peaceful place of wonder for everyone.

The next morning, the phone rang before Sue was out of bed. It was a reporter from the *Asheville Citizen-Times* newspaper in North Carolina. The reporter, who sounded incredibly young, asked Sue if she had any advice for a group of citizens in Asheville who wanted to oppose a local development. Phone calls kept coming, as did the stories. The media reported on Worth Company projects across the country that had filed for bankruptcy or degraded the environment. The stories always mentioned Durango as Worth's next target, and each time a story hit, their donations increased.

Congressman Smythe's story didn't make a dent in the negative media about Worth. Many of the stories, Sue had initially learned from Kira. Sue didn't trust coincidences.

"Kira, is our media person responsible for all these stories?"

"You mean the one you're paying for?"

Well, who the hell else would it be? "Yes," she said.

"The publicist you hired won't focus on damaging someone's reputation. But after the story hit, I gave myself a little gift for all the shit I've been going through and hired a different kind of publicist."

Kira must have seen the concern on Sue's face, because she quickly explained that her publicist would only uncover what was true. He double-checked everything. For Kira, exposing the truth of Harold Worth and the negative impacts of his developments seemed more than fair.

"Do we really need to go this far?" Sue asked.

"Do you want to win?"

She didn't want Worth Winter Wonderland just down the street, but she sure didn't want to play dirty to get there. Maybe she was just naïve. "I've got to go check on the horses." This, she'd need to think about.

Chapter 23

The morning her mom arrived, Sue picked her up at the airport and took her to lunch in town. She had chosen a Mediterranean restaurant because of their amazing appetizer plate and great salads. Another advantage, it was off Main Street and a little quieter than the touristy restaurants. She wanted to have a long, uninterrupted conversation with her mom. It was time.

She wasn't sure where to start, so she gave her mom details about Worth Winter Wonderland, the podcast, and how she enjoyed being involved with something outside the home. A quick smile flitted across her mom's face, and Sue used that as her cue to start the conversation she really wanted to have.

"Mom, what was it like for you when dad left?"

Sue had expected surprise, but her mom acted like she'd asked the time of day. "It was what it was. Divorce isn't fun or easy, but I always thought it was harder on you than anyone else."

"How can you say that? You went from living a privileged life in a big home, not working, to moving into that tiny house and having to work a menial job."

The surprise Sue expected earlier arrived. Her mom sat taller, eyes on fire and cheeks flushed. "Is that how you see me? That's offensive. I have a wonderful life."

"But you lost everything. Dad is still really well off, and you've been struggling for decades."

"I have everything I need." Her mom searched her face, then shook her head. "I'm proud of the life I live. I make my own way in the world, and there's something to be said for that."

Her mother sat back and crossed her arms. Now they had offended each other. How could her mom accuse her of not making her way in the world? She was the one who'd been the career woman, once. Although she didn't start out as a homemaker, Sue stood on the precipice of repeating her mother's life. She teetered on the cusp of losing everything, and all her mother did was criticize her choices.

"I can see you're getting all worked up," her mother said, arms still crossed. "I'm not trying to criticize you. You need to understand that I'm proud of what I've accomplished in my life. I raised you and did a pretty good job of that. I've led a fulfilling life since you left for college. I don't need your dad's money, and that feels good."

"But you let him walk all over you, and you have nothing to show for it." Surely, her mom understood what she had given up, how she had been such a poor role model. Sue had spent decades afraid of following those footsteps.

"How dare you say that to me? You don't know what you're talking about." Her mother's voice was angry and loud.

The outburst came just as the server set the appetizer plate on the table. The woman dropped the plate the last few inches, causing the feta and olives to jump, before she slid away.

"I remember you telling Mrs. Holly to hire a good attorney when she told you she was getting a divorce. Why didn't you do the same thing?" Sue stabbed a piece of cheese with her fork. What a frustrating conversation.

"I did hire a good attorney, and I got exactly what I wanted."

"What are you talking about? From what I can see, you got nothing."

Sue's mother uncrossed her arms and sighed. "I swore I'd go to my grave with this. You were so proud of making your own way in the world, and I thought it would hurt you."

Her mom looked straight into Sue's eyes, worrying a side of her lip before continuing. "As part of the divorce settlement, I got enough money for the down payment on my house and an agreement from your father to pay for your education."

"College? What are you talking about? I was dad's kid. He had to pay for that."

"No, he didn't. You've always thought your dad was better off than he was. He is very good at living at the edge of his means. We had a beautiful home, but the mortgage on that place almost broke him. Sometimes I think the financial pressure got to him and caused other bad habits."

Sue's mind whirled. She had grown up well-off. They had lived in an elegant home in the best part of town with access to the finest schools. She bought clothes at the mall and got a car when she turned sixteen. She never thought money was a problem. That her mom had bargained for her education, first college then an MBA, was almost more than she could bear to think about. The sacrifice was huge. She asked her mom about the bad habits instead.

"He wasn't faithful, and that can be soul crushing, but the biggest problem was the money. He always wanted a new car, a better watch, things he could barely afford. After twenty years, I was happy to get out of the marriage. I only wanted him to pay your tuition on time every year. You were such a smart, independent girl. There was nothing that was more important to me. And I did the right thing. You've gone on to live a wonderful life."

The words were like small knives. Sue had looked down on her mother all these years. She had only been as involved with her as necessary. An education in business had taught her to think of her mom as a terrible negotiator. Instead, her mother's situation was entirely Sue's fault. What a bitch she'd been. Perhaps it wasn't too late to make it up to her.

"Mom, I've got some money saved from when I worked. I would love to give that to you to help you buy a better house."

"I don't want a better house! I love my house. You think my job is terrible. What are you always calling it? Menial labor. It may be menial to you, but it's my passion. I work in a library. Me, who always loved books! I'm surrounded by them every day. And before you offer me money for something else, I don't need your money. I have enough to live on. I have a savings account, and I'll get a pension from the city when I retire. I'm set. Why can't you understand that I'm proud of my life? I'm surrounded by friends, have a job I love, and I live exactly where I want to live. The only things I want from you are time and respect."

No longer little knives, the words had grown bigger and sharper, each cut releasing more shame. In the brief period between appetizer and main course, her world had turned upside down. Sue had picked this restaurant to have a quiet place for a leisurely conversation, and now she wanted to leave before their salads arrived. Running away seemed preferable to facing the way she'd acted.

How was she going to get out of this one? Why was she always out of her element? It wasn't only with her mom that she said the wrong thing. So many times, she'd said something that made someone else feel awkward. She'd done it the other evening with Kira and Amanda.

She had wanted to talk to her mom because she needed help, and instead she'd learned what a horrible person she truly was. She'd wasted thirty years disapproving of her mother. All because of what her mom had given up so Sue could choose her best life. In return, Sue had scorned her mother's choices. Remorse and regret closed her throat, but she pushed the words through them.

"Oh god Mom, I'm so sorry. I didn't know." What else could she say? Words would never be enough.

After a long moment, her mom responded. "Just treat me with a little more respect, and maybe a little more love." The last words weren't more than a whisper.

Sue's constantly spinning, questioning, and blaming inner world stopped, and she realized how much she'd hurt her mom. Just when her mother was embarking on a new life, just when she'd lost her husband, Sue's judgment made sure she lost her daughter as well.

Sue had visited her mom as little as possible. And once she'd had kids, she'd made sure her mom was with them only a couple of times a year. And her kids loved her mom unconditionally. Even Gabe loved her that way. It was Sue who had added conditions. If her marriage did go the way of her parents', she hoped her kids would be more forgiving, more loving, than she'd been of her mother.

"I do love you, Mom. I've been so wrong. I'm sorry."

Her mother said nothing. She didn't even smile. But she did reach across the table and took her daughter's hand.

"I've been a very selfish person," Sue continued, searching for forgiveness. "It seems like all I think about is myself."

"There's nothing wrong with thinking about yourself. That's how you find meaning in your life. It's possible to both think about yourself and give your love to others. They aren't mutually exclusive."

The server came with their salads the moment silent tears started spilling down Sue's cheeks. Of course.

"I'm glad you're here." Sue wiped her eyes and took a long drink of water as she struggled to control her emotions. Finally, she spoke. "I'm glad we're having this conversation. I thought I needed to talk to you about my life, but you've taught me so much I didn't know about yours."

"Sue, I want to help you. I don't think you've realized that I am capable of helping you. Let me in. Let me be a part of your life. If you can stop judging me, that can happen."

"Believe me, I'm done judging you. I wish I'd known earlier about the college thing, and about how proud you are of your life. It would have made a difference."

"I've been telling you how great my life is for years. I just don't think you were ready to hear it. You always thought you were on some better path. So, what has changed? Are you worried about your own choices?"

It was as if her mom saw straight through her. She had been hoping for a few words of wisdom before she shipped her mom back to Arizona. Now, she wanted time to find out who her mom really was, but time was the one thing she didn't have.

"There's so much going on right now. The movement I've started against the development, the kids leaving home, Gabe. I wish we had more time to talk. Can you stay longer?"

"I can't stay longer this trip, but there's this new invention, it's called the telephone. We can talk. And we can make plans to spend more time together. I'd really like that. Now, tell me more about what's happening with Gabe."

No longer surprised at how her mom saw into her deepest thoughts, Sue tried to tell her. In the end, the words didn't come out right. When she said she was afraid her marriage would end like her parents' had, she couldn't explain why. Her mother tried to tell her that Gabe loved her while her own father had been distant. The marriage had ended a decade or more before they split.

"I'm worried because Gabe is in Denver all the time."

"Have you talked to him about it? What's going on in his business that he needs to be in Denver."

"I'm not sure. He's collaborating with a company called MAPTech. I can't imagine what kind of project would take him away so often."

"You met him at work. Don't you talk to him about the company?"

Sue tried to explain why she hadn't stayed involved in Gabe's business. For so many years, it seemed like every waking moment was taken up by the boys. For twelve of the past twenty-two years, she'd had a young child at home. She thought it would get better when they started school, but she'd filled the hours they were away.

Helping in the classroom, preparing for the myriad of school projects, piles of laundry, and endless cleaning and cooking stole time. And when they weren't in school, she needed to clone herself to make sure they were all in the right place at the right time with the right equipment. Not to mention homework, and just finding time to give them love. The last thing she had time for was Gabe's business.

She and Gabe had an unspoken rule. She managed the bulk of their household needs, and he left for work each day and brought home enough money for them to live comfortably. It was only recently, maybe in the last year or two, that she hadn't felt run in twelve directions at once, hadn't been ready to drop with exhaustion. As a stay-at-home mom, it seemed ridiculous to say she didn't have time to stay involved in the business, but life got in the way.

"So, ask him about it now." Her mom made it sound so simple.

"I tried, and it was a disaster." Sue told her mom about the argument when she had accused Gabe of cheating on her. In the open air instead of the tortured confines of her mind, the shameful words prickled her skin. Her fears sounded ridiculous. She had no proof, just a name on his phone that he'd been able to explain. When she told her mom about her trip to Denver where she'd made a scene in front of Gabe and Lucinda, her cheeks seared with regret.

Her mom took the accusation of infidelity seriously. Sue's dad had been wrong to sleep around. It was black and white. Her mom had always kept their house in order, held dinner parties for her dad's business associates, and raised her. Didn't her mom keep her end of the bargain? Hadn't Sue?

"When your dad cheated on me," her mom paused, then looked down at the table as she continued. "He shouldn't have done it. Even today, I wonder why I wasn't enough."

The words gave voice to the kernel at the core of Sue's fear. Gabe had pursued Sue when they met. It took him years to convince her to marry him. But it happened so long ago, Sue barely remembered that version of herself. She wasn't the same person now, that confident, brash young woman making her way in the world. She had loved that version of herself. And she had loved the worn out but loving mom she'd been while her boys grew up. Who was she now?

Her mom was still talking. "In the end, it all worked out for the best. I'm much happier today than I would have been with him. Once you left home, there was no reason to stay. He was mad that I wanted a divorce, but he accepted it once I told him I knew about the affairs. Lots of people were getting divorced then, and I think it was just easier for us than trying to fix things."

Sue had so many questions. She had never imagined her mom had asked for the divorce. She'd always blamed her dad. Technically, she still blamed him, but in a new way. He was the one who'd cheated. She wondered how her dad saw the divorce.

"Sue," her mom said, calling her back to the conversation. "I think you're in a totally different situation. You are so different than I was."

"How? We both basically followed the same path. Got married, had kids, stopped working, then reevaluated when the kids left home." She had lived her mom's life, the life she never wanted to live. She had wanted a career, to control her own destiny, but she'd ended up a homemaker like her mother.

"It wasn't the same at all!" There was anger in her mom's voice. "Yes, I worked, but I was a kindergarten teacher for two years. It was a placeholder, not a job. I was waiting for a husband. That's what women did back then. We were supposed to be homemakers, that was my goal, not teaching. In some ways, I was never my own person until you left home. That was the first time I looked in the mirror and asked myself what I wanted to do for the rest of my life. Until then, I just followed the track I was supposed to follow."

Sue stared at her mom, trying to balance the woman she'd seen as the most put together on the block with someone who had wanted more. Her entire childhood could be seen through multiple mirrors.

"You were totally different," her mom continued. "You always had such fire. You didn't just want a job, you wanted a high-paying job with a big five accounting firm where you'd get to travel. The first time you came home for Christmas, you told me that. You were so specific. That's when I knew you'd be fine, and I could finally end things with your father. And, of course, you went out and got everything you wanted. I have to admit, I was a little surprised when you moved to Seattle for Gabe. You'd always said you'd never get married. But when I saw you guys together, I understood. You two didn't get married because you were supposed to, you were so in love you almost had to. And when you had kids, you didn't expect to stay home, but I knew you would."

"How could you have known that? I hadn't planned on it, in fact, we had already chosen a daycare. I surprised myself with that one." Deciding to stay home had been the turning point of Sue's life. No one could have known that would happen.

"I knew because you never do anything halfway. You've always been the superstar of your own life. There was no way you were going to trust someone else with raising your kids."

The room grew still, and tears rushed to Sue's eyes. She had never felt like a superstar. Well, maybe when she was working, but then she had earned it because she outworked everyone else. Her mom's comment rang true. Daycare was fine in theory, but no one would give her child the love that flowed through every cell in her body. That's when she'd put away her Wonder Woman costume and become a regular mom.

The conversation lulled. Sue's brain hurt from everything she'd learned at lunch. The server came by almost reluctantly, and they ordered coffee and baklava, a sweet end to a revealing meal. It wasn't until halfway through dessert that Sue realized what she needed to say.

"Mom, I'm so sorry. I've spent more than twenty years not treating you the way I should. You called me a superstar, but really, I've led a pretty regular life. I was incredibly fortunate to have my college paid for and not need to work while I raised my kids. I never knew that you were my superstar behind the scenes."

She reached for her mother's hand as tears sprung to her eyes, again. "The deal you made with dad to pay for college gave me an incredible leg up in my life. Because of that, I've led exactly the life I wanted. I have no idea how to thank you."

How could so much love and shame coexist in one body? She'd wasted time thinking her mom wasn't living a life that was good enough. Not only was her mom completely happy, but she had blessed Sue's life with her sacrifice.

An idea formed, a fragile ember that needed protection. She had to honor her mother by being her best self. With or without Gabe, but hopefully with. The time had come to figure out the next phase of her life and make it just as fulfilling as what preceded it, maybe more. In many ways, it was the biggest challenge she'd ever faced.

The preparation for the community event was beyond hectic, leaving Sue little time to think about what her mother had revealed at lunch. Sue had made her mom promise to take some vacation time and return to Durango to help with the event, mostly because she wanted to spend more time with her.

The kitchen had transformed into a war room, and almost any time of the day or night, someone was there going over logistics, talking to nonprofits reps and craft vendors about booths, working with the food trucks, even reviewing the layout and escape routes with the fire department. Chase, Emily, and Colleen were the marketing team, and they were social media machine. They'd even put posters up around town.

The media calls had cooled off, and when they did call, Kira, who'd stayed in town, encouraged them to show up at the event. Amanda had taken a personal day the Friday before and stayed from early until almost midnight, showing up again the next morning. She'd likely be fired if the mayor or city manager found out, regardless of whether Kira said it was legal. Amanda helped anyway. She even brought her kids and husband to help on the weekend.

Everything had fallen into place too easily. She and Gabe had been too busy to have the big talk Sue promised her mother they'd have, but she would the moment the event ended. Sheer work had pushed her worries about Gabe some place too deep to access. It was a relief to ignore them.

The day before the event, Sue wanted nothing more than for it all to be over. They hoped to rally the community and show the city council how many people opposed the development. But nothing guaranteed their efforts would change the minds of the politicians.

Jaxson hadn't come through with the bands he'd promised, but almost everything else had run smoothly. They even solved the band problem, thanks to Jim Beam. It turned out that he frequented the live music venues in town and knew most of the bands. He pulled in a few favors, and they were set.

Lying in bed the night before the event, a combination of nerves and excitement churned Sue's stomach and kept her from sleep. Had they taken care of every detail? Her lists told her they had. Anything that went wrong now was out of her hands. That thought should have brought sleep, but worry that it had all been a little too easy kept her up late into the night.

Chapter 24

It was pitch black predawn when Sue, Amanda, and Kira met the rental company at the fairgrounds. With great relief, Sue let Amanda manage the morning chaos, knowing she would disappear before the sun rose and return as an attendee during opening hours.

Amanda made sure every item they'd ordered had arrived. She sound checked the stage as soon as they set it up and oversaw booth placement for the nonprofit fair. By the time she left at dawn, a mini city had arisen from the parking lot. Amanda even left Sue with a checklist and instructions to ensure the vendors were in their proper booths on time.

Sue and Kira watched her get into her SUV and drive away. Sue's nerves made her wish she had the same option.

"The city sure is lucky to have such a tiger on staff," Kira said.

That was the truth. Amanda had made it a much better, more organized event. Plus, she'd structured it so that the fees paid by the craft vendors and food trucks more than covered their expenses. The event might end up making money.

By nine, Sue had checked in all the vendors. She'd originally planned to go home and change but had run out of time. The public would show up within the hour.

Event planning had never been her forte. The fixed day and time rushed at you like a freight train, and then the event passed. With less than an hour to go, the pressure swirled at tornado strength, but it was too late to stop.

The fairgrounds were nestled into a larger complex that formed a huge semi-circle around the town's two baseball fields. At one end, the Boys & Girls Club anchored the space, followed by the huge city rec center. The fairgrounds sat at the top of the arc, with a large parking lot they used for the booths. The bands would play in the arena that normally housed rodeos and horse shows. The senior center and Durango High School finished the arc back at the main road.

Craft vendors had taken over one side of the parking lot, and the manager ran it almost as a separate event. She expected people to come from up to two hundred miles away just for the crafts. That sounded like a stretch, but Sue wasn't the craft fair type.

She walked through the nonprofit booths one last time. The horse rescue organization had brought in a darling white pony for people to pet. Sue hoped there wasn't any liability there. The animal shelter had half a dozen dogs and cats ready for adoption. When Sue got closer, she found Colleen petting a long-furred, orange cat with huge paws.

Sue worried about the animals as the frosty morning air turned her breath silver. "Do you think they'll be okay in this weather?" she asked a woman who had worked at the shelter for as long as Sue could remember.

"We brought the adult cats and dogs in first. They should be fine. When it warms up, we'll bring in the puppies and kittens."

"Will they all get adopted today?" Sue asked.

"Are you kidding? I've already adopted this one," Colleen said. "Dave is coming down to do the paperwork and take him home."

"You already have two cats." Sue rolled her eyes. To each his own. Now maybe if it were a horse or donkey adoption… Perhaps she'd take home the white pony she passed earlier. One day she'd have grandkids, and no child could resist a white pony.

Despite the chill, the sense of community warmed her. Each booth represented something or someone from this wacky, caring town she called home. She loved the way people brought in animals, books, and crafts. This feeling, these people, this was Durango. Worth Winter Wonderland didn't have a chance.

Sue thought she heard her name and turned around. Sure enough, Chase ran through the booths, calling her.

"Mom! You've got to come see what they did." He pulled up in front of her, panting, the whites of his eyes huge.

"What's going on?"

"Worth, you've got to come see it. They're having their own event."

"What are you talking about?" He had already turned around, so she jogged after him. What kind of event could Worth be having? Chase kept running, past their booth to the far side of the craft fair, and then she saw it. A huge banner, *Worth Winter Wonderland—Here for Durango,* hung across the entire front of the Boys & Girls Club. Instead of the enormous triangular monstrosity of a resort depicted in earlier drawings, this time a photo showed what looked like a charming Swiss chalet. Another photo showed a handsome teen surfing. In a third, a happy family surrounded a little girl blowing out candles on a birthday cake. Every picture screamed wholesome, fun, charming. It was the opposite of the earlier crass depictions of the development.

Sue quit jogging, stunned into rigid stillness. She'd worked so hard on her community event, and this pierced a dagger through her efforts. The building's double doors opened wide, and gorgeous flower arrangements on either side begged you to enter. Chase stood beside her, still panting.

"Let's go in," she said.

"Are you sure? Aren't they the enemy?"

"We are part of this community, and we have every right to go in there." Her insides trembled with anger. She'd been outmaneuvered. The banner made it seem like her event was part of this. She needed to be brave for Chase. She needed to be brave, period. She was the leader of this thing. Chase was right, Worth had become the enemy. She moved forward and crossed the threshold into the lion's den.

"Welcome, welcome." A tall, athletic-looking man with silver-blond hair greeted her. It was the man she'd met when she'd taken photos of the site. "I'm Brendan Callaghan. The Worth Company is happy to have you here."

He seemed incredibly confident, and Sue wondered if recognized her. Velvet ropes like those used at old movie theaters directed her into the gym. The entire space had been carpeted in a sophisticated forest green, and enormous photos hung from every wall. Three repeated those on the sign outside, accompanied by others representing life in Worth Winter Wonderland. Beautiful, luxurious condos with mature, elegant people hosting a party, children running through a field of wildflowers, a beautiful young couple sitting on a park bench. The photos went on and on, showing perfect lives in a perfect community. Even the images of rides or the lazy river made it seem like the people in the photos were having the time of their lives in a beautiful place they truly enjoyed. It was impossible to look at the pictures without wanting to be in them.

"Make yourself at home," Brendan said. "We've got a breakfast bar with local pastries and fresh fruit. Antonio back there in the corner will make you the espresso of your choice. We've also got juices and soft drinks for the young man. I have to warn you that the coffee bar switches over to a regular bar at noon. The menu changes then too. Chet's BBQ will take over for lunch.

"You've got a bar and free food. You're going to go broke." It was the first thing Chase had said since they entered the building.

"Oh, I don't think Mr. Worth will go broke anytime soon. This is just our little way of introducing ourselves to Durango and letting everyone know how much we appreciate being a part of the community. I hope you will get to know us. We are a very different company than the one you've portrayed on your podcast."

Thank god she hadn't gotten coffee, because she'd have spilled it down the front of her shirt. He knew exactly who she was. This really was the lion's den. She didn't know about him, yet he'd recognized her on sight. Everything here was the opposite of the warm community feel she'd had at the nonprofit booths. The big, sophisticated city had come to Durango, and Durango was not prepared. No one entering this room would be against the development. Heck, if they'd presented this at first, she might have been for it.

These are just pretty pictures. Kira had told her once the zoning changed, they'd have the right to build almost anything they wanted, without community input. They still wanted to build the theme park and ill-designed resort she had first seen. The community in these pictures would cost many times as much. This was damage control. Damn, they had mastered damage control.

Just then she saw Tim O'Brien, the director of the Boys & Girls Club. She left Callaghan without a word, having no good comeback for him. Instead, she marched straight toward Tim. Was that fear in his eyes? Satisfaction came with the role of the hunter.

"Tim, what the hell! Why are you doing this?"

"Hi Sue. How's it going?" He shuffled from foot to foot, then belatedly offered his hand to shake.

She ignored the hand. "Tim, why did you let them do this here? You knew we were having the community event today. We even offered you a booth."

He leaned toward her. "Mr. Worth donated ten thousand dollars to the Boys & Girls Club," he said in a low voice.

She backed up to look the shorter man in the eyes. Still hunched, but in a normal voice, he told her it was a lot of money for the club.

"So, you sold out?"

He straightened. "Sue, look at these pictures. This place is going to be great. I think you had the wrong idea. They've talked to me about this. You shouldn't have published those first pictures. They would never have built that. They love Durango."

She hardly knew where to start. Everything she'd worked so hard for would crumble. Then the mayor walked in the door.

He stopped when he saw her and gave her a sideways glance. She could tell he was trying to decide whether to come over. He looked over at the guy from Worth Company and Sue saw the guy look the mayor in the face then tilt his head toward her.

She did not want to talk to him. This whole situation made her stomach hurt. What the hell had she gotten herself into?

"Sue, welcome," Buddy said. He looked like he wanted to talk to her about as much as she wanted to talk to him. It was one of those kindergarten scenes where the teacher tells two kids to kiss and make up after a fight.

"Hi Buddy. I think we can agree this is awkward. It's time for Chase and me to leave." She looked over at Tim. "Good job. Way to be there for the community."

"Now Sue, there's no reason to act like that," Buddy said. "Surely you can see from these pictures that Worth Company wants the best for Durango."

"I can see by what's happening in this room that they've bought off you and the Boys & Girls Club. That's about it."

"Now don't get hysterical. You might not want to say things about people that could get you into trouble." The mayor's voice had the hitch of anger she'd heard on the podcast.

"The first time I say something that's not true, I'll be sure to let you know." She turned toward the door and nodded for Chase to follow.

"Sell out," she said as she was leaving, just loud enough to be heard. Not exactly great behavior to teach your kid, but she had to find some way to stick it to them.

As she made her way out of the gym, she was almost knocked over by a tall blond man with chiseled features rushing in the door. Congressman Cory Smythe. Politicians, gorgeous photos, fancy catered food. She walked outside and looked across the parking lot at the junky craft fair and menagerie of makeshift booths filled with animals and folksy people. They didn't have a chance.

She returned to her event's main tent. Where once she'd thought the Astroturf covering the pavement looked great, now it just seemed tacky. Posters of Worth's original images of Winter Wonderland lined the walls along with aerial photos of the site. Her mom manned a table at the entrance where she encouraged people to sign a petition urging the city council to either stop the development or let the citizens of Durango vote on it.

She'd been so proud of all the work they'd put into the event just minutes ago. Emily sat ready to take donations. Kira waited, phone in hand, for media inquiries. But there was no free food, no slick politicians, no Swiss chalet.

She must have looked as terrible as she felt when she returned to the tent. Gabe had arrived, and he and her mom simultaneously asked what was wrong, while Kira asked how bad it was. It was bad. She told them about seeing the mayor and the congressman, about the ten thousand dollars it had taken to bribe the Boys & Girls Club, and about how appealing they made Worth Winter Wonderland look. Chase brought up the free food, coffee, and booze. Sue didn't know whether to laugh, cry, or give up and go home.

Their reactions were priceless. Her mom grabbed her hand and told her everything would be fine, just the way she had when Sue was little. Kira whipped out her phone and walked away to make a call, and Gabe took out his phone as well. It took him a minute to find the number he was looking for, then he put the phone up to his year.

"Tim, this is Gabe Cleary, I heard Worth offered you ten grand to use the club today. I'll offer you twenty thousand to kick them out right now."

Chase yelped, and Sue's mom started giggling. Sue stood there, mouth open, astonished at his gift. Tim didn't take him up on his offer, but Gabe told him to call back if he changed his mind.

Gabe's offer sent emotion roiling through Sue, gratitude, but also a tinge of resentment. The prince had arrived to save the princess. Part of her wanted to wear the tiara, but a bigger part wanted to save the valley herself.

Stupid fairy tales. She had a real crisis to deal with. Her voice returned, and she heard the edge of hysteria the mayor had accused her of. "What are we going to do? They made Worth Winter Wonderland look like a cool, hip place to hang out with great restaurants and fun activities. When I stepped outside their Shangri-La and looked across the parking lot at our odd assortment of booths, I almost wanted to turn around and go back in."

Gabe put his arm around her and walked her out the tent door. She wrapped an arm around his waist, thankful to have something to hold on to. The sun had begun to warm the day, and the pale blue sky had deepened to turquoise. They looked out over the booths and food trucks.

Even though the event hadn't officially begun, an impromptu tai chi class had started in front of the senior center booth. The Red Cross blood donation van had driven in from another city and parked near the back. The Durango Children's Museum had two tables, one for information and a colorful craft table for kids. Next to them, the Friends of the Durango Library had carts loaded with giveaway children's books.

In keeping with the theme of the event, several environmental organizations had booths, including the Sierra Club and the Environmental Center. At the Durango Birding Group, a man sat cleaning a pair of binoculars, surrounded by gorgeous photos of local birds. A band that didn't sound so great warmed up in the arena.

"It may not be much," Gabe said, "but this is why we came here. We could have had all the slick developments we wanted in Seattle, but we chose Durango because of these people. This is home."

"Some of these people will love the new Worth Winter Wonderland." She'd always felt sorry for the teddy bear forever banished to a shelf by the new toys at Christmas. Worth Winter Wonderland sparkled like the newest gift under the tree.

"Some may like it," Gabe said, "but Durango's a pretty motley crowd. I think most people still won't want a big-city developer telling them what Durango should look like."

"I hope you're right." She didn't believe for a minute that Worth had changed the original concept of the development. He'd just made some pretty pictures hoping to dupe the hicks in Colorado. She was an accountant, and real estate development was a numbers game. He'd put as many hotel rooms, condos, and rides on the property as he could get away with. The more money-makers he fit on the land, the better his bottom line. The pretty new pictures were a decoy, a shiny object to wave in front of people so they'd forget the triangular monstrosity and number of rooms needed to make the project work.

Heck, the Swiss village he'd shown in today's photos wouldn't even fit on the piece of land he was buying, bisected as it was by the river. Not if he was going to build the river attractions, theme park, ski hill, and other amenities in those lovely photos. It would be impossible to make that happen. She turned to Gabe. "I've got an idea. And thanks for trying to buy out the Boys & Girls Club."

That had been an impressive move. He'd tried to stop the bad guys. She turned toward him and lifted her hand to his cheek. Maybe, just maybe, things would work out. Like the town, Gabe was worth holding onto.

Chapter 25

T he morning passed in a whirlwind as Sue talked nonstop to the hundreds of people who walked into their tent. Many were old friends and wanted to catch up as well as talk about the project. Colleen and some of the board members from the Sierra Club conversed with a revolving crowd from Durango.

Even Paula stopped by. She gave Sue a quick hug and whispered, "good luck." As she left the tent, Paula caught up with her husband Denny. The hug meant everything to Sue. Their friendship would survive long past the results of this election. She wouldn't judge her friend for what went on in her marriage. Outsiders rarely glimpsed the complexity of personal relationships.

Gabe and two Sierra Club board members implemented Sue's idea to drive people to the development site. Sue hoped seeing the genuine beauty of the valley would help them recognize what they'd give up if the project went forward. The new Worth photos were beautiful, but they weren't taken in Durango and didn't fit into the reality of the Animas Valley.

At the booth where Emily handled donations, Sue overheard her talking to a crusty older man in a cowboy hat and boots. Sue had seen him staring at the Worth Winter Wonderland photos at the Boys and Girls Club.

"I'd be happy to give to your cause, but I didn't bring my checkbook."

"That's okay. We take cash and credit cards."

"Well, okay then." The man pulled a credit card out of an old leather wallet and handed it to Emily. "You can put two hundred dollars on it."

Sue gaped in amazement before introducing herself to thank him while Emily processed the charge on an iPhone. Emily's boldness in asking for money surpassed what Sue would have done. That girl took care of business! Chase clearly had good taste in women.

Sometime late morning, Sue's mom brought her a cup of coffee and a cinnamon roll from one of the food trucks. She insisted Sue take a break and eat. Sue followed her mom out the back of the tent to a table and two chairs Sue recognized from their tailgating equipment. She wondered when and how her mom had retrieved them. There was so much going on she hadn't even noticed.

It was good to take a break. Talking with people about something she found important filled her with passion, but the long morning had her energy flagging. As she cut into the cinnamon roll, she realized her hands were shaking. This used to happen at work when she had a big presentation and skipped breakfast because she was too nervous to eat.

"Are you doing okay?" her mom asked, sinking into the chair beside her.

"Yes. I'm having fun testing myself to see if I can convince people to oppose the project. There are so many options. They can sign the petition, write or call the mayor, show up at a city council meeting, or donate money. Often, I've got information they haven't heard before, but I also learn so much from everyone I speak with."

"How bad do you think Worth showing up at the Boys and Girls Club will be?"

"I always ask people if they've been there. About half have, and most of the rest are going there next. Almost everyone who's been there liked the new plan a lot better than the original, but many still don't trust Worth. And no one liked the Worth representative. He was too slick for Durango."

"Well, good. You really seem to take to this. You're lit up with energy when you're in there talking to people."

Sue loved chatting with the locals. They were her people, and even when they disagreed, she believed they wanted the best for the community. It surprised her how many people listened to the podcast. Each time someone told her they enjoyed it, an energy filled her that she carried to the next person. A few people thanked her for making a difference, and that made all the hard work worthwhile.

She took her last sip of coffee. Durango needed her, and that satisfaction warmed the pit of her stomach. Worth and his money might win in the end, but Sue wouldn't back down. "Thanks, Mom. I'm glad you knew I needed a break. Time to get back at it."

She walked into the crowded tent and noticed Sam, Kira's Sam, at the entrance. He wasn't supposed to be in Durango until tomorrow. Behind him, a news crew entered. Sue quickly scanned the crowd for Kira as she made her way to front of the tent but didn't see her and lost sight of Sam.

The ABC station director had told her they'd show up sometime today. She wondered if they'd already been to the Worth Company event. A knot of worry dug into her shoulder as she reached her hand toward the young woman holding the microphone.

Then she heard a loud, clear voice ring through the tent. "Kira, Kira are you here?"

It was Sam. Sue turned around, startled. Why was he yelling? Everyone in the tent must have heard him. Then she saw him, several feet above the crowd, slowly turning in a circle. He must be standing on something.

"Kira!" he bellowed as he threw his arms wide. Sue saw the crowd back away from his strange behavior.

"Just a minute," Sue said to the reporter. But the reporter was no longer interested in her. Instead, she led the cameraman toward Sam. Sue made her way through the crowd as well.

By the time she got to him, Sam was no longer on the chair. Instead, he was in front of it, on one knee and facing Kira. No way! This was by far the most exciting thing happening at the community event. Kira stood in front of him, her blue eyes wide and unblinking, her arms stiff beside her. Her light blond hair swayed at her shoulders as if she'd come to a sudden stop.

"Kira, I love you," he started.

His voice carried across the tent. He must have had stage training. Sue saw the reporter gesturing at the cameraman to record.

"I want to spend the rest of my life with you, and I can only think of two ways to do that." He reached into the inner front pocket of his blazer and brought out a piece of paper, rolled and tied with a red ribbon. His hand shook.

Sue wondered if he'd brought a marriage license for her to sign. Not traditional, but perhaps that's what lawyers did. And what about the 'two ways' he'd mentioned? Strange.

He reached into another pocket with his free hand and brought out a small velvet box. It was the perfect size for a wedding ring.

"I want to marry you or start a law firm with you. Or we can do both. If you're not ready to do both right now, then let's at least do one." What had started as a grand gesture lost steam quickly. "Please share your life with me." His final words came out in a cracked whisper.

Sue wanted to tape his mouth closed, afraid all the talking would ruin a good proposal. She'd have stuck with the main question and kept the company stuff for later. And she probably wouldn't have done it in public, especially seeing the look on Kira's face. Whether confusion or fear, it wasn't good.

Sam must have sensed his proposal wasn't going well. He closed the gap, stuffed the ring box and scroll into a pocket and reached for Kira's hands. "Will you marry me?" His voice trembled.

Sue felt the vulnerability as much as she heard it, and her heart ached for him. Everyone else in the tent waited for Kira's response. Sue tried to divine the emotions crossing her face. Sadness, fear, love, trouble, longing. And finally, peace. All the emotions that happened when crossing the threshold from one phase of life to another had been visible, and she had settled on peace, an open door. Her free hand touched his face, drawing it toward her. She kissed him.

"I will marry you," she said after the kiss.

Sam picked up Kira and spun her around, setting her down after one revolution. "Do you want to start a law firm with me? I've got a plan." He pulled the document from his pocket.

"Let's start with one thing at a time."

He put the document away and opened the ring box. At that point, it seemed like the entire crowd rushed in to get a look, and Sue could no longer see them. She wished Gabe had been there. It was such a strange proposal, so public. Gabe had proposed to her on his small boat in the Puget Sound, and it had seemed like they were the only two people in the world when they promised to be with each other forever. Tears pushed their way into her eyes. She wanted that feeling back.

The buzz in the tent lightened after the proposal. Sam beamed. Kira looked a little shell-shocked but happy. Swept up in the happiness, when Gabe walked into the tent to get his next round of passengers, Sue went straight to him and kissed him on the lips, then told him what had happened. The brief look of surprise that crossed his face when she kissed him didn't register until she was halfway through the story. She had forgotten how far away they were from their engagement on the boat.

She shook her head. She had to quit thinking about this stuff. Worry about her marriage and comparison to her parents did nothing to improve her situation. She had to change. Her parents' marriage, the basis for all her fears, hadn't been what she'd imagined. So where did that leave her and all the doubts that had accumulated over the years? And what about the woman in Denver? That was a reality. One that had been explained. It was too much to think about.

She saw Kira halfway across the room and headed toward her to get a look at that rock and see how she was holding up. The ring was beautiful, platinum with a vine design on the band, a small diamond nestled in each leaf. The center stone was sapphire, round, and perfectly sized for Kira's delicate finger. When she looked up to tell Kira how beautiful it was, she saw the representative from Worth Company walking into their tent.

"Uh, oh, this looks like trouble," Sue said. Why had this guy come here to bother them? Hadn't he caused enough trouble with his competing event next door?

Suddenly, Kira squeezed Sue's hand in a death grip. Sue tried to pull away before Kira crushed every bone. She stopped when she saw Kira's shocked expression.

"How dare he?" Kira whispered, her eyes locked on the tall blond.

"That's what I thought," said Sue. "Have you met the guy from Worth Company?"

The man caught Sue's eye and nodded. As he approached, Kira released her hand. Sue tried to rub away the pain.

"Sue, nice to see you again. This is a quaint little affair you've got here. Thanks for doing this. You've shown us the direction we need to take to capture the spirit of the community, adding our own style, of course."

What an ass. She wasn't sure whether to call him out on what sounded like a backhanded compliment or just try to get the visit over as quickly as possible. She squared her shoulders. "We take pride in our community, Mr., um, I'm sorry, I forgot your name. I'd like to introduce you to my colleague, Kira Sutton."

"Hello Brendan, it's been a while."

"Kira, it's great to see you. I heard you were involved in this project. Are you still representing them even though you are no longer with the American Lands Organization?"

Sue wanted to punch the guy. Even though his words weren't wrong, his condescending tone implied Kira had done something wrong to lose her job. Unruffled, Kira calmly told him she was a part of the campaign.

"In that case, we should sit down and talk about the project, attorney to attorney." He looked around the tent, faint derision on his face. "There's no real place to talk here. We can use a private office at the Boys & Girls Club. Would you like to join me?"

"I promise you, I will never be in a room alone with you again. Not after last time." Kira's voice held ice and rage.

Oh my god, oh my god, oh my god. Sue could barely contain her shock. This was him! This must be the jerk who'd assaulted Kira. What should they do? She could barely listen to the conversation, overwhelmed by the past coming back to haunt them.

Brendan's smug face barely registered concern. "I don't know what you're talking about."

"Remember the date you took me on? When we went to that party at the frat house?"

"We had a lot of classes together, but we never dated. No offense, but you're not exactly my type."

Sue's heart went out to Kira. She put her hands on her hips and stepped between them.

"You can pretend you don't remember that night," said Kira, "but we both know what happened in that room."

Kira put her hands on her hips as well, and the women's bodies formed a barrier, keeping the intruder at the tent opening.

"Excuse me." Sue felt a hand on her arm, gently pushing her to the side. It was Sam.

"Brendan Callaghan. I've always wanted to meet you, but I think it's time for you to leave." Sam's voice was ice.

"I don't know who you are, but I have as much right to be here as anyone."

Sam stepped in close to the taller man, and Sue caught the flash of his fist striking the other man's gut. She heard a thud, then Sam backed away quickly as Brendan folded forward in a rush of exhalation. He tried to recover without showing pain, but it was too late.

"What the hell! I'm going to have you arrested for assault," Brendan's voice was hoarse as if he wanted to scream but couldn't draw air.

"You do that," said Sam. "That's exactly what I want. Then we'll get to bring forward the attempted rape allegations. There's nothing I'd like more than to ruin your career."

The men stared at each other, energy crackling between them. Brendan blinked first. "You're going to regret this," he said as he turned and walked toward the exit.

"I doubt it," Sam said. Brendan flinched slightly at the words.

Sue looked around. A few people stared at them, including her mom, but most had no idea what just happened. She turned back to Kira and Sam.

"I didn't need your help," said Kira, hands still on hips, her anger focused on Sam.

"I know. Believe me, I know you don't need my help with a guy like that, but I really, really wanted to hit him."

Kira shook her head, but Sue saw her anger fading, the start of smile at the corner of her friend's lip. "Violence isn't the answer."

"Please, just this one time, let me be your knight in shining armor. I got to fight for my woman." An enormous grin spread across his face.

"You are a Neanderthal, not a knight. You know I am not a romantic like you." Despite the words, her grin spread.

"I'll have to fight for every bit of chivalry you'll let me get away with. You are a completely modern, self-actualized woman. But I still want to be your knight."

"I guess I can put up with it." She waved her fingers in front of him, the ring flashing in the overhead lights. Sam grabbed her in an enormous hug, lifting her off the ground and kissing her.

Sue watched them, brimming with happiness and longing. For a moment, she wished Gabe were here instead of driving people to the site. He was helping her with her project. Perhaps that's what chivalry was once you'd been married twenty-five years.

That night, every muscle ached. Sue hadn't left the fairgrounds until after nine, when the rental company loaded the last of the gear and drove away.

She crawled into bed, aching like she'd run a month of marathons in one day. Gabe had been downstairs watching TV with Chase when she came home. She told them she was going straight to bed after an extra hot shower. He came into the bedroom just as she snuggled under the covers.

"Back rub or foot rub? You've had a long day." He sat beside her, his hand rubbing circles on her back.

"What you're doing feels nice."

"I'm impressed with the event you put together. I think the community needed it."

Sue sank into the comfortable mattress, the friction from his hand adding warmth to the soothing strokes. The pleasant cocoon drew her toward sleep.

"I can't believe everything that happened today," she mumbled. "Kira is getting married, and Sam punched that guy." Better to think about that than the fancy photos and Worth Company bribes. She had loved the event, but they'd definitely outclassed her.

"Kira, Sam, and Worth Company added a little excitement to the day, but you became a community hero," Gabe said.

Hero. What a word. A gentle current ran through her body, and she moved her toes into the tingling feeling. He saw her as a hero. That had to be good. Was that something she could be? She drifted off to sleep before an answer came.

Chapter 26

The next morning Gabe let her sleep late while he fed the horses. The plush bed drew her back toward sleep, but it couldn't compete with the push to get the day started. The paper hadn't done a negative story on Worth yet, and would be bad news, filled with positive coverage of the Worth development. The planning committee would be at the house at ten for a late breakfast and an event postmortem, and they'd have to figure out if they could recover.

She ignored her stiff muscles and pulled on her jeans, the ones with the flannel inside because the ice crystals on the window promised a cold day. She found her fleece-lined moccasins and grabbed her softest sweater. Leftover aches faded with movement, and she practically bounced down the stairs and into the kitchen.

Gabe already had the coffee going and must have gone out to feed the horses. Sue started putting the ingredients together for her favorite green chile and egg casserole. Her worry faded with the pleasant work of preparing a meal. She'd find a way to win this thing, no matter how many beautiful photos the Worth Company produced.

When Gabe came into the kitchen, the memory of yesterday's kiss flitted through her mind. She went straight to him, threw her arms around his neck, and gave him a proper morning kiss. She wouldn't waste how great she felt this morning. The cold air stuck to his jacket and sent a chill through her as his arms encircled her body. His lips were freezing. She kissed them warm.

When enough of her warmth had transferred to him to take the chill off, she looked at her husband. He had that special smile on his face, the dangerous one that led to trysts in the barn.

"No one's up yet," he said.

"We've got a whole house full of people on their way over. Catch me another time."

By the time ten-thirty rolled around, everyone had plates full of food and the noise level in the house had reached an all-time high as a dozen people simultaneously recalled their favorite parts of the prior day. Kira sat so close to Sam she was practically in his lap.

Chase and Emily had left the event last night at dusk to grab burgers, and it seemed like their friendship had reached a new level. Chase kept stealing glances at the girl and smiling a secret smile he didn't know his mom could see. They were also sat hip to hip. She should probably be concerned, but she'd leave the overprotective mom role for another day.

Amanda arrived with her family. Sue had only caught glimpses of her during the event, but they hadn't talked. The only time Amanda had come into the tent, her boss had followed her in and said something to her that caused her to leave. Sue hadn't seen her again the rest of the day.

Amanda beamed as she listened to the story of Kira's engagement and the run-in with Brendan. Behind the smile, Sue saw some tension. Amanda worked her fingers, squeezing them into fists and then stretching them out. Her husband, who sat beside her, covered one of her hands and rubbed his thumb over her palm. Amanda visibly relaxed at his touch. Sue liked this guy. He was a little quiet, like Gabe, but his actions showed how much he cared for Amanda. And he was quite the looker with sandy blond hair, a scruffy beard, and the massive shoulders of someone who worked in construction.

Seeming to find courage with her husband's touch, Amanda explained how when she had tried to find them, her boss had told her he needed to talk to her back at the Boys & Girls Club.

"He said it had come to his attention that I had continued to help you guys. I told him I'd done nothing wrong. I repeated what you said about my having a right to my own opinions outside of the office," she said, turning to Kira.

"Then he warned me that if I didn't improve my performance over the next sixty days I would be terminated. He actually used that word, terminated, as if he were going to kill me, not just take away my job."

Kira puffed up with anger, ready to go on the attack, but Sue deflated, upset by more bad behavior from city leaders. At yesterday's event, people told her they had seen the representative, the mayor, and the city manager at the Worth Company event. What made it okay for them to take sides so obviously and then threaten Amanda's job because she had helped them? The more she learned about local politics, the more she thought it needed to change.

She turned her attention back to the table, surprised to hear Kira telling Amanda not to worry, that she had a feeling that everything was about to change.

"What do you mean?" asked Sue.

"I can't talk about it yet. My guy in D.C. is still working on it. But there's a story brewing."

Several people pressed her for more information, but Kira wouldn't say anything else. Sue hoped whatever Kira had, it would help them combat the glowing stories from the local paper and the centerfold collage of beautiful Worth Winter Wonderland photos.

Finally, Jim Beam cleared his throat and announced that Emily had something to share with the group. Chase beamed at the girl beside him as she spoke.

"Yesterday we raised over thirty-five thousand dollars in donations. One guy gave us five thousand dollars."

"That's amazing," said Sue. "We also cleared over twenty-five thousand in profits from the event. The craft fair and food trucks brought in an astounding amount of money. If I'm doing my math right, we've raised over a hundred thousand dollars for the valley since we started. What are we going to do with all this money?"

"It's time to start a nonprofit," Kira said. She looked at Sam. "You said you were taking this week off. Why don't we do the legal work and set up a permanent nonprofit?"

"That sounds great," Sam said. "Also, Gabe invited me to Denver with him to meet with the guys from MAPTech. The software they're working on could probably be modified to help manage land conservation. It sounds like an incredible product."

"But how will a nonprofit help us stop the development?" Sue asked. "Besides, yesterday two of the council members assured us they hated the development, and I think a third is leaning our way."

"Don't count your votes until they've been cast in a public forum." Kira crossed her arms. "What council members say and what they end up doing can be completely different."

"Doing what's right for the community is a long game." Amanda's nervousness had disappeared. "If we stop Worth, that's great. But we may lose, and money will help fight him if this battle continues. Not to mention other developers will threaten the valley. If we had an organization in place to care for what's great about Durango, it could change everything."

The conversation moved on to the details of founding a nonprofit. Sue was interested, kind of, but lacked the passion of the others at the table. They discussed goals, determined to make sure it didn't overlap with the activities of the Sierra Club. Amanda got so excited talking about trails and picnic tables at overlooks that Sue was afraid she'd fall out of her chair, perched on it and bouncing the way she was. Amanda had one great idea after another, and suddenly Sue realized that was what the new organization needed most, Amanda.

It was perfect, but how on earth were they going to make it happen? Sue wasn't sure how the finances would work. They were raising money now, but once the Worth project was resolved one way or another, would it have sustainable income? She had to find out. She jumped up, her chair scraping across the floor. Everyone turned to look at her.

She smiled at them awkwardly. "Just going to the porch for a minute. Kira, can you help me with something?" She had meant to be smooth but ended up sounding like she was hiding some big secret.

Kira followed her outside. Sue turned to face her. "Amanda should lead the new organization."

Kira looked a little guilty. "I thought you would want to lead it, after all you started this movement. And you've been looking for something to do once your kids leave."

Ouch. Was she really that transparent? She had to admit she had considered it, and for a hot second it had seemed like the right thing to do. But, watching Amanda, she knew she didn't have the long-term passion needed to run an organization like that.

"I thought about it," she admitted. "But I could never match Amanda's love for this stuff, or her expertise. I just can't figure out the long-term finances. Won't the money dry up once the Worth project is no longer in the headlines?"

"I work with organizations like this all the time. There are lots of potential income streams. The money we've raised so far can be used as working capital. Grants are often available for land purchases and programs. We'd need to take a good look at the expenses because it's Amanda's livelihood at stake. I wouldn't be comfortable with less than three years of working capital."

"You've done a lot of thinking about this," Sue said, already worried about how they'd raise the rest of the money.

"I have. I may have gotten into this for revenge, but I believe in this project."

Sue noticed a new glint in Kira's eyes. They were a little softer, a little less fierce. She nodded, warmed by the other woman's words. "I believe in it too. Let's figure out how to make this happen." She reached forward to hug Kira. It was a little clumsy since she wasn't sure either of them was the hugging type. But as awkward as she'd often acted over the past few weeks, it hadn't impeded her accomplishing more than she could have imagined. She could live with the flaw.

Sue liked the idea of a solid number to work towards. Amanda should run the organization, and Sue would raise money. She'd always been a numbers girl, and it was far more interesting to her than park benches. Fundraising would draw on a lot more skills than arithmetic, but she'd honed her persuasion skills working to stop the development. That just might translate to raising money.

Before she returned to the living room, she snuck upstairs. In the office/studio, she sat down at the computer and ran the numbers. She looked up office rental rates, found Amanda's salary online, and got estimates for furniture and insurance. It would cost at least one hundred and fifty thousand per year to run the organization. Then she did a different calculation.

She had built up quite a nest egg by saving every penny possible from each paycheck for over a dozen years. A woman at a college lecture had spoken about the importance of a woman having her own stash of money. After her parents' divorce, it had seemed like sound advice.

She'd told Gabe about the money before they were married, but he always insisted she keep it separate from the family funds to use however she wished. At night and on weekends, she'd studied investments, and she'd made some good ones. The money meant safety. If everything went wrong, she could take care of herself.

She ran a few more numbers. She opened the project website and went to the donations page, doing math in her head the whole time. Her hands shook as she marked the $100,000 donation box. Her conservative accounting mind would never have considered this a month ago. But today was different. Worth had played dirty ball yesterday, but even so, her event had raised money to save the valley. The public relations investment had paid off. A room full of people sat in her kitchen planning a better future. She trusted their belief that money would help secure the valley's future. And Sue could make a difference.

She didn't have to end up like her mom, or like the person she used to think her mom was. Her mom's life fulfilled her. That was the key. Sue would do the same, regardless of what was thrown at her. She got to decide her future. She didn't have to wait for it to happen to her.

Her finger hovered over the keyboard, part of her still not wanting to click the button. She did it anyway. This was about creating opportunities for the valley, for Amanda, and for herself. Hope opened before her as big as the whole Animas Valley and the mountains beyond. She couldn't even see the horizon.

Truths came with the opportunities. Gabe wasn't responsible for the rest of her life, the rest of her happiness. She was. Her parents' marriage hadn't set her own marriage in stone. Her life was hers. She needed to make the most of every moment she had left.

With one donation, she had set the future in motion. She leaned back in the chair, wanting to revel in her newfound power, but buyer's remorse set in quickly.

Hot with oncoming panic, she left the office, slunk downstairs, and headed to the barn. She wanted to go on a ride. This would be the third day in a row she'd missed. Planning and putting on the event had taken all her time. She wouldn't ride now, not with a house full of guests. She could, however, sneak out for a few minutes of alone time.

As soon as she walked in the barn, she saw her mother halfway down the aisle feeding a carrot to the donkey. Her mom turned to her with a conspiratorial smile. "I was a little tired of being around people, especially after yesterday, so I came to see the animals."

"How can you work at a library if you get tired of being around people?" Sue asked.

"Well, I've lived alone ever since I started working at the library, so I have a nice balance now. I love to help people, but I also need my alone time." She stroked the donkey's long nose as he stretched for another treat.

"I kind of needed to get away too." Sue walked to Samson's stall and clucked at him. The big horse nickered when he saw her, sticking his blazed head out of the Dutch door.

"I just gave a hundred thousand dollars to the valley project. We're going to start a nonprofit, and I want Amanda to run it." Her words sounded more confident than she felt. Inside, she worried about funding a future for someone else when her own was so muddy. She had to stabilize these swinging emotions.

"Gosh, that's a lot of money." Her mother's eyebrows arched in a way that suggested appreciation more than surprise.

She wondered how much her mom had in savings. How much did one hundred thousand dollars mean to her? But for once she didn't comment, judge, or ask about what her mom did or didn't have. Maybe she needed her mom's help more than her mom needed her money.

"I have the money. It's from what I earned when I worked. Plus, I've made some good investments since then." She walked over to the donkey. In a soft voice, she shared her concerns with her mom. "I'm in limbo. I really don't know what I want to do next. I want to stay involved in important issues, but I don't want to run the organization."

"I'm sure you'll find the right thing for you."

"But I have no idea what that should be."

"Is there any reason you need to decide this today?"

Sue rubbed the donkey's fuzzy neck. "I need direction, something to plan for. I know there are opportunities out there, but how do I find the right one?" She couldn't explain the need pressing on her chest. Every year the pressure increased a little more.

She had to find her purpose. She'd raise money for the valley, for now. But what else was there? It sounded so trite to tell her mother that she needed to figure out what to do next with her life, but it overwhelmed her.

She walked across the barn aisle and sat on a bale of hay with her head in her hands. "I think I'm having a panic attack. There's just so much pressure. I need to know what's next, but I can't see what's coming. Honestly, sometimes I create scenarios in my head, worrying about things that might not even happen, just so I can plan my response."

Her mother sat beside her on the hay and took her hand. "I know that feeling. Don't be afraid of what's next, and don't rush."

"But I can't stand that the future is so unclear. I'm the ultimate list maker. I need to prepare, but how can I get ready for something when I can't even decide what I want to do?" The frustration added to the pressure. Finding direction used to be easy.

"Sue, the next part is the best part." Her mother stared straight into her eyes. "In many ways, nothing is more rewarding than raising kids. I loved being your mom. But over the last twenty years, I've finally built my own life. I do exactly what I want to do, learn what I want to learn, and I only have friends I truly enjoy. You tolerate a lot less bull when you're older, and that makes life better. You also learn who to hold on to and who to let go. That was a huge lesson for me. I wish I'd held on to you a little tighter."

"That was my fault."

"Stop blaming yourself for things. Stop overthinking. The future is going to come whether you want it to or not, and I promise, you're going to be ready for it."

"I don't think so. Everything is up in the air."

"You're entering a transition period. You're not even there yet, Chase won't leave for a few more years. Stop worrying. I know you. The right thing will come along, and you'll be ready for it. My biggest concern is that you'll get desperate and choose the wrong thing just because you think you have to choose something." Her mom squeezed her hand.

"Great. One more thing to worry about." Her attempt at levity fell flat.

"Even if you choose wrong, you'll be fine. You'll have the freedom to change your mind and try something else. Besides, if you can afford to give away a hundred thousand dollars, then you probably don't have to worry about money. Think of the next few years as a gift. Next year Chase will be the only boy at home, so you'll have more time to spend on you, to figure out what you want the next step to be. I envy where you are in your life."

Sue laughed. "Sometimes I'm such a mess. No one should envy that." Despite the joking, the conversation had helped. Heck, it might be fun to test drive a few different careers, the same way the valley project had been fun.

She had enjoyed the spark of the idea and then making something that would exist beyond her. Perhaps she'd figure out how to replicate that success with other community issues. Although, it was hard to imagine ever having an enemy as clearly drawn as Harold Worth. He represented something so many in America hated, and that brought in all those donations.

Lost in thought, she felt her mother squeeze her hand again. "Sue, we have to talk about Gabe."

Sue dropped her head. Just when things had started to look up. The pain of losing him took her breath away.

"Sue, look at me."

She raised her head and looked into her mother's pale blue eyes. Her mom touched her cheek.

"I think the problems in your marriage are in here." Her mother's hand moved from her cheek to the top of her head. "I've watched you two together. There's still a lot of love there. Heck, every time I looked up yesterday, you guys were kissing."

"Oh Mom." Tears and bitterness rose in her throat. "When he's here, things are good. But he's always gone. Sometimes I get a surprise message that he's on his way to Denver and I don't see him for days. I'm so afraid he's found someone else. I just don't know what to do."

"He doesn't act like a man who's not in love with his wife. You've always been a take-charge person. Just tell him you need him home more."

Sue chuckled through her tears. "Just like that. Hey Gabe, I want you to stay home more. And while we're at it, if you're seeing anyone else, I'd like you to stop."

"Well, I probably wouldn't add that last part since he told you he's not. But if you feel this bad, he needs to be home more."

"And if he won't agree?" The words sounded small when she said them out loud.

"Well, then you'll know." Her mom wrapped her arms around her, embracing her in a protective hug. "Wouldn't that be better?"

Sue cried in her mother's arms, swept up in emotion and the exhaustion from the last few weeks. The child she used to be clung tight, despite how old and worn out she felt. She closed her eyes and relaxed into her mom's embrace.

Her mother tensed and pulled back. Sue let go and followed her mother's gaze toward the front of the barn. Gabe stood in the doorway.

"Talk to him," her mother said, rising from the hay bale.

He came to her and sat beside her on the hay. He had to see she'd been crying. Her scratchy eyes must be red. She saw the concern on his face and knew she couldn't chicken out.

"I need you to be home more."

"Okay."

She watched him. She could tell he was thinking by the way he cocked his head, but he didn't seem angry, or guilty.

"I was going to take Sam to Denver this week. If I can be gone three days, I can wrap things up there. I promise I'll travel a lot less after that."

"Okay," she said.

They sat in the barn, sharing a bale of straw but not touching. Things didn't seem okay, but they didn't seem any worse.

"I just gave a hundred thousand dollars of my savings to the valley project. I want to create an organization that will last, and I hope Amanda will quit her job to run it."

He looked startled for a moment. "You don't want to run it yourself?"

"No, I really don't. Amanda will do a better job. She's got more experience."

"I think you would have been great, but I trust your judgment. I can give a donation from the company. We'll use it as a tax write off."

She didn't hold back her smile. This time he followed her lead and matched her action instead of trying to save her. "Thanks, I'm going to go tell them about the new donations." She hugged him, then paused before getting up. "Thanks for everything." Her mom was right. She was a step closer to knowing the future.

"There's something I need to talk to you about," he said.

She looked at him, waiting, but the words seemed stuck. Was this it? Was this the moment he'd tell her he'd found someone else?

"I'm The Professor."

It took her a moment to catch up with this unexpected turn. "You're my troll?"

"I didn't mean it that way. I thought I was helping. You hadn't done anything like this before."

"What the hell? You haven't done anything like this before either. Yet somehow, you're a font of knowledge who can lecture me on a public forum. My public forum." Ice ran up her spine, straightening her while he seemed to shrink.

"I'm sorry," he said. "I wanted to help you get better, and I thought it would be easier that way. I didn't want to hurt your feelings. I didn't understand how everyone was taking it until Chase said something the other day." His forlorn look and pleading eyes begged for forgiveness.

Sue stood, shocked at the unexpected betrayal, and left the barn.

Chapter 27

"Jackpot," Kira said, hanging up the phone.

Sue looked up from her computer. "What's up?"

Kira looked tense with excitement, her blue eyes big. "We've got photos of Representative Smythe and his family at the Worth Waikiki Beach Resort."

"What? Is he there right now?" Sue asked.

"Ten months ago, he took his family to Hawaii. I'm betting he got some freebies from Harold Worth since he stayed at his resort." Kira had a Cheshire cat grin.

Sue grew still, trying to understand Kira's excitement, while an undercurrent of dread tugged at her. "How do you know this?"

"I told you I'd hired someone to find out what the good representative has been up to, especially since he's been so vocal and visible regarding this project. You wouldn't believe how unsophisticated some politicians are."

"Are you having him followed?"

"Not exactly, that would be too expensive. My friend just dug stuff up online. The mayor seems clean, but this morning the guy I hired found out about the congressman and Hawaii. He's going to take a closer look at what Mr. Smythe paid for on the trip."

"It sounds like you're trying to trap him." Sue watched her words change Kira's face, first to confusion and then indignation.

"No, Sue, but if he traps himself, I'll make sure we know about it." A long moment of silence passed between them. Kira's blue eyes locked on Sue. Finally, Kira continued. "If he and his family accepted gifts from Worth Company, like airfare, meals, and lodging, that is illegal. The people of Colorado need to know if their politicians are on the take. Do you agree?"

Sue hated unseemly partisan politics. She had tried to keep her head down and stay out of the disappointing vitriol between the right and the left. She now realized she couldn't wait for things to change, she had to change them. Damn it. Why didn't politicians just do the job they were elected to do? So many people put their trust in these people, only to have them fall from grace. It shouldn't be like that. Americans, everyone, deserved politicians with the community's best interest at heart, not their own pockets.

"You're right. If he's done something illegal, we need to know. Everyone needs to know." She wished she could spit the conversation's unpleasant taste out of her mouth.

"Listen," Kira said, reaching for Sue's hand. "We'll be careful and not go public with anything unless we can prove he's done something wrong. But if he has, I expect it will be quite a story."

"I'm sure it will be," said Sue. "One more politician caught with his hand in the till. At least they didn't catch him at a local KKK rally or with his pants around his ankles. Is it me, or are politicians worse than ever? I'm just so tired of it."

Kira sat up straighter. "I think politics is improving. A lot of new people ran for office last time around. More Muslims, Blacks, veterans, and teachers ran than ever before. People are fed up."

Kira had a strange light in her eyes as she stared at Sue. "You could do it," Kira whispered.

"Do what?" asked Sue, afraid of the answer.

"Run for office. You could run for city council, or even for Smythe's congressional seat, should it become vacant." A smile played at the corners of her mouth.

Sue's stomach lurched as if a trap door had opened in front of her, one she shouldn't look into. But she was curious. It was a path she'd never considered.

"You could do it. You'd be great."

Sue knew the size of the congressional district. It sprawled across southwest Colorado, encompassing towns she loved to visit. Ouray perched high in the

Rockies where snow-capped peaks sheltered a darling main street and the world's best pie shop. Cortez sat on the high plains where the mountains fell into the desert. The people were as varied as the landscape. The number of tech geeks Gabe found in small Colorado towns had always surprised her. She'd visited craft shops and ma and pa eateries and passed huge agricultural and mining companies that took miles to drive by. She loved this part of the world, her Colorado. But what did she know about politics?

"I'm not a politician. That's not anything I've ever wanted to do." She jumped out of her chair. "I need to go check on the horses." At the door, she turned back and looked at Kira. Part of her wanted to continue the conversation, but instead she put on her parka and stepped into the sunlight.

Sue tromped to the barn, full of inexplicable nervousness. She checked on the horses and donkey, who were, of course, fine and only wanted a nuzzle. Finally, she went out the barn's back door and stood facing the mountains with the late morning sun in her face. The door had baked warm in the sun, and she leaned against it, a pocket of comfort in the cool day. The ridge loomed in front of her hiding the mountains beyond.

In a way, this was what she had been waiting for. She had been thinking about a future career as a do-over. Accounting was too far gone to recover. Running a company, even a nonprofit, had never held much appeal. She liked to fix things, not endlessly manage them.

Politics. As much as she wanted to hate that option, since she'd never exactly respected politicians, it appealed to her. It was the one thing that drew something from every aspect of her life. The accountant who divined the truth from numbers, the mother who understood what families and children needed, the community member who'd sparked an idea for change. Deep in her bones she understood what was important for the citizens of Colorado, what needed to change, and as with Worth Winter Wonderland, what didn't. As terrifying as it was to consider, it was a place she could make a difference.

Kira had mentioned city council, but Sue didn't want to spend time in meetings arguing about what to name a street or whether the tourism marketing budget was adequate. She didn't want to sit in meetings with the mayor, although she was sure she would meet his type many times over if she chose politics. The county made more sense for her, with its focus on health and human services. She surprised herself by her knowledge of which branch of government handled what. She had always thought that Gabe was the one who cared about politics, but it turned out she'd been listening.

Could she start with state politics? There she'd get to deal with higher education and broad economic initiatives. A federal congressional seat, Cory Smythe's seat, glimmered in the distance, perhaps real, perhaps fool's gold. Federal politics was big and ugly and needed the most help.

Eventually, she went back inside the barn, the sun already burning her face in the thin mountain air. She had a brief conversation with Samson, asking him what he thought. He bobbed his head in agreement without whispering a word of opposition. The perfect constituent.

The hope and longing that filled her made her think of Gabe. This was big. She might fail. She would need his help. Goose bumps rose on her arms and spread across her body like fire. She needed him. She wanted a big future, and she needed him to be a part of it. Their relationship wasn't something she might lose, but something she could gain.

If he wanted to be her partner stepping into this venture, there wouldn't be anyone better. Politics was something he'd always loved and understood, and he'd loved and understood her too. It'd be interesting to see what he thought of meshing his hobby and his love life. She smiled. This was going to be fun.

She was still smiling when she walked back into the kitchen. It didn't look like Kira had moved. When she raised her face, Sue saw victory.

"We got him! We really got him!" Kira waived her phone at Sue, not that she could see what was on the screen from across the room. "He flew to Hawaii in a Worth Company plane. I can't believe he was so stupid! Even if he paid for the flight, which I highly doubt, the optics of it are terrible. He stayed in the Ocean Penthouse, a four thousand dollar a night room. Who knows what else we'll find, but it doesn't look good."

"What a bonehead," Sue said. Seriously, the guy had been on the national news stumping for Worth. His face had shown up on a Worth Company flyer in her mailbox. He had to have known how the vacation would look, not to mention that it was likely illegal.

"Some people think they're above the law. I'm sure he'll try to find some way to wiggle out of it, but this will devastate his career."

Devastate. Such a loaded word. If he had illegally accepted gifts, it would devastate his family. Sue had seen the perfect wife and blond children on TV. But wasn't that what he deserved? What Coloradans deserved? Politics was a dangerous game.

When the proof came in, Kira's contact turned the lead over to the media. Photos of the representative and his family on a Worth yacht played on screens across America, and a hotel clerk had confirmed that Smythe and his family were comped at the hotel. They had all flown back to Denver on a Worth company jet.

A reporter caught the Smythe family leaving a performance at a Denver playhouse. Camera lights lit the shocked faces of the handsome family. Representative Smythe was tall, blond, athletic looking. His wife was beautiful in an unassuming, conservative way. They had two teenage boys, both on their way to being as tall and handsome as their father. The only girl, eight-years-old, had long blonde curls falling over a white parka and pink dress.

Smythe's face went from relaxed to suspicious to angry in a matter of seconds when he saw the cameras. He gathered his family behind him as the reporter approached.

"Did you repay Harold Worth for your trip to Hawaii?"

Cory Smythe, with a stony face and stern tone, told the reporter that he would not answer questions while he was with his family. In the same breath, he assured them that his trip met or exceeded all ethical standards. Saying he'd be happy to comment later, he shuffled his family to a nearby car. The reporter followed him, shouting questions, but he didn't look back.

Kira seemed satisfied that she'd caught her prey, but Sue imagined what Smythe's kids would go through. She hated having anything to do with it. Her disgust with Smythe didn't ease her own guilt. This debacle would crush those kids and his wife whose eyes had widened with fear when her husband addressed the reporter.

Unfortunately, for the representative, the story spread from one network to another like a virus. By the time he held a press conference the next day, dozens of media outlets had covered the story. He'd gone home to Grand Junction, perhaps hoping the media wouldn't follow him to the remote city. They did. It was night by the time he addressed the press from his campaign office in a nondescript office building.

There wasn't much to be learned. He told them he had been on official business, attending a military event in Honolulu, home to many active servicemen and retirees. He reminded them he had served in the marines and had been stationed in Hawaii. Of course, he would reimburse Mr. Worth for the expenses.

Sue and Kira watched CNN as a panel of experts broke down the press conference almost as soon as it ended. There was wide agreement that accepting plane flights, hotel stays, and other gifts was wildly illegal. Even if Smythe paid Worth back, Congress would censure him for his actions. One pundit believed Smythe would resign quickly. It would be impossible to overcome the scandal. Sue noticed the media's glee at reporting on the politician, scarcely mentioning Worth's role.

"What happens to someone who screws up their life in such a spectacular way?" Sue wondered aloud.

"He may go to jail, but I wouldn't worry too much about him," Kira said. "His wife's family has lots of money. If her father hadn't funded his campaigns, he wouldn't be your representative. They're not going to starve."

"That's good. Those kids will have enough to go through without having to worry about paying for college."

"Hey, are you okay?" Kira asked.

"I'm just so mad. We're America. We've got to be better than this."

Kira looked at her for a long time. "We need better politicians," she finally said.

"Yeah, I'm figuring that out."

"You know, the scandal has caused a spike in donations. When do you think you'll talk to Amanda?"

"I want to have three years of revenue in place. My target is half a million."

Sue's phone rang, and she found herself speaking with the assistant to a major Hollywood star. The man and his wife had vacationed in Durango and wanted to support the movement.

Sue passed Kira a note with the amount and name on it. Sue's excitement over the money, twenty-five thousand dollars, didn't compare to Kira's glee about the celebrity. At first, Sue didn't understand why Kira demanded the phone, but she politely asked if the woman would mind speaking to the project's legal counsel. Sue listened to the one-sided conversation as Kira asked if they could publicize the donation. The assistant agreed to promote the star's generosity on social media.

Kira's insight was masterful. Within twenty-four hours, other stars had joined the cause, resulting in a whirlwind of social media promotion that swept up fans. Sue loved reading the pro-Durango tweets, but the anti-Worth posts far outnumbered positive news. Mr. Worth's reputation had returned to haunt him. Now if only the politicians would vote against the project.

The next morning, Sue, Kira, and Amanda discussed whether they should spend some of the new organization's money on mailers. They might not outspend Worth, but Sue thought it could make a difference. Amanda voted no, saying Worth's mailers were an act of desperation.

"We've got a huge following," Amanda said. "I think we've turned the corner. There are new rumblings at city hall about getting this over quickly. No one wants Smythe's mistake to tarnish Durango's reputation. Even your troll has gone away."

"About that," said Sue, her cheeks growing hot. "It was Gabe."

Silence followed as Sue looked into her friends' round-eyed stares. A giggle rose from her chest. In the end, she didn't know who started laughing first. At some point, Kira screeched out, "The Professor," and they fell into fits of laughter again.

"Men are such idiots," Amanda said once they could all breathe.

"Here's to that," said Sue, raising a glass of iced tea. A thousand pounds of weight had been laughed away. Gabe had made a stupid, endearing mistake. She might never let him forget it, but it no longer hurt.

Chapter 28

Several days after the Smythe story broke, Gabe and Sam returned from Denver, and Kira and Sue met them in town for lunch. They'd hardly been seated five minutes before the subject of Representative Smythe surfaced. While Gabe and Sam had seen the news, the women told them that the publicity had resulted in donations nearing the half-million mark.

"Sue should run for Smythe's seat," Kira said.

Sue's face went hot, unsure she wanted to share this potential desire. What if they thought it was ridiculous?

"You should go for it," Sam said. "I figure Coloradans will want a completely different kind of politician after this." His head cocked as he gazed at her as if evaluating her for the first time. "You're a mom and an environmental activist, but in a local, save Colorado kind of way, and your husband is a respected business owner. I think you've got a shot."

"I'm not sure I'd be interested in something like that," she stammered. She was curious, well, equal parts curious and terrified. The table was quiet, everyone waiting for someone else to speak.

Gabe looked right at Sue and spoke into the quiet. "I think you'd be great."

Time slowed. While it was probably the answer she wanted, her chest and throat constricted with dread. It was one thing to want to do more, to want more out of life. It was another thing to get agreement, encouragement even, to act on your dreams. A distant opportunity had become real. Was this what she wanted? It would be so much work. She'd have to put herself out there in a way she'd never considered before. Look what had happened to Smythe. It was equally scary and exciting.

She sat up a little straighter, her practical mind coming in to steady her. "I've got a lot of research to do before I seriously think about running for office. I also need to consider the impact it would have on our family. But I want to look into it." The last sentence filled her with unexpected joy. She had cemented what she wanted to herself as much as to the others.

Later that night, after the kids went upstairs to study, she pulled two chairs and a side table close to the fireplace. She had told Gabe she wanted to meet him in the living room at nine o'clock for wine and a talk. She opened a bottle of red she'd saved for a special occasion and set two glasses on the small table between the chairs. The crackle of the wood and smell of pine burning made the space homey and romantic.

She poured herself a glass. Shot through with flames of gold from the fire, the garnet liquid trembled in the glass as she raised it to her lips. The dry and robust liquid filled her mouth with berries and oak. She closed her eyes and enjoyed the flavor and the warmth from the fire.

"Hey," Gabe said as he sat down next to her and picked up the bottle. He glanced at the label. "The good stuff." He poured himself a glass, then reached out to clink hers in a toast.

"I love you," she said. "We've got a lot to talk about."

He nodded at her, his eyes crinkling at the corners, not in a smile, exactly, but in agreement. "Like about my being your troll?"

"No, that's behind us. Just don't ever do it again. And promise me you'll talk to me if you've got an issue in the future." She arched an eyebrow at him.

"I promise I will never, ever do that again." He raised his glass, and she touched hers to his to seal the promise.

"I'm not sure where to begin," she said. "I want to talk to you about our argument when I accused you of cheating. I want to talk about why you've spent so much time in Denver. I want to talk about our future, and the things I'm afraid of. And I want to talk about the conversation we had at lunch, about the prospect of my running for office." She had told him she didn't know where to begin, and she'd ended up beginning everywhere.

"Okay," he said. He set his glass down and took her glass from her and set it on the table as well. He leaned forward, taking both her hands in his. "I love you. I haven't had an affair. You are the only woman I want to be with."

His hands were warm, his green eyes tender. She could hardly breathe. He almost never spoke so openly. Hope clutched her heart. Tonight, everything would be resolved.

"I have a confession to make," he said. "For a while now, I've been thinking about the boys leaving, wondering what it was going to be like in the house without them around. So, I started working on something. I probably should have talked to you about it, but you've never seemed interested in the business, well, not in a long time."

For the first time since she'd known him, she wished he would quit talking and get to the point. What was his confession? What had she missed because of her disinterest in the business? Perhaps he wanted to move back to Seattle. But she loved it here! Her mind raced through scenarios.

"I'm selling the company."

Sue sat back and stared into the fire. This was the last thing in the world she expected. She'd never known him without his business. It was a part of him.

"I didn't think you'd object. I mean, you haven't been interested in the company in decades." She heard the worry in his voice. When she looked at him, deep lines crossed his brow.

"I don't care," she said. "Not if that's what you want to do, but I am surprised. I thought that business meant everything to you."

Now it was his turn to sit back. His hand released hers. "No, you and the boys mean everything to me. I've missed so much. Two of them are already gone. Soon they'll start their own lives and won't even be home for holidays. The business doesn't mean anything to me compared to family."

How did she always say the wrong thing! "I didn't mean it like that, I know our family is the most important thing in your life. You're a great dad."

"But not a great husband?" He waved his hand as if trying to erase his comment. "Sue, that's what I'm trying to tell you. I want to spend more time here, with you. And with the boys while they're still around."

"Why now?" she asked.

He sighed, suddenly looking tired. "I've run this business since I was twenty-three. I've nurtured it, watched it grow. It's taken a lot of energy, a lot of hours. I don't want to die an old man sitting at his desk. I want to enjoy my life and my family. Before it's too late."

All this time she'd worried about what to do with the rest of her life, and he'd been wrestling with the same emotions. What do you do when you realize your time is finite? Just when she was looking to go out in the world, he wanted to come home. Somehow that didn't seem fair to either of them.

"Wow," she said, buying time. "So, now that I'm thinking about getting a job or running for office, you want to sell the company and stay at home?" She hadn't meant for it to be a question. He'd been pretty clear, but it came out as one anyway.

"Don't you see?" he said. "It's perfect. I can support you the way you've supported me all these years. I can be there for the boys, and you can finally have the time you need to do what you want."

He thought this was the solution? It made her head hurt. Would reversing roles solve anything? Then her accounting brain kicked in.

"I just gave a ton of money to fight the Worth development, and whatever I choose to do won't replace what you've been making. Will money be an issue?" Every step forward was a giant leap back.

He chuckled. At first, she thought he was laughing because of the financial pickle she'd put them in just when he wanted to stop working.

"Sue, we are not going to have to worry about money. MAPTech is buying the company, for a lot. We'll also own a portion of MAPTech, and I'll get paid as an advisor."

Sue shook her head. It was a lot to take in. "So, you'll be working?"

A smile crossed his face, excitement replacing worry. "I'll probably work about twenty hours a week. I may have to go to Denver a few times a year. I'd planned on working from the house, but we'll have to figure out something different now that my office is a podcast studio." The smile crept from his grin to his eyes.

She started to say something, to apologize for taking over his office, but he put his hand up. "I'm not worried about the office. I can work from anywhere. Mostly I'll just be researching new products and new markets. No meeting with clients or managing employees. It's going to be all the stuff I love and none of the stuff I dread. I feel like a kid again."

He looked like a kid with that enormous smile plastered on his face. When had he last been so happy? Maybe at the hockey tournament last year when Jaxson won most valuable player. But this was even better because of the relief in his eyes. She wished she'd known what he'd been going through. For as long as she'd been married, she still had a lot to learn.

"Tell me about your plans," he said. "Are you serious about running for office?"

She took a deep breath, needing to tell him everything, all her hopes and fears, then took another sip of the rich wine. There was no reason to rush. Her mind usually worked at warp speed, her mouth bumping over the road it left behind. Tonight, she needed to slow down and be careful about what she said. "I might be. It was interesting hearing you talk about how the prospect of the boys leaving made you consider what to do with the rest of your life. I've been doing the same thing, for years now."

The memory of sitting on the second-floor landing listening to her mother's book club flashed through her mind. "I've always been afraid of repeating my mother's mistakes. I'd have a happy marriage, take care of the kids, and then as soon as they left everything would fall apart, and I'd be left to start over. So, for years, I've been trying to figure out what to do about that." She held the glass of wine with both hands, afraid the trembling would show.

"You were afraid we'd break up?"

"I had so many things wrong. My parents' marriage didn't end the way I'd thought. My mom told me she wanted the divorce. I always thought he'd left her." She looked at Gabe, saw the confusion on his face. "That's why I was so upset when Lucinda kept popping up on your phone."

"I didn't know." His voice scratched with pain.

"I didn't talk about it. Over the past few years, I've lost some of the confidence I used to have. When I worked, I knew who I was and where I was going. When I became a mom, I completely invested in that. Now that the boys are almost grown, I've had to figure out who I am again, what I want for the future." She brought the wine to her lips.

"Please want me."

His words shot straight to her heart and lodged there, releasing guilt, love, and desire that overflowed and spilled out her eyes. "The best thing I can imagine is us staying together."

He took her glass from her hands and pulled her into a hug. "I've planned my whole future around you. I need you."

"I need you too, and I'm sorry I didn't bring this up earlier." She hugged him hard. Knowing he wanted her as much as ever made the earth solid beneath her feet after years of wading through quicksand. She pulled back from him. "Thank you for putting up with my self-esteem issues."

"Of all the people I know, you should never have low self-esteem. You came in and told me exactly what I should do with my company. You built a career fixing companies. When you became a mom, I knew you'd be great at it, and look how our boys turned out. That's your doing. Whatever you want to do next, you'll be great." He leaned forward and touched his lips to hers.

She kissed him back, then asked him to sit. For once, she would not leave things half done. "Let's talk about what's next. Working to stop the development has been amazing. I've put something in place that will make a difference in the community. Not all of it was fun, dealing with the mayor certainly wasn't. But I enjoyed meeting people at the event, hosting the podcast, and reaching people through the podcast and social media."

"I've loved seeing that fire in you again."

She took one more sip of wine for courage. "Thank you. I do want to consider politics, although Smythe's office seems like a pretty big lift for a first try. I want to learn more about opportunities at all levels." The statement ran through her warmer than wine or fire.

Gabe didn't speak for a long minute. When he did, his words surprised her. "Lucinda is a player in state politics. If you're interested in running for office, you need to meet her. I'm sure she'd make some introductions for you."

A remnant of embarrassment from their first meetings shot through her. "Would she talk to me after our bizarre, um, meeting in Denver?"

"I'm sure she would. I think you'd like her if you got to know her. Think of it as part of your research."

She nodded. A flicker of excitement took hold. Regardless of what she ultimately decided, exploring politics with Gabe would be fun.

"This is going to be fun for me," he said, echoing her thoughts. "I love politics, but I wasn't built to be out there in front of people. You're great at that."

"With your help, I can be." And with that, she released the doubt and worry and concerns. A surge of confidence lifted her to her feet. Together, they were a great team.

"Come on," she said, taking his hand and pulling gently. "Tonight, you have the opportunity to make love with a future U.S. congresswoman."

Chapter 29

The next morning, the phone woke Sue before five a.m. Representative Smythe was hitting the Sunday morning political news circuit, and she'd already received her first call for an interview.

Full of nerves and anticipation, she barely choked down the coffee Gabe made before he went to feed the horses. She had nothing to wear, and her hair needed to be done, but those weren't the big worries. Two items topped her list for the day: not to make an ass of herself, and to convince people to save the valley. For all she knew, her audience would be in the millions, but she'd pretend only the city council could hear her.

The publicist quickly set up three interviews. Kira helped Sue dress, picking out an indigo cashmere sweater. Two of the three interviews were on camera. Fortunately, she had the phone interview first.

She told the reporter how the Worth Company had shown up in Durango, at their event, with prettier pictures of what they said they were going to build, but they had not changed the proposal they'd submitted to the city.

She confirmed that Representative Smythe had been at the Worth exhibit that day. "People need to demand more from their politicians," she said on more than one occasion. After the first interview, she grew more comfortable. She only needed to tell the truth.

At one point, Chase came down in his boxers, sleepy but excited, to show her something on his laptop. She stopped him at the bottom of the stairs and sent him up to put clothes on, since Kira and Sam were at the kitchen table. She shook her head as the crazy boy retreated up the stairs but hugged him two minutes later when he came back down and showed her donations had topped half a million dollars.

It was time to tell Amanda about the job. Kira and Sam had written the bylaws for the new organization. They had also created a job description for the executive director. Between media interviews, they picked the board members: Sue, Kira, Colleen, and Jim Beam.

Amanda stopped by after work that evening. Sue and Kira sat her down at the table and tried to be more serious than excited as they told her about the money and the job.

"You want me to run the nonprofit? But I already have a job."

Amanda's smile didn't reach her worried eyes, but Sue had already had a day full of convincing people. "We've already set up the organization, and Sam and Gabe have volunteered to help through the startup phase. We'll pay you what you're making currently, and we'll guarantee health insurance for your family and a 401K program. I know that's important to you." Sue spoke with authority, but excitement tinged her voice.

"You really want me to do this, to be the one to lead it?" Amanda's asked, then shook her head. "This is your baby, you started it."

"This isn't my calling," Sue said. "But you're going to be great."

Amanda looked at them and shook her head again. "I appreciate your faith in me, but I love my job."

"But what about how the mayor and city manager have treated you?" Sue was incredulous.

"Every day I go to work and make a difference in the community in so many ways. It's what I want to do with my life. I appreciate the opportunity, but I can't leave."

"We understand," Kira said. "We'll have to work together to find the right person for the job."

"You've got to do what's best for you. I'm just happy for all the help you've given us so far." Sue followed Kira's lead and tried to sound gracious. She admired Amanda, but the disappointment and worry stung. Her plan foiled, she started to make a list of what they'd need to do next.

Sue and Kira recorded a podcast episode announcing the new organization. On air, they talked about how donations from across the country had supplemented the money raised locally. They were now able to form a permanent organization to protect the Animas Valley for the enjoyment of all. Sue mentioned they'd be looking for a director.

At one point, Sue saw Chase look up, then walk across the room behind her, out of view. A couple of seconds later, she heard the door close softly. He walked back to the table and laid a note in front of her.

Worth Company would like to call in to the podcast. Now.

Sue felt her eyes go wide and tilted the note slightly so that Kira could read it. Kira nodded and mouthed yes.

Sue looked up at Chase and nodded. Worth Company had been absent from the media since the Smythe story broke. Chase took her phone off the table and left the room. Sue and Kira kept talking, searching for topics amid worry about the coming interview.

A few minutes later, Chase came back in and hooked the cell phone to his laptop. He set the phone in front of Sue, the name Brendan Callaghan displayed across the top of the phone.

"We have a special caller," she said. "Brendan Callaghan from Worth Company is on the line. Thank you for joining us, Mr. Callaghan."

"Call me Brendan. It's nice to be here ladies. Thank you for having me on today. I wanted to start by—"

Kira interrupted. "Mr. Callaghan, I'm surprised you called in today. Can you tell us a little more about Representative Smythe accepting travel expenses from Worth Company for a family vacation?"

"As I'm sure you've heard, the representative was on official business, and he has already reimbursed the Worth Company for the costs of his visit to our troops and veterans stationed in Hawaii. The Worth Company is proud of our association with such a noble effort."

Kira leaned forward over the table, staring at the phone like a hawk about to attack. "I'm also sure you realize it was illegal for the representative to accept these gifts."

"As I said, there was nothing improper, and the records will show that." He sounded testy. "The reason I called today was to talk about the Worth Development in Durango. I believe that is what this program is about?"

"It certainly is," said Kira, "and I think the public connects Representative Smythe's travel with that development. After all, Representative Smythe was part of the Worth Company presentation in Durango."

"Yes, that was a spectacular event, although Mr. Smythe did not attend in an official capacity. We are proud of our work in Durango. Fortunately, we showed the public what a first-class development truly looks like. I know the people I spoke with were excited about the prospect of Worth Winter Wonderland enhancing the valley."

Anger roared through Sue's ears. What an ass to think Worth would make Durango something better than it already was. "Well, you certainly showed up with prettier pictures than the originals." Sue heard the sneer in her voice, and for once, didn't mind.

"I can promise you that Worth Company will build a classy, sophisticated development that you will be proud of. The people of Durango are fortunate to have someone as important as Mr. Worth investing in their community."

"I don't know if you actually looked around during your visit, but we've got a pretty great community here already." Sue said.

"The public needs to understand that Worth Company will make Durango better, improve its reputation, and turn it into a world-class destination. We have the money to make Durango a truly phenomenal experience. Once this development is built, the people will thank us."

"So, your approach is to take what you want from this town and tell them to sit back and enjoy it?" A quiet anger fueled Kira's voice. "This is exactly what is wrong with America right now. The people of Durango should control their own destiny."

For a long moment, no one spoke. Sue couldn't think of how to fill the dead air.

"Look, we're not trying to force anything on anyone," said Brendan. "If Durango doesn't want us, we'll take our money and go elsewhere. There are plenty of communities that would pay to bring this development to town. Places where people understand what's important."

"And there you have it," Sue jumped in. "I've lived in this community for twenty years. I've raised four boys here. Heck, we came here because we thought this would be a great place to raise our kids. I guarantee you that parents in Durango think about what's important every day. So do the environmentalists and outdoor enthusiasts who flock here to take advantage of the natural wonderland in our mountains and valleys. I don't need a fancy developer to tell me what's important for my community. I need my neighbors. I need elected officials we can believe in, and I need the great people of this town. That's who gets to decide the future of Durango. Worth cannot threaten us or hold us hostage. Mr. Callaghan, thank you for joining us today, but I think we've heard enough." She nodded at Chase, and he ended the call.

Sue leaned into the mic. "To our city council members, if you're listening, we have entrusted you with making the right decision on this project. Please listen to the people in Durango instead of outside developers. It's up to you."

She thanked Kira, then signed off. The broadcast had ended, but the fight in Sue remained. Enough. Enough of corrupt politicians and greedy developers. Enough of people thinking they could take whatever they wanted. The time for change had arrived.

"This feels like the end," Kira said. "All the cards are on the table."

"No," Sue said. "This feels like the beginning." Whether they would prevail was unknown. But regardless of the outcome, this was a new beginning.

Sue had just given her first political speech. Yes, she had more research to do. Yes, the city still needed to vote on the project. But the direction had been set. It was funny. In a way, Worth Company had already changed Durango. It had made people reconsider what was valuable. It had made Sue reconsider the value in her life, and in herself.

The broadcast made the national news. The next day, a city council member added the Worth Winter Wonderland development to the next city council meeting agenda. That same day, Gabe received a notice that the chamber of commerce had called an emergency meeting of the board of directors.

Gabe called her from the meeting. "I'm sorry. The board voted to support the development. The vote split the board, with twelve of twenty-one board members voting for the development and the remaining nine voting against it. I voted no, but it wasn't enough."

"Gabe, it was more than enough. Thank you."

That night, the crowd at city hall was larger than the council chambers could accommodate, and rows of chairs lined a broad hallway, along with a television showing the council meeting. Sue had arrived early enough to get a seat in the main meeting room.

When the meeting started, the mayor announced that one hundred and six people wanted to speak publicly about Worth Winter Wonderland. Sue looked for Brendan Callaghan but didn't see him.

Drew Polowski, CEO of the chamber of commerce spoke first. He told the council that his board of directors supported the Worth Winter Wonderland project. The mayor thanked him for his support. One of the council members asked Drew if the vote had been close, and Drew had to admit the truth.

Pride filled Sue's chest as an overwhelming majority spoke against turning the natural beauty of their valley into a "monster-sized playground for a bunch of out-of-towners" according to one speaker. A few supported the development, especially people looking for work. For Sue, their words pointed to a larger community problem.

When she finally took the stand, as the seventy-fourth speaker, she shared the numbers Chase had prepared. "In an online poll, seventy-four percent of respondents opposed the development, not because they are against progress, or money, or jobs but because they believe Durango's future should be built on the things that make the community great today."

Cheers filled the room, and the mayor slammed down his gavel and asked for quiet.

"Good has come out of this fight over the Worth Winter Wonderland development," Sue continued. "We have founded an organization to preserve Durango's natural environment and create new ways for the public to enjoy the valley. I'd like to thank the people in Durango and beyond who have raised their voices and committed dollars and time to the future of this community. I'd like to thank you, our council members, for your consideration and ask that you vote against the Worth Winter Wonderland project."

She returned to her seat during another standing ovation. The mayor called the chamber to order again, and the remaining speakers had their say.

The mayor opened the council discussion with his own speech. "I believe we are voting on this item too early. I believe councilman Rogers placed this item on the agenda today to take advantage of current events."

A rumble from the audience crossed the room. Sue assumed he was talking about the news surrounding Representative Smythe, and the crowd didn't seem to like the mayor's accusation.

"However," Buddy continued, "I see how deeply the community cares about the project given the comments here tonight. While I would prefer to wait until all the information on the project was in, since we must vote this evening, I will cast the first vote against the Worth Winter Wonderland development."

Amanda had warned Sue this would happen. Even if the mayor wanted the project, he needed to be on the winning side of the vote if he wanted to be re-elected. Sue tried to give him the side-eye, but he didn't look her way.

After a moment of shocked silence, the building erupted in cheers. The mayor tried to gavel the audience back to order, but no one listened. People swarmed Sue, congratulating her. She'd never been hugged so much in her life, and she smiled so hard her face hurt.

"Don't stop the podcast," someone called.

No, she wouldn't stop the podcast. It would change, become more hers and not solely exist to fight the development. She'd focus on broader issues, ones that affected the entire western slope of the state. She'd talk to experts, find her footing, and do more, on a bigger scale. One taste of making a difference, and she knew exactly what she wanted her future to hold.

The room calmed, and the mayor gaveled the meeting back to order so the vote could continue. Sue's phone buzzed in her pocket. She looked at Gabe's brief text. *Great job. What's next?* She smiled again as the meeting restarted.

One council member talked about how the Worth project came to them because it didn't conform to the very zoning laws that made Durango special. "I'd like to thank Sue Cleary for her podcast and for making sure the community knew about this issue." He nodded at Sue, then moved to deny the project. The remaining council members quickly voted unanimously in opposition to Worth Winter Wonderland.

The council chamber erupted again. Sue hugged a few more people and then escaped. She wanted to celebrate with family tonight. They were her support, her future.

But most of all, she wanted to be with Gabe. He wasn't just her past or her future. He was a part of her, a part of every breath she took, every decision she made. Once she had worried whether she was good enough, whether he'd choose her again for the next part of life. Now she understood the difference between need and want. She could live a life without him, but it would be half a life. She wanted the whole thing, the family, the career, and the man. And she was going to get it all.

THE END

***

Thank you for reading *THE PODCAST CHRONICLES*! I hope you loved it. For another story about friendship and women of a certain age finding their passion, try the following titles from Kathryn Dodson:

A Powerful Season

Five Tries to Get It Right

About the Author

Kathryn Dodson grew up writing and riding horses in far West Texas. She graduated from SMU in English/Creative Writing and went on to get an MBA from Thunderbird and a PhD from Clemson.

She has worked on both sides of the US/Mexico border and has held jobs with governments, chambers of commerce, and other businesses. Now she spends her days writing about interesting women in fascinating places.

Join Kathryn for updates and extras at www.KathrynDodson.com.

NOVELS

Tequila Midnight
The Podcast Chronicles
Portrait of Deception

Acknowledgements

I'd first like to acknowledge everyone who found this book, and especially those of you who read to the very end. Without readers, novels are just dreams. It's the readers who make them real. Thank you.

This novel is about friendship, and I've been fortunate to have incredible friends. My high school best friend, Lisa Ulrich, remains a best friend. When we're together, I swear we pick up mid-sentence from our last conversation. I have great memories from college (relatively few of them from the classroom), most of them with Cara Williams. My friends from the Santa Monica Chamber of Commerce, the City of El Paso, and the City of Carlsbad (California) have been a huge part of my life. My writing friends are the most supportive people I know. None of this would have happened without them. I'm also incredibly lucky to have neighborhood friends who show up in the front yard every Friday for cocktails and stories. Finally, my book club friends have been together since our kids were little. We're sending them off to college this year–yet one more phase we'll go through hanging onto each other.

Finally, I'd like to thank my family. I am rich with the support of parents, inlaws, and a bevy of aunts. I married my husband in Durango almost thirty years ago, and it was the best decision I've ever made. I'm also incredibly lucky to have a kid who is my greatest supporter and who inspires me every day.

9 789898 787851449